First Test

Surely, Cassandra thought, she could remain immune to the Marquess of Blytheland's seductive charms alone with him in the garden. A ball was going on in the mansion but a few yards away, and she could return to it if danger dictated flight. Besides, this was her chance to show the marquess how properly pure she was.

But she was not prepared for how disturbingly soft his voice was when he asked, "Will you kiss me, Cassandra?"

The best she could do was reply, "I--I have not given you permission to use . . . my Christian name, sir."

"Then give it to me now."

"I—"

"Please."

Her only answer was a sigh—answer enough for Blytheland's lips to come down on hers, swiftly, firmly, gently. Without thinking, a small gasp opening her mouth, she leaned forward, her passion matching his.

This was the first test of her virtue—and the only question now was how badly she would fail it. . . .

Cupid's Mistake

Karen Harbaugh

A SIGNET BOOK

SIGNET
Published by the Penguin Group
Penguin Books USA Inc., 375 Hudson Street,
New York, New York 10014, U.S.A.
Penguin Books Ltd, 27 Wrights Lane,
London W8 5TZ, England
Penguin Books Australia Ltd,
Ringwood, Victoria, Australia
Penguin Books Canada Ltd, 10 Alcorn Avenue,
Toronto, Ontario, Canada M4V 3B2
Penguin Books (N.Z.) Ltd, 182-190 Wairau Road,
Auckland 10, New England

Penguin Books Ltd, Registered Offices:
Harmondsworth, Middlesex, England

First published by Signet, an imprint of Dutton Signet,
a division of Penguin Books USA Inc.

First Printing, February, 1997
10 9 8 7 6 5 4 3 2 1

Prologue

Paul Templeton, Marquess of Blytheland, stared at the fire before him but did not see it. He sat, his fists clenched on his knees, and saw only the face of his wife as she was when he first met her. He remembered her as she was long before this night, not as she was now, lying in her room next to his, giving birth to the child of another man.

A loud groan came from the other room, and he raised his head briefly, listening. But it was only a groan and not her voice calling out for him. He turned his head away from the connecting door, despising himself for listening, for even being here, waiting. His love for Chloe had not quite died yet—he could tell by the persistent ache in his chest as he listened to her laboring to bring forth the child. He had given up too much of himself when he married her and even now it was hard to pull away, hard to admit that all the love he had invested in her had brought such bitter returns.

He looked into the grate again, and saw in the flickering red flames the color of her hair and the bright laughter she had always brought when she entered a room. He had fallen in love with her for that, and for her superior intellect; stupid women had always bored him. Chloe had excited his mind with her radical ideas and wide-ranging thoughts, and the wildness of her passion had excited him in the marriage bed.

He had been mad for her, though his friends had told him he was mad for marrying her. He should have listened. He should have heeded Lord Eldon, his best friend, when the man had shaken his head and said Chloe Fenwick was not a woman to marry but to bed. Blytheland had almost called Eldon out for that. Was she not a well-chaperoned and therefore innocent young lady, after all?

A high scream sounded from the other room, and then there was silence. The marquess tightened his fists, closed his eyes, straining to hear more. There was no other sound. Even now he wished to go to her, but he would not. He would wait for the news to come to him. He was tired of being a lapdog, running when called. He had been a fool, and he would be so no longer.

He had felt quite vindicated on their wedding night three years ago, for she had indeed been a virgin. She'd not repulsed his advances either after that, not until last year. He had not known what had changed . . . she had continued to hold her salons, writing her papers and discussing her ideas with her guests. Chloe had been well occupied, he had thought. He should have known better, once she had started to espouse the ideas from that Wollstonecraft woman's books. He'd seen too many people copy the style of life of the philosophers and teachers they'd admired, but he had thought Chloe more clear-minded than that. But she was as unoriginal as the others . . . Wollstonecraft had taken lovers, and Chloe had adopted that philosophy as well.

He could not, in the end, reason it away. He had enjoyed philosophical discussions himself, had enjoyed the talks he had had with Chloe. But when she had cheerfully come home one day, telling him she had taken a lover, he had felt as if he had received a blow to the gut. She could not even understand why he had grown so angry—did he not understand the principle of it?

He had not, and could not, though there was a space of time where he had actually tried. And yet . . . and yet, here he was, waiting for another man's child to be born, despising himself for a fool.

There was still no sound from the next room. A distant clock tolled the hour—it was two in the morning. He almost rose to go to the next room, but forced himself to sit where he was. At last a knock sounded on the door to his chamber, and he stood up at last and opened it.

It was Dr. Jenkins. The man's gray hair was tousled, his eyes tired and sad. He glanced at Lord Blytheland then looked away, clearing his throat.

"My lord . . . It is not good—"

"Chloe?"

"Her ladyship did not —she is—" The doctor straightened himself and looked Blytheland in the eyes. "She is dead, my lord."

Blytheland closed his eyes briefly and swallowed down the hot rage and sorrow that filled his throat. "The child?" he asked after a moment.

"It, also."

"I see." Blytheland turned and gazed into the fire again and tried not to see the image of his dead wife in the flames.

"My lord, what do you wish me to do?"

"What you usually do in these cases, I suppose. If you need anything, you may speak with my solicitors and tell them you have my approval." He glanced over his shoulder at Dr. Jenkins. "You may go." He heard the doctor step away from him.

He could not help himself and turned swiftly, impulsively holding out his hand. "Stop! I would like to know . . ." The doctor looked at him in inquiry. "Did she—did she ask for me at all? Say my name?"

A look of profound pity entered the doctor's eyes, and the marquess hated himself for being so weak as to ask. "No, my lord," the doctor said. "No, I am afraid she did not."

"I see," Blytheland said again, and turned away.

"I am sorry . . . she was a lovely lady."

"Yes."

There was only silence, then he heard the doctor's foot-steps go away from him and the door close, and for a few minutes he did not move. The long sigh that came from him echoed in the room, and he rose at last. He wandered around his room and randomly picked up different items in it, looking at them and putting them down again. An odd blankness was in him, an aimlessness—he did not know what to do. Moving about seemed better somehow than simply sitting.

He came around at last to the trunk at the foot of his bed, and hesitated. Slowly he kneeled and opened it and took a leather violin case from it. He ran his hands over it slowly, feeling the smoothness of the leather. His hands hesitated for a moment, then he unlatched the case and brought out the instrument.

It was a beautiful thing, still polished and shining; he had not touched it in years. His music was another thing he had given up when he married Chloe. She had, for all her intel-ligence and education, not liked music much—he knew now it was because she did not have an ear for it. Anything in which she was not accomplished, she generally despised, but it was not something he realized until much, much later. But her reason for being against his playing had seemed so sensible—gentlemen did not take playing instruments with much seriousness; that was a thing for hired musicians only. Other people had thought the same thing—it had been his father's opinion, too. It was one more thing he had given up, a thing he had once thought had been an insepara-ble part of himself.

Could he still play it? He took the violin from its case, settled it against his chest, and drew the bow across the strings. A long wail came from the instrument—it needed tuning, of course.

His hands shook, and the violin dropped into the trunk. Not even this. He had given Chloe everything he could think of to keep her with him, had given up his music, too. Now it was all gone from him—he had no wife, no child, no music—and he had lost himself, somehow. Blytheland sank to his knees against his bed and pushed his palms against his eyes, pushing back the weeping he knew would come if he let it.

He took in a long, shuddering breath and rose to his feet. When he put out his hand to close the lid of the trunk, however, he hesitated. He still had the violin, and he remembered all the music he had ever played—it had been his special talent. Could a talent disappear if one did not practice it? He was not sure.

Blytheland brought out the violin again and carefully placed it back in its case. He would find out if he could still play, and if he got his music back, he would never let it go. He would never lose that part of him again, not to anyone.

The latches clicked in place, and the violin was protected once again inside its leather case. Blytheland pressed his lips together tightly. He would do as *he* wished from now on, and surround himself with people with whom *he* wished to associate, and do things that *he* pleased. Did he not still have his estates, his title, his fortune, things most men would envy? Was he not still young—only four-and-twenty years old—? Chloe was gone now, and she had been unfaithful to him. All his giving had been for nothing.

It would not happen again. He would make sure of it.

A sudden shuffling, fluttering noise made him look up, then he shrugged. It was no doubt the doctor in the next room attending to . . . his duties. A rising nausea filled Blytheland's throat and he closed his eyes tightly. He could not stay here, not tonight. He would go out—there were gaming hells enough where he could occupy his mind with either wagers or drink.

The marquess gazed around his room once again. It

seemed dark and empty and cold. Quickly he stood and pulled on the coat he had discarded earlier. He strode to the door of his chamber and for one moment his steps faltered as the grief and anger threatened to surface again.

No!

He shut the door firmly behind him.

There was no noise now except the ticking of the clock on the mantelpiece . . . and then a flutter, as if a bird had settled itself into the room. A slight glow moved from one corner of the marquess's chamber, and slowly, cautiously, the glow took shape: a face, shoulders, hands, torso, legs, and feet. And then, with another flutter, wings.

The boy who materialized gazed at the closed door with a slightly guilty look on his face. He had made a terrible mistake. He was usually very accurate with his arrows and his darts, and his timing had always been impeccable, but this time he had erred badly. He had meant to shoot Lord Blytheland when he was looking at another young lady, but the marquess had suddenly shifted his gaze at the last moment and had looked at Chloe Fenwick instead, falling desperately in love with her. The boy had hoped that it would work out anyway—often it did; for being loved to distraction was often irresistible to men and women alike and softened their hearts to love in return. But Chloe Fenwick had not been like that—she had been all mind and little heart.

The boy took in a breath and let it out again in a resolute burst of air. Well, there was nothing for it but for him to remedy the mistake. Now that the woman had died, the marquess was free once more to follow his heart. The boy suddenly felt uncertain. Lord Blytheland's face had looked as if he had decided to encase his heart in a steel cage, rather than let it free to love again. The boy hoped it was not too late. He frowned. He had never made a mistake before, except perhaps once; it was nonsense to think he might not remedy this situation. In all the millennia of his existence, his arrows had always shot with purpose and extreme accuracy, moving his victims—that is, targets—to love, to revulsion, or indifference, depending on if they needed a lesson in love or humility. He was Eros, the God of Love, and took whatever shape he needed to accomplish his goals—successfully. There was no reason to think he would make another mistake again.

The frown turned into a considering expression, and Eros reached over his shoulder to the quiver between the wings on his back and pulled out an arrow. He ran his thumb against the edge of the arrowhead in a contemplative manner. A slow, mischievous smile grew on his lips and a silent laugh shook his shoulders. The young lady he had first intended for Lord Blytheland would be in town the next year or two for her first Season. She was a little different now than she was when she and Lord Blytheland had passed in a crowd at a country fair, but not much; the two would still suit very well. Neither one remembered the other. He could start fresh: it would be as if the whole incident with Chloe had never happened, he was sure.

The boy turned to look out the window of the room, down at the tall figure walking purposefully down the street beneath the light of the full moon. Eros sighed, then slowly his form faded to a faint glow again. The windows of the room opened, and a breeze stirred the bed curtains. Then the windows closed, as if an invisible hand had moved them, and the room was silent and still once more.

Chapter 1

"Heavens, Cassandra, could you not have held your tongue?" cried Lady Hathaway. She pulled her shawl fretfully about her shoulders and eyed her oldest daughter with deep discontent. "I devoutly pray that you do not speak so—so unbecomingly when we go to the musicale tonight as you did just now!"

"But, Mama, I could not let people speak so harshly of Miss Matchett. Granted, Miss Matchett's style of dress is slightly dowdy, but she cannot help that. She does the best she can on the income she receives." Miss Cassandra Hathaway moved gracefully into the parlor with her mother and draped her own shawl upon the back of a chair before she sat down.

"I do not know how I shall show my face at Lady Amberley's ball next week," replied Lady Hathaway mournfully. She gazed at her daughter and sighed. At three-and-twenty, Cassandra was all that a mother could want in a daughter: accomplished, modest, good-hearted, and lovely to look upon. But she was also painfully blunt, and it was already bruited about that she was a bluestocking. It wanted but a week to the Season, and already Cassandra had attracted some male attention—from afar. Lady Hathaway greatly feared that Cassandra's impetuous speech and lack of dissembling would keep them there.

A concerned look crossed Cassandra's face and she leaned over and patted her mother on the arm in a comforting manner. "Never fear, Mama. I shall apologize for speaking so forwardly, and you may hold up your head with the best of them."

"And say you were much mistaken, too?" Lady Hathaway asked tentatively.

Her daughter looked at her, and a crease formed between her brows. "Whatever for? I believe I am not mistaken at all, and to say so would be a lie."

"Yes, well, my dear, sometimes one must make allowances—"

Cassandra's gaze turned reproachful. "Must I make allowances for cruelty? Have you and Papa not said many times that lying is wrong and cruelty worse?"

"Yes, of course, Cassandra, but, but . . ." Lady Hathaway drew to a faltering stop in the face of her daughter's attentive and inquiring expression. She sighed. How did one explain the need for discretion in society? It was not something her daughter had learned in the country or in all the lessons taught at her father's knee. "Well, I suppose I should be grateful that you remembered not to talk of your climbing boys."

Her daughter shifted in her seat and looked away.

"Oh, Cassandra! You have not taken in yet another one?"

Cassandra rose and her hands twisted together anxiously. "But, Mama, he was so little, and so hurt! He had sores on his feet and could hardly walk!" Tears formed in her eyes and she swallowed. "I have only sent four to the Dower house at home. Only four! And it does not take a great deal to feed and clothe them, I am sure."

Lady Hathaway gazed at her daughter, exasperated. "You have no idea how much it takes to feed children, especially boys! Why, I often feared your brother would eat us out of house and home when he was a child!" She pulled her shawl closer around her and sighed. "I suppose you are completely out of your pin money this quarter, too?"

Cassandra looked up at her mother and smiled. "Oh, no!

I have thought of a famous scheme! I wrote to our vicar last month and enlisted his aid. He was very approving of it, and so has got up a collection for the boys. So I only spent what it took to send little Tommy home."

Lady Hathaway groaned and sank into a chair.

"Is there something the matter, Mama?" Cassandra asked, a worried frown creasing her brow.

"No, of course not," Lady Hathaway replied, and she could not help the irony that crept into her voice. "Only that Vicar Thomason is one of the worst gossips in our county. I can depend upon him to spread the news of your generosity all over the village, and everyone will think you more of an eccentric than before. Heavens, why *do* you do these things, girl?"

Cassandra looked at her mother earnestly. "But if you had only seen little Tommy, Mama! He was so thin, and shaking with cold and pain. And that monster of a chimney sweep! He asked the most exorbitant price for him, and then he *hit* Tommy when the child did not come to me straightaway!"

Lady Hathaway's heart melted, though she kept her face stern. "Well . . . well, I suppose in this instance it would have been difficult to ignore. But, Cassandra, do try not to be so impulsive! And *don't* mention your activities to anyone in the *ton,* if you please!"

"But I do not see—"

The door opened, and Sir John wandered in, spectacles at the end of his nose, brandishing a dry quill. He looked vaguely about, and then his gaze sharpened as he spied his quarry. "Ah! Thucydides! Now how did it come to be in the parlor, and on this table? I know I had the book in my study yesterday." He gazed severely at his wife and daughter, as if somehow they had stolen into his inner sanctum and taken it for some nefarious purpose.

Lady Hathaway felt bewildered, but Cassandra smiled fondly at her father. "Papa, you know you brought it down this morning. You were looking for Euripides, and exchanged Thucydides for it."

"Oh, is that how it was?" Sir John's brow cleared, and his smile encompassed both Lady Hathaway and Cassandra in its beam. "Well, then, I shall be more careful, and not leave my books laying about." He put down his quill on the table, and picking up the book, he opened it. "Yes. Here it is . . ." he mused, and walked in the direction of the parlor door, leaving his quill behind.

"Oh, my love!" Lady Hathaway called to him.

"Eh?"

"I wish you would speak to your daughter!"

Sir John looked at his wife over his spectacles. "But I just did speak to her, my dear," he said reasonably.

"No, no! About her forwardness! Her lack of discretion!"

"What is this, my girl? Have you been seeing some man clandestinely?" He turned to Cassandra, his voice stern.

"Heavens, John!"

"Oh, no, Papa!"

"Well, what is it, then?" Sir John said impatiently.

"She is so . . . so impetuous in her speech!" Lady Hathaway said.

"And—?"

"Papa, I have taken in another climbing boy," Cassandra confessed. She looked at him earnestly and told him of her encounter with the chimney sweep. "Truly, I could not ignore his plight!"

Sir John's brow creased as he bent his powerful brain to the question. "Of course, you could not!" he said at last, and smiled proudly at his daughter. "That's my good girl!"

"But what of her reputation? Do you really think a well-connected gentleman would wish to marry a young woman who spends all her money on such things? It is not as if Cassandra's dowry were a fortune, after all!" Lady Hathaway protested.

Both husband and daughter looked at her with clear in-comprehension.

Lady Hathaway let loose a sigh that was almost a moan of despair. How was she to tame Cassandra's impulses when Sir John agreed with her? There were a number of re-formers amongst the *ton,* but they were people with a great deal of money and could afford such things. If it came to anyone's ears that Cassandra spent her allowance on climb-ing boys as if she considered them her sole responsibility, she would not only be seen as an eccentric but possibly a li-ability. Who would wish to marry a girl who would no doubt insist on bringing her charity cases along with her? Face, figure, and a good dowry would be as nothing com-pared with the burden of the climbing boys. It would be worse than marrying a young woman with a poverty-stricken family. Certainly it would be seen as a drain on the estate and the future of one's own family.

"Oh, heavens!" Lady Hathaway said, irritated. "You may do as you like, Cassandra, with your charity cases. But *don't* speak of them, if you please. It is not considered . . . polite conversation." Inspiration suddenly struck her and she smiled triumphantly. "Indeed, it would seem much like boasting of one's virtues, and you cannot think that would be at all becoming!"

Cassandra blushed and stared at her mother in consterna-tion. "Oh, no! I would never, never wish to puff myself off in that manner!"

"See that you do not, then," Lady Hathaway said sternly. She sighed in relief. Thank goodness! It was one less thing to worry about in company. She glanced at the clock on the mantelpiece and rose from her chair. "We will need to be at the musicale in the next hour. Do go up and ready your-selves for it—hurry! And don't forget your quill, husband, for you will come wandering down again and lose yourself for at least a half hour looking for it."

An hour later her irritation faded completely when she gazed at her eldest child. Cassandra's green eyes sparkled, her cheeks glowed, and her lips were parted with eagerness. And nothing could have been more demure or ladylike than her demeanor upon entering Mrs. Bostitch's house. Lady Hathaway bit her lower lip anxiously. Perhaps this time all would go well. Cassandra's bluntness and scholarship were only known at home, around and about Tunbridge Wells, and not yet in London. Surely, she had talked stringently enough with Cassandra so that she would guard her tongue and not speak with such alarming forthrightness. But Lady Hathaway remembered how her daughter had reprimanded Lady Amberly and could not dismiss her uneasiness. Well, Cassandra had not precisely reprimanded—perhaps "corrected" was the more accurate word. Lady Hathaway winced. "Corrected" was no better.

But there had been sympathetic looks from some of the other ladies. Perhaps the display of Cassandra's warmth of heart and sense of Christian charity for Miss Matchett had found favor with a few of the ladies who were Lady Amberley's equals. Who, after all, could fault a generous impulse?

Lady Hathaway sighed and could not help the uneasiness that lodged itself in her heart. She knew London society far better than either her husband or her daughter, and well knew that diplomacy often took one farther than honesty and good-heartedness.

The first faint sounds of the musicians tuning their instruments floated down the hall as the Bostitchs' butler led her, Sir John, and Cassandra to the conservatory. Cassandra looked up at her mother, anticipation clearly in her smile, and Lady Hathaway smiled in return. Perhaps it would not be so bad, she thought. Perhaps Cassandra would occupy her mind with the music and keep her comments to musical appreciation and away from any other subject.

Lady Hathaway sighed again. One could always hope.

Paul, Marquess of Blytheland, brushed the air in front of him with his hand, as if brushing away an annoying fly. He frowned. This had happened before. It was as if a warm draft of air briefly blew upon his face. Sometimes it was accompanied by a soft sound, like the fluttering of wings. He would not have thought much of it had it occurred out of doors, but it had lately happened indoors, at night, and now mostly just before a performance. Perhaps someone had opened a window. He shrugged and bent his attention upon his violin again.

An odd, sharp ache suddenly struck his chest, a sudden weeping agony, and the image of Chloe flashed before him. He drew in a long, slow breath, and then it disappeared. This was another thing that had happened before. He knew what this was, however. Every once in a while, when he was preparing to play his violin, the anticipated emotion of the music opened the wounds of the past, and painful memories of his wife would try to surface once again. He had always been successful in suppressing them—better now, for she had died more than two years ago. But that was the danger of playing music, was it not? Music was an emotional thing, after all. In fact, he had lately been very successful at using that emotion and putting it into his performances. That was the secret of an artist, a great musician once told him: using one's own pain and making it sing in one's music. Lord Blytheland smiled and raised his eyes to the guests waiting in front of him.

And his fingers failed on the strings of his violin. The instrument let out a small moan at being so mishandled, but the marquess ignored it.

She was not the most beautiful lady he had ever seen, but she was, indeed, very lovely. The lady caught him staring, blushed, then looked away. Blytheland recovered himself. He concentrated on tuning his violin, and accidentally twisted a pin too far. He cursed under his breath and glanced toward the lady again. She walked into the room with a slightly familiar, graying gentleman and a middle-aged lady who bore a strong resemblance to the young woman—her parents, no doubt. He would recall the name of the gentleman if he gave himself time to think of it. He twisted the pin again, and now it was too loose.

"May I be of assistance, my lord?" asked one of the musicians politely.

"What? Oh, no, my good man, just a little nervous."

The musician smiled as he bowed in assent. Blytheland at last tuned his violin correctly and tried not to look at the young woman in the audience.

He failed. She seemed almost to float within her dress, like a fairy woman walking through a mist of rose silk and silver net. She glanced at him from across the room, and there was something at once innocent and frank in her gaze. He wondered who she was.

He smiled to himself. It was often thus just before and during a performance. He had often thought the anticipation and sizzling energy he always felt as he prepared to play and when he was in the midst of a performance was similar to that of seduction. Music was a sensual thing that made the heart beat faster and made the mind fly in wild imaginings. It was easy to be influenced by the sight of a lovely woman when in such a state.

His smile turned bitter. Still, after two years, after his experience with Chloe, he was susceptible. How contemptible and weak he was! But he had learned to be discriminating, at least. All he needed was to find some fault with the woman and concentrate on that, and he would grow bored or contemptuous. There was nothing better than boredom or contempt to obliterate the beginnings of any interest he might feel. If his attention was still tied to the young woman by the end of the piece, he would be sure to obliterate it quite thoroughly.

I will be on my best behavior, Cassandra thought to herself, and will not worry Mama again. She sat down with her parents, fairly close to the musicians, feeling slightly em-

barrassed at her own behavior, but could not help glancing
from time to time at the violinist who had stared at her so
when she first came in. She gave herself a pinch. There!
You will *not* stare, because you know it is rude, and heaven
help you if Mama catches you doing it. She smiled, satisfied. She *could* be vigilant of her own behavior.

She rewarded herself with another glance at the violinist—it was just a glance, after all, not a stare. Of course, he
was not one of the professional musicians, for his clothes
were too fine for that. He affected a slightly more colorful
raiment than most other gentlemen she'd seen so far, but it
suited him. His golden hair was swept back and he wore a
coat of Bath superfine. His waistcoat was blue-and-silver
chased, and in the intricate folds of his neckcloth sparkled a
sapphire pin. If his collar was not so high as some she had
seen, perhaps it was because it would interfere with the
playing of his violin. Was he a dandy, perhaps? She saw
none of the padding to broaden the shoulders that so many
dandies used, however, and his knee breeches outlined his
legs—Cassandra looked away, blushing, and gave herself
another admonishing pinch. She was not merely glancing,
but *staring* again, and she must not do so, for she had
promised her mother to pay strict attention to her manners.

A tapping of the baton brought Cassandra's attention to
the musicians again. She felt irritated at herself. She had
been so intent on not looking at the man that she had
missed hearing who he was, and what the musicians would
play. Perhaps it was a piece she had heard before—she had
a good memory for music, and she would know the title as
soon as she heard the first few notes.

It was a Mozart divertimento. Cassandra sighed and
lifted her eyes to the violinist again; surely it was proper to
look at him while he was playing.

He was looking at her, and she could feel her face become warm. Once again she looked away, but not before
she noticed that he had blue eyes. The music! That is why

you came to the musicale, Cassandra told herself sternly.
Do pay attention!

The music flowed around her, and the high, sweet notes
pulsed an alluring andante beat. Once again she looked up,
and to her relief she saw the violinist was not looking at
her. Cassandra allowed herself to be pulled into the music,
as she always had in the past. And yet she could not feel
comfortable. The music seemed different somehow—that
was why she was feeling so strange. The rhythm became
slow, but at the end of the movement she felt breathless, as
if she had been running, and that had never happened to her
before. The violinist was a virtuoso, it was clear; it was the
skill and intensity of his performance that made her feel so.

And yet, the divertimento finished before she was quite
aware it had come near the end. Cassandra applauded politely, again annoyed at herself. She had not listened closely
as she had always done, but had been partly caught up in
watching the violinist. How stupid she was being! One
came to a musicale to listen to music, not to stare at the
company or the musicians.

The violinist bowed very elegantly to the crowd, and
then once again in her direction. Cassandra blushed and
looked down at her lap. Did he mean to do that?

"Quite excellent," Lady Hathaway commented. "It is almost a pity young Blytheland is a marquess. His talent out-
shines most professionals."

So, he is the Marquess of Blytheland, thought Cassandra.
And it seems Mama knows him—or knows of him. She
shook herself mentally. Really! Her thoughts were quite
wayward this evening. She looked up again and saw that
the marquess was no longer with the musicians. She firmly
tamped down a spark of disappointment. She was here to
listen to music, not think of possible beaux. Cassandra
smiled wryly to herself. As if someone as talented and
handsome as the marquess could be one of hers! She understood by now that she could not rate her attractions high at

all; to think that Lord Blytheland would—Sheer foolishness!

"Ah, Sir John! I hope I find you well?" said a soft baritone voice next to her. Cassandra looked up. It was the marquess.

"Eh? Oh, yes, Blytheland!" Sir John wiped his spectacles with the end of his neckcloth and put them on his nose again. "Quite well, quite well! And how does the duke, your father? I understand he has found a manuscript of great antiquity—an Arabic translation of *De Res Medicos*. I am not at all proficient in Arabic, however—Eh, what was that, my love?"

Lady Hathaway smiled sweetly at her husband. "My dear, I am sure Lord Blytheland would like to discuss his father's discovery at length—*later*."

Sir John's eyes focused at last upon his wife and daughter. "Ah, of course! Not enough time at a musicale."

"But perhaps at supper?" said the marquess. His gaze went to Cassandra, and he smiled at her. Cassandra could feel her face grow warm, but she could not help responding with one of her own. His smile was truly charming—it lifted up on one side of his mouth more than the other and gave him a slightly boyish look.

At his wife's nudge, Sir John looked at the marquess and his daughter. "Ah, yes! If you would permit me to introduce my wife and daughter . . ."

The marquess bowed most elegantly over Lady Hathaway's hand and Cassandra's. Perhaps it was her imagination, but did he linger just a little more over her hand than her mother's? His lips hovered just a few inches above her fingers before he rose from his bow. She could feel the warmth of his hand through her gloves, and when he released her hand she felt, almost, as if the warmth remained.

"I am most pleased to meet you, my lord," said Cassandra.

"And I, also. But I would be further pleased if you ac-

companied me to the supper later—if you would do me the
honor?" He looked to Sir John and Lady Hathaway for permission. Lady Hathaway smiled and nodded.

"Oh, yes!" Cassandra said, then blushed. "That is, I am
flattered that you ask me, sir. I would be happy to accompany you."

The marquess smiled at her again, bowed to Sir John and
Lady Hathaway, and left. Cassandra watched his passage
through the crowd. Could it be that he found her attractive?
It seemed that some men had found her so, since her arrival
in London. However, they never did call again after the
first couple of meetings. It was a surface, transitory thing
then, this apparent attraction, and not to be taken seriously,
she was sure.

She had never considered her looks before—it never
seemed important, and Papa had always taught her that true
beauty came from the mind and heart. But since they'd
come to town, the notion that one's physical appearance
had more than ordinary significance—aside from sheer aesthetic appreciation—to the world at large, kept intruding
upon her attention. Indeed, she was nigh infected with the
idea. Certainly, the marquess's appearance seemed to have
affected her in more than a purely aesthetic way. She shook
her head. How odd it was!

She felt a touch on her arm and found her mother gazing
sternly at her. "Now, Cassandra, when Lord Blytheland
comes to take you into supper, you must be all that is amiable and pleasant. And please do not blurt out every
thought that comes to your mind. Gentlemen do not find
that way of speaking at all attractive."

"Yes, Mama," Cassandra said.

A look of deep misgiving came over Lady Hathaway's
face.

"I will *try*, Mama!" Cassandra exclaimed. "Truly! Have I
not tried these past weeks?"

Lady Hathaway's expression softened. "I know you have

tried, my dear, and you have improved. But really, do be careful."

The sound of tuning instruments made Cassandra glance eagerly at the musicians again, and she gave her mother a hasty yes in reply. This time she heard the name of the piece—a violin sonata by Herr von Beethoven.

For the first time in her life, Cassandra could not keep her mind on the music playing before her. It was as if each sweet note conspired to make her think of Lord Blytheland and the way he looked, and smiled, and held her hand. It did not help at all when it was time for him to play the solo. His manner was cool and polite as he stood by the orchestra. But once he put the violin against his chest it seemed as if some otherworldly spirit seized him, for his bow and fingers attacked and caressed the strings and brought forth music that sang from heaven or cried up from hell—she knew not which.

Finally, after what seemed an age, the music stopped. Cassandra found she could breathe again in a normal fashion. She still looked at him, and it appeared as if his smile was just a little warmer in her direction when he bowed to the audience. She looked away, irritated at herself for blushing. How silly she was being! She was acting no differently than the shallow schoolgirls she'd known at the Bath girl's school she had stayed in—until, thankfully, Papa had rescued her. There was no education to gain there, Papa had said, and he was in the right of it.

She would speak honestly when they went into supper, she thought, determined to rid herself of the silliness that threatened to overcome her. If the marquess did not like it, why then she was certain Papa would say the man was unworthy of a man's—or woman's—esteem.

Cassandra felt a moment's unease when she remembered her mother's dictum. It was true she tended to speak before she thought. But this time, she would be careful of that. She would think through her responses before she spoke and make certain she spoke as carefully—as truly—as she could. There could be no offense in that.

Perhaps it was a slight noise or a little breeze stirred by his movement toward her, but Cassandra was suddenly aware of the marquess's presence. She looked up and found him smiling down at her.

"Shall we go in to supper, Miss Hathaway?"

Cassandra looked uncertainly at her mother, for her father had left her side to talk with an acquaintance, but Lady Hathaway merely smiled and nodded. "Of course, my dear, do go. Your father and I will follow you, as soon as I can tear him away from discussing his musical theories."

"Thank you, my lord, I shall be pleased to accompany you." Cassandra glanced at him. The marquess was still smiling at her, and she could not help smiling back. He took her hand in his own—gently, caressingly, as if it were some rare treasure. She rose, and he led her to the supper room.

Mrs. Bostitch had set up an informal supper, with little tables in the middle of the room and sideboards filled with delicacies next to the walls. The marquess led Cassandra to a small table set behind some palm fronds. Though the table was otherwise not secluded in any way, Cassandra felt as if the plants lent the table a certain intimacy. She smiled at herself. How fanciful she was becoming! Her parents were clearly in sight—she could see her mother standing patiently next to her father as he talked with his friend. Yet when she looked up at Lord Blytheland, she felt almost as if she were alone in a small room with him. There was something about his deep blue eyes, whose penetrating look seemed to read her heart as well as he surely read music. He said nothing, but seemed content for the while to look at her. His gaze seemed almost assessing—then he glanced away briefly, and she was sure she fancied the whole of it.

"You play beautifully, my lord," Cassandra said. She felt

she must say something, for his gaze and the silence had stretched out to an uncomfortable length. "I think the second movement of the sonata was especially well done."

"You are musical, then, Miss Hathaway?"

"Oh, I play the pianoforte, but I am in no way the virtuoso you are."

"You flatter me, ma'am."

Cassandra raised her eyes to his. "Oh, no, I never flatter. You must be quite an acclaimed musician, for I have heard many violinists, but you are far better than any I have heard so far."

Blytheland began to feel a touch of boredom. He had heard these words before, from other quite insipid misses. That was why he generally kept himself to older, much more sophisticated women—fast widows preferably. He wondered if Miss Hathaway was going to gush out further tedious little phrases. It was just as well if she did—that would be the flaw he would concentrate upon, and thus banish any incipient interest he might have. He let his gaze wander away from her.

"However, I did think you could have added a little more forte in the middle phrases of the first movement."

Blytheland returned his gaze swiftly to Miss Hathaway's face. Her expression was open and clear of guile or coquetry. Indeed, her brow creased in thought, and her eyes seemed to consider the subject seriously.

"How so?" He wondered how much of music Miss Hathaway really knew.

"Well, I have always believed that Herr Beethoven favored the pianoforte above any other instrument, and it is clear even in this sonata. However, it *is* a piano and *violin* sonata, and the composer gave the violin the opportunity to express itself in the middle phrases of the first movement by having the pianoforte play a less complex melody than the violin there. It was your opportunity to establish that this, indeed, was the violin's place. I felt you did not take complete advantage of the opportunity."

The marquess did not know whether to feel delighted or annoyed. He looked at her large green eyes, her soft pink lips, and delicate skin. She dressed in good taste and becomingly—not daringly—but well enough to enhance her charms and hint at more intriguing assets.

For now it could not hurt to be delighted, he decided.

"You are quite right, Miss Hathaway. That passage has always been a difficult one for me, and I tend to take it with more caution and less spirit than I should."

Miss Hathaway looked at him in a considering manner. "But you are clearly a most excellent musician. I would think you could easily overcome any difficulty and play it with ease."

He now saw she said this with no intention to flatter. She furrowed her brow as if she were working out a puzzle, and she stated her opinion simply, as if she expected her reasoning would be taken seriously.

Blytheland smiled. "I fear you vastly overrate my abilities."

She gazed at him, her eyes earnest. "Oh, no, my lord. I fear *you* vastly *underrate* your abilities. I am excessively fond of music, and I have never heard anyone quite as proficient as you are." She reached over in an impulsive gesture and pressed his hand. "You really should have more confidence in yourself, Lord Blytheland," she said kindly. "How else can you continue to improve?"

The marquess opened his mouth and then shut it, suddenly bereft of words. He wondered if she was aware that she praised and insulted in the same breath. And yet, he felt he could not take offense, for clearly she spoke nothing but what she perceived to be the truth, and clearly she meant well. A mischievous part of his mind wondered how other people took her blunt statements. It would be very, very amusing to see.

"Improve?" he said. "and I thought you said I was of virtuoso status! I am sorely cast down, Miss Hathaway." He
put on a look of extreme dejection.

He noticed she blushed wonderfully. "I did not mean—
That is to say—" She stopped, looked at him straightly, and
lifted her chin. "You, my lord, are a terrible tease."

"I?" He put on a wounded expression and spread his
hand over his heart. "My dear Miss Hathaway, how can
you say so?"

"Very easily! Do you have sisters?"

"Yes, I do."

"Then I daresay you were a menace to them."

"Not I! Rather the opposite. Never was a poor, helpless
boy so besieged by his termagant sisters."

"With reason, I am sure!" But her lips quivered upward.

"Ah, there you are!"

Blytheland turned to find that Lady Hathaway had arrived with Sir John in tow. Sir John had an abstracted air
about him, as if he were in profound thought. The lady
smiled benevolently at her daughter and the marquess.

"I am terribly sorry we were delayed," she said. "I hope
Cassandra has been keeping you entertained." Blytheland
noted wryly that she did not look sorry in the least. No
doubt she considered him a good "catch" for her daughter.
He would put an end to that notion, and soon . . . although
it could not hurt to linger in Miss Hathaway's presence for
just a little longer.

"Quite," he replied. "Miss Hathaway, I find, is a music
connoisseur." He turned to Miss Hathaway. "Do you play
your pianoforte often, ma'am?"

"Oh, I try, but it is nothing—not with the skill you have
at the violin, my lord." Miss Hathaway blushed, but the
marquess felt perhaps this was not false modesty. There
were very few ladies who played with much skill or talent,
after all.

"Perhaps I may ask that you play for me at some time,

Miss Hathaway?" Blytheland surprised himself. He did not
intend to say that at all. But as he looked into her beautiful
eyes, he could not help but continue. "Tomorrow, if it is not
inconvenient?"

Lord Blytheland cursed himself roundly as he put away
his violin and made ready to leave Mrs. Bostitch's house. If
he had any sense at all, he'd quit society and become a
monk. He'd only meant to seek out some flaw in Miss
Hathaway when he had introduced himself to her and her
family. Well, he'd found one, but had he concentrated upon
it and politely detached himself from her and his attraction
to her? No, he had not. Instead, he had asked to call upon
the Hathaways and asked to listen to Miss Hathaway play
the piano.

An image of Lady Hathaway's smug smile and eager
agreement that Miss Hathaway should play for him came
before him. He grimaced. Not only had he allowed himself
to be drawn into the Miss Hathaway's company, he had
raised Lady Hathaway's matrimonial hopes for her daughter. He sincerely hoped Miss Cassandra Hathaway was a
wretched pianist and he could depress any pretensions in
that quarter, and in her mother. He closed and latched his
violin case with a decided snap.

"Hit a sour note, old man?" said a familiar voice.

Blytheland looked up to see his friend Lord Eldon, and
he grinned. "No. Not that you'd notice if I did—which
makes me wonder why you are here, El."

"Oh, you know how it is with m'sister and the mater. It
isn't enough to have my younger brother caught in the parson's mousetrap—although I must say Susan is quite a
pretty little thing—they must have me caught, too." Lord
Eldon held up a hand. "And before you accuse me of being
led around by the nose by the females in my family, I came
only because St. Vire's here—damnably fond of music

these days, it seems—he told me he'd reveal the trick to trying a perfect Mathematical."

Blytheland eyed the impeccably tied neckcloth around his friend's collar. "Seems like you already know the trick, El."

Eldon looked pained. "One may always improve. A man of fashion does not rest on his laurels."

"Nor does he ignore the ladies when his mother tells him he needs to produce heirs."

Eldon gave a disappointed sigh. "How you malign me—" But a grin broke out on his face. "Well, there it is. If I don't see what's available in the marriage market this year, I'll never hear the last of it from the mater, and will have to leave town just to get out of earshot. Damned awkward, that, especially when I need to replenish my supply of waistcoats." He shrugged. "I'll just cast a glance at the usual gaggle at Almack's, tell the mater they're not worthy of the Eldon name, then spend the rest of my time at White's." He lifted an eyebrow at Blytheland. "Although I must say, the lady to whom you were so attentive was above the usual run of misses one sees in London these days. Thinking of giving another try at a nursery, Blythe?"

The marquess turned a sardonic eye to his friend. "Misery loves company, is that it? A nursery—hardly. Why you should think so is beyond me. Just because a man speaks with a young woman, it does not mean he's thinking of matrimony."

"True, true. But it seems she was accompanied by her parents . . . and I've not seen you go near a marriageable young thing in a while."

Blytheland shrugged. "Sir John Hathaway is a classical scholar, as is my father, and they are acquainted. Sir John wished to ask after an ancient manuscript, that is all."

"Of course." Lord Eldon grinned widely.

"Stubble it, El." The marquess picked up his violin case

and gave his friend an irritated glance before stalking from the room.

"Anything you say, Blythe," Eldon called after him and chuckled.

Eros kept himself fairly insubstantial and hovered near the ceiling so that his glow would blend with that of the chandelier's candlelight. Well, he had done it, and he was quite satisfied. He had known for a long time that Miss Cassandra Hathaway would be the right mate for Lord Blythcland, although it had taken him three tries to do it. He had hit the marquess each time, but for some reason, the man had seemed unmoved, as if he had not seen Cassandra at all. Instead, he had had a brief affair with some other woman, over in less than a month.

The thought that something was quite wrong with the marquess had definitely occurred to Eros, and even now made him feel a little uneasy. He shook his head and grinned. Well, it was of no matter now; Lord Blytheland had seen Cassandra at last, and certainly must have fallen in love with her.

Chapter 2

"Cassandra," said Psyche, "do listen to me."

Cassandra turned slowly toward her younger sister as if pulled unwillingly from a delightful dream. She looked at the girl blankly.

"I am sorry, Psyche. Did you say something?"

"Only that you have knotted your fringe in a terrible tangle."

"Oh, have I?" Cassandra looked down in her lap at the fringe she was trying to make. Her face suddenly lost its dreamlike expression and she let out an exasperated sigh. "Oh, good heavens! So I have." She turned a rueful smile to her sister. "Dear Psyche, do be a good child and unknot this for me. You know how terrible I am at fringing, and you are so good at disentangling things."

"I don't know why you even try fringing at all, Cassandra," Psyche said, taking the piecework from her sister and curling up in an armchair by the parlor fire. She carefully started picking it apart. "I thought you had given it up long ago."

"Well, I thought it might be good for me. Mama says that fine work helps keep one even-tempered."

"I do not see how she can say that," Psyche replied, cocking her head to one side in a considering manner. "I have always been good at needlework, but Mama always says I am too unruly for words." She gazed assessingly at Cassandra. "And why do you need to be even-tempered?"

Psyche had always thought that Cassandra must be the best-behaved young lady ever, for she never got into trouble like she herself did.

"Oh, goodness, I don't know! I truly do not know what came over me—I detest fringing." Cassandra rose from her chair and poked at the fire in the grate.

"Harry says it's the marquess." Psyche nodded her head wisely.

"Really, Psyche, how can you say so?" She turned around and faced her sister. Psyche smiled privately to herself. She'd be willing to wager that the pink in Cassandra's cheeks was *not* caused by the heat of the fire alone.

"Well, Cassandra, I don't. That's what *Harry* says."

"You know very well that your Harry is purely imaginary. And you also know Mama does not like you to speak about him—it! You are all of twelve, Psyche, and should have outgrown your pretend playmate long ago."

"He isn't pretend. Besides, Papa believes me."

"Oh, I daresay Papa thinks you are speaking in metaphors." Cassandra walked to the pianoforte and absently toyed with a melody.

"No he doesn't, and Papa does believe me—he told me so!" Psyche retorted. "Not only that, but Harry is here right this minute, turning the pages of—what is it? Oh, it's Aristophanes."

Cassandra turned to look at the open book Psyche pointed to across the room. It sat on a table close to the window. As she watched, a page flipped over. She started, but then recovered.

"Oh, nonsense, Psyche! It is only that this house is dreadfully drafty. It is merely a breeze—and yes, look here—someone's left the window open." Cassandra closed it with a snap.

"Window or no, Cassandra, you must admit that some things have come about that you couldn't account for."

"Such as—?"

"Our butler and housekeeper. They used to have dreadful rows belowstairs, and now the maids say the Thrimbles act like a new-wed pair. Harry told me he detested their noise and so he shot his arrows at them."

Cassandra smiled kindly. "I think it was more the books on marriage Vicar Thomason asked me to give them, Psyche, than any of Harry's arrows." She let out an exasperated breath. "Oh, now you have me talking of him—it!—as if Harry were real!" Her eyes settled on the clock upon the mantelpiece. "Oh, heavens! I must change my dress! I think the mar—That is, we will be having callers soon." Gathering up her skirts, Cassandra rushed out the door.

"I told you."

Psyche put down the fringe and looked at the boy sitting on the table near the window. She made a face at him. "So you did. But I really wish you would let another one of my family see you, too!"

Harry leaned back, clasping one knee in his hands, and his wings waved lazily. He grinned. "You needn't talk about me, you know. Then there would be nothing for them to disbelieve."

"How can I stop when you pinch housemaids, for instance? And Kenneth was unjustly accused of it, too!"

"I do not pinch housemaids," Harry replied loftily. "It was only *one* housemaid. Besides, it is not as if your brother hasn't pinched housemaids himself—and got away with it."

"Well, I think it's beastly of you—whatever did that poor maid do to you?"

"Oh, nothing—more's the pity," Harry said. He looked up at the ceiling, folded his wings, and looked quite angelic.

Psyche put her hands on her waist. "Don't come the innocent with me, Harry! I know you must have been up to mischief!"

"Not I! I was only seeing that justice was done."

"What, by pinching the maid?"

"No, by seeing that your brother was accused of it. I find it unfair that any number of housemaids have fallen head-over-tails in love with Kenneth, and all he does is steal a kiss and pinch them."

"I should hope that is all he does with them! Mama and Papa would be quite angry if he fell in love and ran off with one of them!"

Harry smiled in a superior manner. "You are such an innocent, Psyche. But never fear. I will make sure he will do nothing scandalous."

She looked at him suspiciously, then sighed. "Well, at least Papa likes to hear of you."

"He likes to hear *stories* of me, you mean."

"Do you think, then, that he does not believe me, either?" Psyche felt a little bereft at that. It was a lonesome sort of thing to have a dear friend and not be able to introduce him to anyone else.

"Oh, he would like to, but he believes you have a fine imagination and would make a good writer of improving tales for children someday." Harry grinned mischievously. Psyche looked reprovingly at him. He had been eavesdropping again, she was certain, and she never did feel quite right about it—although she had to admit it did have its uses.

"Well, I cannot see why he should think that," Psyche replied, wrinkling her nose. "I detest improving tales." She sighed. "But Papa does like to believe the best of us, and so perhaps he has forgotten that I do not like such stories." Psyche gazed at Harry questioningly, hoping that he might enlighten her as to her father's state of mind.

Harry shrugged his shoulders and looked bored. He opened the window that Cassandra had just closed and looked out at the street. A small breeze lifted one lock of his golden hair and a ray of sun suddenly broke through the clouds to shine upon his face. He glanced at her and smiled.

Psyche smiled back. She was glad he had decided to come with her to London, for otherwise she'd be bored to tears. Sometimes she would accompany Mama and Cassandra on a shopping expedition or drive to one of the parks. But aside from these activities and her discovery of many delightful Minerva Press novels, as well as attending to Cassandra giving her lessons in geography and the Italian language, there was little for Psyche to do. So she was thankful that Harry was here. There is nothing like a change in one's circumstances, she thought, to make one appreciate one's friends. And Harry was her very best friend, for she had known him ever since she was a very little girl.

She'd been about seven years old at the time—really not much more than a baby. She'd been with her older brother Kenneth near the lake at their country home. Awaking from a doze in the sun, she had found that Kenneth had either hidden himself or had left her alone, and it was growing quite dark. Crying because she could not find her way back home, she stumbled into the woods that circled part of the lake and grew more frightened.

And then there he was. Psyche had thought he was one of those angels her nurse had told her about, for he had white wings and wore white clothing. But he had laughed at her and shook his head when she asked him this, and he told her his name. Well, it was hard to get her tongue around it then, so she had called him Harry instead, and never bothered to change it.

He grew up, as she did, although he seemed always to be a few years older than she was—he looked to be twelve or thirteen years of age now, although he would never tell her how old he actually was. She had learned more about him, however, not so much from Harry, for he found such things tedious to relate—but from her father's books. He looked a little like the pictures in those books, although his nose didn't come down straight from his forehead like the people depicted in them had, but it looked like her own quite normal one.

She wished the rest of her resembled Harry, for she was short rather than tall, and instead of blue eyes and blond hair, she had a mop of unruly red curls and large, undistinguished gray eyes. She'd learned that his dress—for it looked like a very short dress, indeed—was called a chiton. Psyche thought that perhaps she should have been embarrassed that his bare legs showed, or when he'd unpin one shoulder of his chiton when he shot his arrows, but he was Harry, and she'd known him for so long that it did not matter. But his arrows! Those were another thing altogether.

In fact, Harry was pulling one from his ever-present quiver right now, his gaze intent on something in the street below. A wide, crooked grin was forming on his lips. Psyche knew that grin, and alarm flashed through her.

"Harry, what *are* you doing? Get away from that window!"

It was too late. He drew back his bow and loosed the arrow before she could rush to his side.

"A hit!" he crowed. "Two with one shot!"

"Oh, Harry!" Psyche cried.

She leaned out the window to see whom he had struck. There! A tall young man held a fainting lady in his arms. The arrow had apparently hit the young man through the arm and scratched the lady as well. Psyche could see the arrow fading from sight as she watched.

"*Ma chère* Stephanie!"

"Oh, Phillipe, Phillipe!"

They kissed passionately while onlookers made a wide berth around them. Some people cheered. Psyche blushed and covered her eyes.

"Oh, Harry, how could you? In broad daylight and in the middle of the street as well!" She looked at him reproachfully through her fingers.

"*They* don't seem to mind," Harry said carelessly. He

twirled another arrow between his fingers in a negligent manner, a lazy smile on his face.

Psyche peeked between her fingers at the entwined couple again, this time with more interest. She had rarely seen Harry shoot people or the immediate after-effects of one of his arrows; it had been very embarrassing to watch usually well-behaved people kiss and act in a very silly manner. She'd mostly only seen Harry's complacent reaction after he'd made a successful hit. She had become a little curious lately, however, for she had once caught her parents kissing—briefly—and she supposed it was something adults did from time to time. "Did it hurt them? Your arrows do look sharp, you know."

"Mortals are too dense to feel much. They felt nothing— not the arrows, that is."

"My, it did act quickly, didn't it?"

"I've told you it does."

"Well, you are wont to boast, Harry, you know you are!"

"Not I! I am in general very truthful."

She made a face at him, then leaned against the windowsill next to him to get a better look at the pair outside. "Do they breathe much when they do that, Harry?"

"Very much. They usually gasp like fish."

"Good heavens, Psyche! Stop acting like a hoyden and remove yourself from that window!"

Psyche jerked upright immediately at her mother's voice and bumped her head on the casement handle. She rubbed her temple gingerly. "Yes, Mama," she said and stepped quickly away from the window. She could not help casting a glance at Harry, who was still watching the scene below.

"What *were* you looking at?" Lady Hathaway said, going to where Psyche had stood. She leaned over and peered out the window, then straightened herself suddenly. "Scandalous! In broad daylight! I do believe it is—My word. Mademoiselle Lavoisin and the Comte de la Fer. I never would have thought it, although they do make a handsome couple. The last I heard, they were at daggers drawn with each other! One would think that well-born emigrés would comport themselves with more discretion! However, they *are* French." Lady Hathaway turned, a small smile of triumph on her lips. "And Hetty Chatwick is out of town today! Well, I shall have something to tell *her* for a change!"

Lady Hathaway's gaze encountered her youngest daughter, and her smile abruptly disappeared. Her eyes became stern. "And what, may I ask, were you doing staring—yes, staring!—at such shocking behavior?"

"Well, Har—" began Psyche, but Harry shook his head at her. "That is, I heard a scream, and I thought someone was injured! So naturally, I looked to see if someone was indeed hurt, so I could call for help if it were needed."

Her mother's eyes narrowed in a considering manner. Psyche held her breath.

Lady Hathaway smiled then, though her eyes still held a bit of sternness. "I shall let it go this time, child, for I know you are a good girl at heart. But please! You *must* try to comport yourself with more decorum, and *not* stare or lean out of the window no matter what may be occurring in the streets! Although, I must say," Lady Hathaway mused, "that such shocking behavior would make anyone stare, to be sure! The Comte de la Fer, of all things! And I had thought him very ancient regime in his manners."

"Oh, Mama, I am so sorry!" cried Psyche, feeling tears come to her eyes. She ran to her mother and put her arms around her. She felt terrible that she had lied, for she never liked to do so. She cast Harry a burning look, and he had the grace to look ashamed.

"Now, now, my dear girl, there is nothing to cry about. You take these things too much to heart, Psyche." Lady Hathaway smiled and smoothed her daughter's hair back fondly. "My, your hair does go every which way, does it not? Do go up and get it brushed properly, love. The Marquess of Blytheland is calling on Cassandra! Can you believe it? I shall allow you to come for a short while, but you must only speak when spoken to! He has come to see Cassandra, and I do hope she minds her tongue for once."

"I am very glad Cassandra has an admirer, Mama. She is a very good girl, isn't she? So she deserves someone who will love her as we do," Psyche said loyally.

Lady Hathaway sighed. "I certainly hope so. Now do go, Psyche and tidy yourself."

Psyche went out of the parlor, with Harry trailing behind. She did not look at him.

"Psyche."

Silence.

"Psyche, don't be angry with me."

The girl turned and looked at her friend. "You made me lie to Mama."

"You know it was for the best, Psyche! You would have received a terrible scold about making up stories, and you would have been sent up to your room."

Harry's face looked solemn and sad. Psyche's heart melted. She could never stay angry with him for long. "Well, I suppose it wasn't so horrid. Let's go up, then."

"May I come to see this marquess of Cassandra's?"

Psyche looked warily at him.

"It's only to see what sort of man he is—if he truly deserves to be Cassandra's suitor."

"Oh . . . very well, then. But no tricks! And promise you will leave your arrows behind."

"I? Tricks?"

"Harry!"

Harry sighed. "I promise."

Chapter 3

When Thrimble, the butler, announced the marquess, my lord saw no one in the parlor except a young, mop-haired girl. He felt slightly put out, even though he was only a little earlier than usual for the *ton's* afternoon calling hours. Then he remembered that Sir John was considered rather provincial in his habits and perhaps kept different hours. Annoying, that, but understandable.

He looked at the girl, who had stood up from her chair at his entrance. He thought she must be Miss Hathaway's sister, for though her hair was a decided red, her eyes and nose had the same shape as the elder Miss Hathaway's. She looked at him, her expression uncertain and shy. He wondered if she was mute, for she simply stared at him, and as the minutes ticked by on the mantelpiece clock, her face grew anxious and urgent. She wriggled her nose and grimaced, as if she had something to say but could not. Well, the least he could do was introduce himself and see if she responded.

"The younger Miss Hathaway, I presume?" Lord Blytheland said, smiling, and bowed. "I am Paul Templeton, Marquess of Blytheland, here to call upon your mother and sister."

An expression of profound relief crossed the girl's face, and she sketched a competent curtsy. "Yes, sir—that is, my lord. I am Psyche Hathaway. Please be seated. Mama and Cassandra should be here shortly."

His smile turned into a wide grin. "I see your father is truly the complete classicist." He sat down in a comfortable chair by the window.

The girl rolled her eyes toward the ceiling. "Yes, my lord."

Blytheland chuckled. "Fathers can be a burden, can they not? My father is also fond of the classics."

"But *you* do not have to suffer under a name like mine!"

"Ah, but here's something I do not tell everyone: my middle name is Xanthus."

"Oh, dear." Psyche made a face, then looked contrite. "It is not a terrible name, about as bad as my own, really. But at least it's not your *first* name," she said consolingly.

"Certainly, I may be thankful for that!" Blytheland laughed, reflecting that the elder Miss Hathaway was not the only blunt one in the family. A slight noise made him look up and he rose immediately, for the door opened and Cassandra entered, Lady Hathaway following her. He caught his breath.

He had thought perhaps his perception of Miss Hathaway's charms might have been partly due to his imagination. Blytheland had known times when, caught up in the afterglow of a successful violin piece, he'd overestimate the attractions of a woman. He had not done so this time. Indeed, the sun that had finally broken through the clouds shone through the windows and showed all that the dim lights of candles might have hidden—but there was nothing to hide. The soft curve of her cheek, the large and dark-fringed eyes, the pink lips, and the long, smooth column of her throat seemed to glow as she moved gracefully through the sunlight toward him.

"Your servant, Miss Hathaway," the marquess breathed, and raised her hand to his lips.

She blushed and glanced at her mother, who raised her brows but smiled nevertheless. Blytheland felt annoyed at himself for going so far as to kiss her hand, and was glad at his annoyance. It gave him a measure of control over his reactions, and he vowed he'd not give Lady Hathaway reason to raise her brows or smile in that matchmaking way again. He would keep in mind that Miss Hathaway was a bluestocking, perhaps even as extreme in her views as Chloe had been. He'd finish calling upon the Hathaways, and never come near Miss Cassandra Hathaway again.

Bowing to Lady Hathaway, he said, "I find you and your family well, ma'am?"

"Quite well, thank you, my lord. I see you have been talking with Psyche. I hope she has not prattled on too long." She gave an inquiring look at her youngest daughter.

"Oh, no, Mama. I did just as you said. I did not say a word when Lord Blytheland came in until I was spoken to," Psyche said earnestly.

"Oh, for goodness sakes, child!" Lady Hathaway exclaimed, flustered. "Did you not even greet him? I certainly did not mean—Oh, heavens!"

The marquess grinned. "She was not to speak until spoken to, eh? So that was what all your silent grimacing was about. You looked as if you were about to burst, Miss Psyche!"

A choking sound caught his ear, and he looked at Cassandra. Her shoulders were shaking, and she had her hand over her mouth to stifle her giggles. Her laughing eyes met his, and there was no self-consciousness there, but an invitation to laugh along with her at her sister's literal interpretation of Lady Hathaway's dictum.

"Well, I *felt* I was about to burst, my lord," Psyche replied. "I wished so badly to make you welcome, but Mama said not to speak until—"

"Yes, yes, I do remember what I said," her mother said hastily. "My word, child, must you take me so literally?"

"But I—"

"Perhaps you should go upstairs now. I am sure there are some lessons for which you need to study."

"But I thought Cassandra was going to play the pianoforte. Could I not stay for that—just for a little while?" Psyche looked hopefully at Lord Blytheland and Cassandra, obviously abandoning any hope of support from her mother.

"Of course," Lord Blytheland said, earning a grateful smile from Psyche.

"Oh, do let her stay, Mama," Cassandra entreated. "You know how quiet she is when there is any music. I know she will behave quite properly."

"Very well, then. But mind, Psyche, no fidgeting or interruptions!" Lady Hathaway settled herself in a chair and bade her guest to choose a comfortable seat.

"Oh, no, Mama!" Psyche said, all smiles.

The conversation before the music would normally have been tedious for Psyche, for it was all about people she did not know. She glanced at Harry, glad for his presence, for she would have been hard put to keep her promise not to fidget otherwise.

"Harry," she murmured almost under her breath, even though she was at quite a distance from her mother, "what do you think of him?"

Harry looked at her admiringly. "You become better and better at not moving your lips at all when you speak."

"Do I?" Psyche said, pleased.

"Yes. I remember a man once who could do that. He could even make his voice seem to come from objects at a distance from him."

"No, really? I should like to do that someday."

"What was interesting," Harry continued, "was that he had two heads and traveled about in a raree show." He gave her a wicked smile.

"You are the most detestable boy imaginable! I do not have two heads!"

"I never said you did!"

"Did you say something, Psyche?" Lady Hathaway called.

Harry shot Psyche a warning look.

"No, Mama." Psyche made herself look as innocent as possible. She sighed and sipped the tea the butler had brought in. Telling lies was becoming quite easy lately. Her mother smiled at her and returned to the conversation.

"Really, Harry, you are provoking!" Psyche whispered. He opened his mouth to retort, but she shook her head slightly. "Now enough! What do you think of Lord Blytheland?"

Her friend, wings motionless from concentration, stared at the marquess, then frowned. "I can't have made another mistake . . . no, there must be something wrong with him."

"Whatever can you mean?"

"Only look at him. He is obviously attracted to your sister, but he resists it. It is not something I like at all."

Psyche felt uneasy. Harry could be the most amiable boy imaginable, but he took certain things quite personally, especially when it came to the way gentlemen and ladies behaved toward one another. He was staring at both Cassandra and Lord Blytheland in a most intent way, as if trying to solve a puzzle. His frown deepened.

"Perhaps we should tell Mama that he is not really a good match for Cassandra," Psyche said. She felt a little uneasy. Harry could be very persistent if things did not go the way he wished.

Harry shook his head. "He *is* a good match. I never make a mistake about such things." A brief, uncomfortable look flashed across his face, but he continued. "He is arrogant, Psyche. It's hubris, and *that* is always offensive to me."

Psyche was not entirely sure what hubris was, but it was not something one did or had without getting Harry and his relatives irritated. Her uneasiness grew. She remembered the stories her father had told her about Harry's relatives, and began to wonder if the marquess would end up turned into a tree, or chained to a rock and eaten by vultures. However, she was certain there were no vultures in England, so perhaps his punishment would not be so very severe. There were ducks, though. She tried to envision death by duck, but it did not seem very much the same as death by vulture, somehow.

Harry made a short, angry sound, so startling Psyche out of her thoughts that she almost upset her tea. She looked at him and watched his expression grow more stormy as he gazed at Lord Blytheland.

"He believes he is invulnerable when he truly is not. In a way, he is a little like your brother Kenneth, who pinches maids and kisses them, but never does anything else. Blytheland tells himself he does not need a wife, is not in love with your sister, and that he is looking for more than what she has to offer as either wife or lover." He looked solemnly at her.

"Are you saying he will pinch Cassandra?" Psyche gnawed her lower lip. She had thought the marquess a very amiable sort of gentleman. She could not imagine him pinching anyone, much less her sister.

Harry suddenly grinned. "If only he would! Then I would not need to give him the punishment he deserves for his arrogance. Your sister would give him such a set-down that he would need a shovel to dig himself out of the ground."

"Then where is the trouble?"

"Look at Cassandra."

Psyche turned in her chair. Her sister's gaze was intent on Lord Blytheland's face, drinking up his words as if they were some life-sustaining elixir.

"Is she in love with him?"

"Of course, though she does not know it quite yet."

"Of course? Why is that?" Psyche looked suspiciously at him. "You didn't!"

"No, I did not shoot any of my arrows at her!" Harry said

indignantly. "Your sister doesn't need any. I shot my arrows at *him*. And he has such arrogance that he refuses to give in to them."

Psyche looked at him, horrified. "You *didn't*!"

"Yes I did." Harry smiled in a satisfied way. "It was when your sister and your parents went to the musicale. I'm certain he fell instantly in love with your sister, but he is a stubborn case. He has overcome my arrows before, but this time I'll make certain he does not."

"You *always* think people are arrogant when they resist you, Harry! You *shall* change him back!"

Harry frowned. "Why should I? He's eligible enough, and Cassandra is not opposed to his attentions at all. Only look at him! Would he not make a perfect husband for her? He is handsome, plays exquisite music, and is quite intelligent. Also, he is wealthy and has a title. Few females can resist that."

"Cassandra is *not* mercenary!"

"But you cannot deny his other assets would influence her."

Psyche looked at the marquess again. She had to admit he was quite handsome, and Cassandra was excessively fond of music. She creased her brow in thought. "He *is* amiable, even if he is rather old. He must be all of thirty. Hmm. It is not as if she would know the difference, after all." She shook her head. "No, I cannot like it, Harry. You must change him back. I am quite right about such things."

"He is six-and-twenty. *That* is not old, Psyche," Harry replied, smiling. "At least, not for your sister."

"No. Mama thinks that Cassandra is nearly on the shelf, so she must be getting a bit on, don't you think?"

Harry's smile widened into a grin. "Not really. You will understand when you are turned three-and-twenty."

Psyche made a face. "I do wish you wouldn't talk to me as if you were so much older than I am. *You* can't be any more than fourteen, if that."

"But I am much—".

"And I still think you should change him back." Psyche stared at him sternly. Harry was very good at distracting her from her purpose, and she knew he was doing it now, but she knew better than to let it go too far.

"No." He stared back at her, his chin thrust out stubbornly.

"Then I will tell Cassandra what you have done."

Harry smiled sweetly at her. "She won't believe you."

Psyche stared at him again, but he only stared back defiantly. She could try not talking to him again, but sooner or later he'd say something and she'd forget about it. Perhaps she could think of a way of persuading him later. She sighed and shrugged her shoulders.

"Well, for now, let us listen to the music. Cassandra has learned a new piece by Herr von Beethoven. She told me it is called 'Sonata in F minor,' " she said, proud that she had remembered it.

When the first notes broke the parlor's silence, Blytheland sat up abruptly, recognizing the music at once: the "Appassionata." It was not at all a feminine piece to play, and when he glanced at Lady Hathaway's disapproving face, he saw that she thought so, too. And yet, gazing at Miss Hathaway, he felt not disapproval but despair that he had come to listen to her play, and that she had chosen this music.

Cassandra's eyes had widened, absorbed and intent upon the keyboard. Blytheland watched her fingers fly over the keyboard, sure and practiced. Her technique was excellent, her talent superior to any young lady's he had heard so far. He had hoped that she would play poorly, that her apparent knowledge of music was false.

But it was not so. For she was clearly caught up in the music, as he often was himself when he bowed his violin. And passion! Her hands pounded it from the keyboard, and her fingers coaxed it out to shimmer hotly in the air. A single curl fell forward onto her brow, and Blytheland closed his hands against the feeling that he must brush it back. He made his body still and forced himself to sit in a negligent manner on his chair. But his mind was not still and he envisioned himself brushing back the curl, his fingers feathering across her cheek and tracing the outline of her lips before his own lips followed. Her mouth would open under his, and she'd respond with, yes, passion. Her slender fingers that now slipped amongst the keys would slip downward from his chest and—

With a last flourish, Miss Hathaway was done, and the pianoforte fell silent. Blytheland blinked, suddenly released from his imaginings, and drew in a deep breath. He saw Cassandra cast an uncertain glance at Lady Hathaway, and at her mother's meaningful look, she bit her lip and looked worried. He stood up abruptly.

"Truly masterful, Miss Hathaway! An excellent rendition of the sonata." Before Lord Blytheland could stop himself, he strode to her and lifted her fingers to his lips. He did not need to look up to see Lady Hathaway's smug look—he could well imagine it was there. He mentally cursed himself, but put a smile on his face. "It is not what I would expect a young lady to play, but it was very well done."

Instantly, Miss Hathaway's look of pleasure at his words faded, and he regretted his words. After she gave another apologetic glance at her mother, she smiled briefly and murmured, "You are too kind, my lord."

An odd, twisting sensation went through his chest for a moment as he looked into her eyes. "No, I am far too moderate. In truth, you are an excellent musician, and I would welcome a chance to play a duet with you." The words came from his mouth before he could stop himself. It does not matter, he told himself, gazing at Miss Hathaway's now sparkling eyes and softly smiling mouth. Besides, it was not as if he were declaring himself by wishing to play a duet with the chit. It was merely that she was an excellent musician. He would want to play a duet with any musician of her caliber.

Miss Hathaway blushed and pulled her hand from his, and he mentally cursed himself again for holding her hand for so long. "Oh, to be sure I—that is to say—you flatter me. I would be pleased to join you in—in practicing music."

He raised his eyes and caught Lady Hathaway's not-quite-concealed look of triumph. However, it would not do to seem too eager. He smiled coolly at them both and bowed to Lady Hathaway.

"I hope I do not impose, ma'am."

"Oh, heavens, no, Lord Blytheland. Why, you need only say when you wish to practice with Cassandra, and I shall set aside the time." Lady Hathaway's face was wreathed in smiles.

Of course you will, he thought wryly, and ignored her expectant look. Really, it seemed he was digging a deeper hole for himself than he had thought he would. Well, it was not as if he hadn't got himself out of worse situations. He turned to Miss Hathaway.

"Do you go to Lady Marchmont's ball, Miss Hathaway?"

"Why yes, I believe we do." Cassandra smiled shyly up at him. "Shall we see you there, my lord?"

He picked up his hat, bowed over Lady Hathaway's hand, and then Cassandra's. "Perhaps," he said, and smiled. There. He had promised nothing, and when he did not appear at the Marchmonts' ball, both the Hathaway ladies would have no one to blame but their own expectations for any disappointment they might feel.

If he had thought Miss Hathaway beautiful before, he was mistaken. The smile that parted her lips also delicately blushed her cheeks and seemed to light her eyes from within, and he could not help staring at her again.

"Oh, Lord Blytheland, I do hope I—we shall see you there."

Her voice made him blink and he hastily released her hand. He really should try not to be so influenced by music. He smiled once more and bowed before he left.

Chapter 4

"Oh, heavens, Cassandra, do hurry and change your dress!" cried Lady Hathaway two days after, waving a calling card at her daughter. Cassandra looked at her mother, startled. "He has come to ask you for a drive in the park—Blytheland!"

"Oh!" Cassandra's heart beat a little faster and an odd confused feeling came over her.

Lady Hathaway turned to the butler. "And, Thrimble, take Lord Blytheland to the drawing room and offer him refreshment while he waits. I shall be down as soon as I tidy myself." The butler left and Lady Hathaway glanced at Cassandra. "What, are you still here? Silly girl! Go up, quickly! I will be with you directly to see that you dress as you ought."

"But, Mama, my errand—"

"Never mind, Psyche and I will attend to it. Just *go*!"

Cassandra hurried up the stairs, wondering why her mother seemed so impatient of late. Her mother rarely dictated what she wore, for she trusted that Cassandra would choose her clothes carefully, and with an eye to modesty. Well, she would be careful to do just that; surely Mama would be pleased.

But she was quite wrong. She had chosen a simple walking dress with a light woolen pelisse, which covered her from chin to toe, very pretty, too. But the moment Lady

Hathaway caught sight of Cassandra's clothes, she frowned.

"No, no, Cassandra, not that one! You must wear your new walking dress, the one with the frill at the collar."

Cassandra glanced out the window at the partly cloudy sky and looked at her mother doubtfully. "But, Mama, I thought that one might be a little light for this weather."

"Nonsense!" Lady Hathaway said firmly. "You can see the clouds disappearing. And if you think you will feel a chill, you may wear this black velvet spencer on top of it."

"But it buttons only underneath the bosom! What if a wind should come up?"

"If a wind comes up, you may wrap yourself with your shawl."

"Mama, I do not think the dress quite matches the spencer," Cassandra replied, gazing at her mother and feeling very puzzled. How odd! She could not account for it. Mama had told her all her life to wrap herself up warmly in case a chill breeze should arise, but now she was insisting on a dress and spencer that was not as appropriate as what she had been wearing.

"Well, then, you shall start a fashion," Lady Hathaway said firmly.

Cassandra cast her mother another puzzled look, then sighed and turned to her maid to change her dress.

At last she was done dressing, and Cassandra could not help glancing at her mother a little suspiciously. The green walking dress was well enough; it had a large white frill that draped around the back collar of the dress and outlined the low neckline in front. But the spencer was a little smaller than she remembered it to be and felt tight about her chest. There must be a reason she was told to wear these clothes, but Cassandra could not tell what it could be from Lady Hathaway's proud and satisfied gaze. She smiled at her mother. Surely it was nothing, and surely she must appear quite well; her mother would not look so proud, else.

But then they entered the parlor, and after Lord Blytheland smiled, stood, and bowed over Lady Hathaway's hand, he bowed over Cassandra's as she curtsied . . . and he seemed to stop breathing for a moment before he rose, slowly. Then he met her eyes.

His eyes should not be blue, Cassandra thought as she looked into them. Blue was a cold color, and the emotion that showed in his eyes was hot, and caused heat to rise from the pit of her stomach to her face. It frightened her a little, for she did not want to turn away; she wanted to stare and stare at him, and it was a strange, unfamiliar feeling. His smile faded, and his gaze traveled slowly down from her face and up again.

Cassandra looked down as well, and her face heated even more. He was still holding her hand and—oh, heavens! Her spencer, which had seemed perfectly respectable when she had first put it on, had shifted her dress about during her descent to the parlor, and now gaped open more than it ever used to. She shot an agonized glance at her mother, but all she received in return was a smile and a nod, as if Lady Hathaway was oblivious to her state of dress.

"Please . . ." she whispered and tugged at her hand. A startled look crossed the marquess's face and he hastily released her. Lord Blytheland smiled again, but his mouth looked a little strained at the corners. He took a step back, putting his hands behind him.

He cleared his throat. "I am happy, Miss Hathaway, that you were able to accept my invitation on such short notice."

Cassandra made herself smile. "Yes, I was going to run an errand, but Mama told me she and Psyche could just as well do it, and that I was free to go with you if I wished."

She heard an exasperated breath from her mother, and wondered if she had said something she should not have.

Cassandra swallowed. She was not doing as she ought, that was clear, but she did not know quite how to remedy it. However, the marquess smiled at her again, and this time it was wide enough to be a grin. Cassandra almost sighed in relief. At least *he* was not displeased with her, and perhaps he did not mind her spencer fitting improperly.

"And did you wish it?" he asked.

Cassandra smiled, relieved. "Why, of course! I have never been in a high-perch phaeton before, and should like to try it. I used to think it a frightening thing to be up so high, but I am sure you are a competent driver and will not overturn us."

"Really, Cassandra!" Lady Hathaway's voice was reproving. "You must know that Lord Blytheland belongs to the Four-in-Hand Club!"

"Does he?" replied Cassandra, not entirely sure of the significance of this. She had heard it mentioned from time to time, but since she was not particularly interested in driving carriages she had not paid much attention to what was said about the club. "I suppose that must be a good thing, then." Her mother gave her an exasperated look, and Cassandra bit her lip. How she wished she had listened! But she had always gone to balls to dance and to musicales to listen to music—that was what they were for, after all—and so had never thought she ought to do more than that.

She saw Lord Blytheland's smile turn wry. "It *is* a good thing," he said. "It is almost a guarantee that I will not overturn us." He moved forward and bowed to Lady Hathaway, then turned to Cassandra. "Shall we go?"

"Yes, please," Cassandra said. She glanced at her mother and an embarrassed irritation grew in her. Mama was looking positively smug, and Cassandra was sure now that Mama meant to try to push her and the marquess together as much as possible. It was clear now why her mother acted strangely, and not as dignified as Cassandra was used to seeing her act. It disturbed her, and the idea that her mother was being mercenary on her behalf suddenly came to her. Perhaps she was wrong. . . . But even though she tried not to listen to gossip, she could not help hearing of estates and dowries, of incomes and titles when sitting amongst other ladies. It did not sit well with her; how her mother could wish for a monied marriage when she herself had married for love, Cassandra did not know.

Lord Blytheland took her hand and placed it on his arm and drew her to the parlor door. His arm felt firm underneath her hand, and she felt, somehow, more confident. *She* would not be swayed by monetary considerations. No, when—*if* she fell in love with Lord Blytheland, or any other man, for that matter—it would be a true meeting of minds, for how could anyone live one's whole life with someone who did not enter into one's interests or beliefs?

She would be sensible, and not let her mother's efforts on her behalf—and she was certain her mother meant well, for did she not love all her children dearly?—blind her to a man's true virtue. All she needed was to find out if the man was truly compatible in mind and spirit. She thought of the philosophies she had discussed with her father, and her spirits lightened. She would be scientific about it—did not her father say that logic would someday solve all questions? She would think of it as a scientific experiment, and then she would know to whom she'd give her heart.

Lord Blytheland was almost certain he would overturn the carriage. For all that Miss Hathaway's dress was modest in its basic lines, the tantalizing glimpse of her bosom revealed between the frills whenever she turned to speak with him distracted him. Twice he had to rein in his horses sharply before he ran into a pedestrian or passed too close to a cart.

"Is my mother right, saying you belong to the Four-in-Hand Club?" Cassandra asked after he had missed the cart.

"Yes."

"Are only the best carriage drivers allowed in it?"

Lord Blytheland glanced down at her and saw she had pulled her shawl close to her chin. "Yes," he said again and breathed a sigh of relief.

She gave him a quizzical smile. "I would not have known it just now."

"I am, however," he said stiffly.

"Oh, you need not poker up, my lord! I can see you are quite a good whip." Cassandra smiled kindly at him. "I was only teasing you."

"Really." He stared straight ahead at the traffic, concentrating on squeezing his phaeton between a curricle and a barouche. A good whip. He was, actually, known as one of the best. Irritation twisted within him, and then he felt relieved. There, that was another flaw in Miss Hathaway. She was ignorant of society ways, and therefore not at all the sort of woman he admired. She had no finesse whatsoever. Oddly, a sinking feeling went through him at the thought.

"Ah, I see!" Miss Hathaway's voice was contrite. "You are offended, are you not? I am sorry, but I did not realize you could not take a joke," she said.

Blytheland stared at her, but she had turned away and her bonnet obscured her face. How did she do it? She apologized, apparently sincere, but in the same breath strongly implied she found him humorless.

"Miss Hathaway, I can indeed take a joke."

"Really."

He shot her a keen glance and glimpsed her smile and the mischievous sparkle in her eyes before she turned away again. He burst out laughing. "You are a minx, Miss Hathaway! How is it that you have escaped strangulation at the hands of your siblings?"

"Oh, we have a rule at home, my lord, that speaking the truth does not constitute grounds for execution." This time she smiled widely.

Blytheland laughed again and caught up her hand and kissed it. "Why *is* it that I have not met you until now?"

Miss Hathaway blushed. "Well, I—This is my first Season, my lord."

He watched how the blush fired her cheeks and then descended to her neck—and then a shout caught his attention. He quickly reined in his horses before he touched wheels with another carriage, and was glad he could concentrate on something that needed his immediate attention. He grimaced. Miss Hathaway was right; no one could tell by his driving today that he belonged to the Four-in-Hand Club.

He glanced at her still-pink face and knew he had gone too far—he had kissed her hand again, perhaps raising her expectations. Or did she have expectations? Certainly, she seemed not to employ any of the tricks young ladies did when trying to attract a man. He took in a deep breath and let it out again.

"You astonish me," he said, making his voice more cool than before. "Since we are trading frank words, I would guess you to be at least one-and-twenty."

"I am three-and-twenty and more," Cassandra said primly. "Practically on the shelf, or so my mother says."

"And your parents did not want you to leave their home so early?"

"No . . ." For one moment she hesitated, and then smiled at him. "I did not want to leave at first. My life has always been comfortable and useful at home; why should I wish to change it? Why should anyone?"

Blytheland felt much in charity with this attitude, and nodded. He, too, had a pleasant life now, and did as he wished; why *should* he want to change? But she had hesitated. . . .

"But what of marriage and children?" he asked. That was not an unusual question to ask, surely, especially since she had revealed a reluctance to change her life.

Cassandra blushed again, but looked at him. "I think I

could be just as happy caring for my parents in their old age, if I cannot find love as they have. Then, too, I can easily occupy myself in such pursuits as my—in my charitable pursuits."

Blytheland gazed at Miss Hathaway for a moment and smiled slightly. He was certain she had just caught herself before blurting something she shouldn't. Should he try to find out what had changed her mind? A brief, anxious look crossed her face, and he decided he would not pry. If she wished to talk of charities, so be it. It was a safe enough topic, after all.

"And to what charities do you contribute?" He watched her as she looked even more anxious.

"I . . . the usual ones, my lord."

He smiled. "I am afraid I will sound like a selfish fellow if I say I do not know what the 'usual' charities are. But I do contribute to a few as well."

Cassandra cast him a glance that was clearly relieved. "I am so glad you do!" she said, then looked worried. "Oh dear. I did not mean to imply that I thought you uncharitable! It is just that talking of one's charities is akin to talking of one's virtues, and *that* is a prideful thing. I don't wish to seem prideful."

What knots she seemed to tie herself into! Blytheland could not help feeling a little sorry for her. Her bluntness was clearly often at war with her wish to be virtuous, and it was just as clear she knew she blundered—after the fact, unfortunately. He smiled widely at her.

"I promise I will not think you prideful, Miss Hathaway." He turned the carriage on to Hyde Park, then glanced down at her.

Her lips were slightly parted in a smile of gratitude and the sun chose just then to peep from behind the clouds and shine upon her hair, making her curls seem like the waves of the sea at night. The light kissed her cheek and chin and brushed her lips with the color of coral. Suddenly he wanted to plunge his hands into her hair and kiss those lips as the sun had kissed them, to see if they were as warm as they looked.

And then the sun hid behind the clouds again. He grew conscious of the silence between them, how her eyes seemed at once confused and lost, and how he held the reins so tightly that the horses stopped. *She must not fall in love with me, for her own sake. I do not have what she needs for me to give.* He looked away from her and concentrated on his horses.

What nonsense! He took a deep breath, and it cleared his mind. He did not know the state of her heart and would prefer not to think of it. He smiled wryly to himself. Indeed, what arrogance it was for him to think she might love him! No woman really had before, or not that he could tell, not even Chloe. And truly, it was better that way. He'd best tend to his own unruly passions instead of pondering the doubtless nonexistent ones of Miss Hathaway, and think in a more rational vein than he had lately.

"Did I say something amiss, my lord?" Cassandra's voice was uncertain.

He smiled at her. "No. Or rather, because you have not yet told me what charities you sponsor, I was left to my own imaginings. For all I know, you are devoted to the reclamation of abused coal scuttles." Cassandra laughed. "One never knows what charity will be in fashion next," he said.

She frowned for a moment, then said, "I suppose there are many who contribute because it is fashionable to do so. And though it is not the best reason to do so, one must be practical about these things."

"You, of course, have chosen a far more practical one than coal scuttles, I imagine?"

Cassandra smiled briefly, then pressed her lips together for a moment. "Yes. I . . . there are various parishes that need help. Food, clothing, blankets—I try to provide them."

She seemed to watch him for some reaction, and her voice was hesitant, as if expecting a reprimand. He wondered for a moment who it was had told her it was not a thing to mention in society. Her mother, probably. Perhaps it was not something most young ladies indulged in, but it was not a socially damning thing after all. He felt a slight touch on his sleeve and looked down at Cassandra's earnest face.

"It is a terrible thing, the way the poor ch—people live, Lord Blytheland—often abused and starved. No one who has seen one can help but be moved to one's very heart."

He raised his brows. "You have seen them?" he was accustomed to people who gave to charities and spared themselves the sight of the recipient.

Cassandra bit her lip. "I . . . I have seen some at the meetings I go to."

Shown off like a freak at a raree-show, Blytheland thought with distaste. But he supposed it was an effective way of eliciting sympathy for one's cause. He nodded.

"A worthy cause, Miss Hathaway. I commend you."

Her smile lit up her face, and it was as if the sun had come out from the clouds again. Again, he nearly touched wheels with another carriage, and exasperated, gave it up.

He turned to Cassandra. "Would you like to walk a little? I believe the ground is not damp."

"Yes, please," Cassandra said.

"Tim, take the reins," he said to the tiger sitting behind them as he slowed, then stopped the phaeton. They descended the carriage and walked next to the line of trees next to the roadway.

He took Miss Hathaway's hand and put it on his arm, and they walked in silence for a moment. He heard her sigh and he looked down at her. She had a speculative look on her face as she gazed at him, and at once he felt wary. He'd seen that look before on women's faces, and it usually meant they wished to entrap him in some manner. Was she, after all, like other young ladies with an eye toward marriage? He felt some disappointment, though, really, he should be pleased she was not above the ordinary.

"Is there something you wish to say, Miss Hathaway?" he said. He thought of a number of set-downs he could use if she decided to flirt with him after all.

"I was wondering . . . if, well . . ." She hesitated, and a slight blush appeared on her cheeks.

If she asked him if he would attend some social function or other, he would definitely say no. He had too many commitments as it was. "Yes, Miss Hathaway?"

"I was wondering if perhaps you might be interested in contributing to our charity," she said all in a rush, and her cheeks grew even more pink.

Lord Blytheland could not help feeling some chagrin. She was not, apparently, interested in his presence anywhere at all. He felt quite the fool, thinking that she might. He wondered if perhaps he was becoming arrogant, and if it showed.

"The poor ch—people,they are so hungry!" Cassandra looked at him pleadingly. "You don't know how horribly they've been treated, and some of them so very young, only babies!" He saw her swallow, and turn away, taking a deep breath before she continued. "Some of them fear even the kindest of approaches, thinking we come to cause them harm." She gazed at him, and he could see her eyes, wide and with a hint of tears. She touched his sleeve. "Please . . . it is a terrible thing, and should happen to no child—no one in England."

"But of course, Miss Hathaway," he said, before he could stop himself.

She gave him another smile of clear gratitude, and pressed his arm. A speculative look entered her eyes, and she said tentatively, "And do you think perhaps you can persuade your father to speak on the matter when he goes to Parliament?"

Blytheland gave her a sharp look. She immediately hung

her head as if in chagrin, then peeped up at him from beneath her lashes. She looked very much like a puppy who wanted to play but had gone beyond the line, Blytheland thought. And then she grinned and shrugged her shoulders.

Blytheland burst into laughter. "You are incorrigible, Miss Hathaway!"

"Ah, well. I thought I ought to try."

Blytheland opened his mouth to speak, but hesitated. He wondered what her reaction would be if he did as she asked. She would smile at him again. He realized suddenly that he liked to see her smile; her mouth curved in at the corners in a slight curl and made him want to kiss her. It was pleasant to have such an attractive companion, of course, but it was a trying thing to walk beside her and not give in to his impulse to—He let out a slow breath and tried not to think of his impulses.

Well, it would not hurt to approach his father about the poverty in the parishes about town . . . and it was not as if the duke was opposed to such things, after all. "You are very devoted to your cause, I see," he said.

Cassandra's expression sobered. "One cannot help being so, after seeing the poverty."

"I suppose I could speak to my father upon the matter . . ."

A tiny shriek made him look down at her, and he found his hands seized in hers and squeezed tightly. Cassandra's face was alight with joy, and she gave a little jump, almost seeming about to dance. But she bit her lip instead, clearly restraining herself, then raised his hand to her cheek. "How good you are!" she exclaimed.

Blytheland stared at her, feeling the warmth of her cheek against his hand. If she moved her head but a fraction of an inch, he'd feel her lips against his hand, and he could not help imagining what it would feel like. Warm, of course, but nothing compared to what it would probably feel like if it were his lips instead of his hand. He looked into her eyes and found she was staring at him. A blush rose in her cheeks and she hastily released him, and he was able to look away at last. He sighed. In a way, he wished she would not smile at him. It was her best feature, and it distracted him.

"I am not as good as you think, Miss Hathaway," he said. "Besides, I cannot guarantee my father will agree to speak on the matter at all."

"It is enough that you ask him—and I know I was impertinent to ask it of you, so I think you are indeed very good to agree." She gave a happy sigh. "It is more than anyone else has agreed to do."

Blytheland grinned at her. "Do you always go about impertinently demanding support for your charities?"

"No, because I have learned that it puts off a great many people when I do. But you looked as if you understood about the—parishes, and then your eyes were smiling in *such* a way that I thought you would not mind."

"Do my thoughts show that much, then?" He did not like the idea that they might.

Cassandra pursed her lips in a thoughtful manner and swung her reticule to and fro as she walked beside him. "No . . . no, not really. I doubt most would be able to discern your state of mind. But I have had to watch people carefully—I suppose you have noticed that I sometimes say things I ought not?"

Blytheland could not help laughing. "Yes, I am afraid I have."

"You should not laugh at me, my lord," Cassandra said, her voice solemn, but then she sighed. "Well, I suppose it is something I must become used to, for I forget, you know, and cannot keep from saying what I think, though I do try! And it is certainly better than being angry at me. But one good thing I have learned is to watch people carefully, so that I may discern whether they are angry or not. I think I have become fairly good at reading countenances."

He nodded, thinking that perhaps it was necessary for someone as defenseless as Miss Hathaway to find some way of dealing with others. He hadn't thought of it before, but he supposed she was rather defenseless, since she seemed to have very little notion as to how to navigate through the *ton*. It was an uncomfortable thought and nothing he should be concerned about, certainly.

The wind picked up and blew against Miss Hathaway's bonnet, and Lord Blytheland looked up to see that heavier clouds were forming above them. "I think we should return to the carriage," he said.

They hurried their steps and found Blytheland's tiger bringing up the carriage. Hastily they ascended and seated themselves.

"But all of this—your charitable pursuits—should be no barrier to marriage, Miss Hathaway," Blytheland said, taking up the reins again. "You could just as easily do them if you married." The horses moved forward.

She hesitated, looking oddly . . . bereft, was the closest he could come to a description, then said, "I have no guarantee that my husband would be a good man. Why should I risk possible unhappiness when I can logically, sensibly choose the happy life I already know?"

"And where did you get such ideas, Miss Hathaway?"

"Oh, from a book I read by Mrs. Wollstonecraft." Her voice faltered slightly at the end.

A hard, hot anger seized Blytheland's gut, and his hands clenched, bringing the horses to a stop.

"Lord Blytheland?" Cassandra's voice sounded tentative.

His fingers were digging into his gloved palms. He loosened them, and the horses went forward again.

"Your father allowed you to read such nonsense?" He could not help the sneer that came to his voice.

An angry light entered Cassandra's eyes. "It is *not* nonsense—not all of it. You need only look about you to see that there are people who are not happy in their marriages."

"It is not necessary that people be happy or unhappy in their marriages. It is a thing one does to continue the family."

Cassandra felt as if a chill had come over her, and she pulled her shawl tighter around her. "I daresay many people think that. But I believe it is best that a marriage be a loving one. If one cannot have one such, it is better to remain unwed, and even better, find a useful occupation so as not to be a burden on anyone."

For one moment an uncertain expression crossed Lord Blytheland's face. Then he smiled coolly.

"You are an idealist, Miss Hathaway. As you said, there are no guarantees about one's husband or wife. The best anyone can do is to rub along amiably."

Cassandra gazed at him doubtfully. Before the uncertainty, anger had marred his expression. Something she had said had caused him to be angry, but she did not know what it was.

"And how would you know, Lord Blytheland?" she asked. She supposed he must base his opinion upon his own family, but she had heard nothing scandalous of either his father the Duke of Beaumont, or his mother the duchess. The reports were that they were always amiably disposed toward each other, at least in company. Although, this was not saying much, to be sure, for she rarely listened to gossip and probably would not have remembered if she had heard it.

He smiled coolly, then looked past her. "Ah, I see Lady Amberley waving to me, and her most charming daughter is with her." He nodded to a carriage coming toward them.

Cassandra smiled to herself. So, that was one of his setdowns. It comforted her in a way, for it was one more puzzle piece she had gathered for a better picture of his nature. Lord Blytheland was not the sort of person she was used to . . . there was a part of him that seemed hidden somehow. She was used to being able to assess easily those she met and pin down the pattern of their behavior. Once she understood, it was a little easier to refrain from saying things that would offend them. She sighed. But oh, people did become offended at the most innocent things! And the fact that the marquess was not so easily assessed, disconcerted her. How was she to know what would offend him or not? The only way was to speak what she thought and see how he responded. If he became offended, then she would know enough not to speak of things that offended him.

Cassandra made herself smile in a friendly manner at Lady Amberley and her daughter Sophia when Lord Blytheland introduced them, though she felt rather abstracted. She was still puzzling over the marquess. For one moment she felt a little guilty. Perhaps it was not a very well-mannered thing to do, making people reveal themselves. She sighed. But what else was she to do? Men, she found, were the most contrary sort of people of all. One could not always use much logic with them, for all their claim to be the more logical sex. They tended to become quite emotional when one reasoned with them—and how logical was that? Not at all, to be sure.

But it did seem, at least, that in such things as discussions, Lord Blytheland was as other men. As a result, she was that much closer to knowing more of him. And she did so wish to know more of Lord Blytheland. Not, of course, because she wished . . . well, what she wished, she was not certain.

"Do you stay in London long, Miss Hathaway?"

Cassandra turned her attention to the young woman in the barouche next to her. Miss Sophia Amberley was beautiful and had large blue eyes. Cassandra would almost have thought they were innocent eyes, but the sharp, speculative look Miss Amberley gave her and the marquess was not innocent at all. Cassandra's face became warm. Surely Miss Amberley was not thinking that Lord Blytheland could be very much interested in her, Cassandra? No other gentleman had this Season, and there was no reason why he should either.

Stop it! Cassandra scolded herself, and made herself smile at Miss Amberley. "Oh, only until the end of the Season, for there is not much more left to do after that."

A satisfied expression came to Miss Amberley's face. "That is too bad. There are dozens of diversions in London after the Season is over, you know. We often stay into the summer."

Cassandra nodded, pleased that there was something upon which she could converse. "Oh, yes! But it gets terribly warm here in the city by then, and I cannot think the miasma that rises from the river at that time is at all healthy. It could make one look quite sickly.

"That is to say," Cassandra said hurriedly into the silence that ensued, "the fresh country air in the summer is bound to bring a healthy glow to one's complexion—not that *you* do not have a healthy complexion, Miss Amberley! Or you, Lady Amberley!"

"I am glad to know you think our complexions quite . . . healthy, Miss Hathaway," Lady Amberley said, her voice chilly. "Well, Sophia. I do believe I see Lady Stonebaugh a little farther along the road." She nodded her head to the marquess and barely glanced at Cassandra. "My lord, Miss . . . Hathaway. Good day to you both." She signaled to the coachman, and the barouche went forward.

Cassandra's heart sank. She looked down at her tightly closed hands, then flattened them on her lap. She must have insulted Lady Amberley and her daughter. She glanced at Lord Blytheland. He was not looking at her, but ahead as he slackened the reins, moving the horses forward. For a moment, a small smile played about his mouth and relief flowed into her. Perhaps she had not totally ruined this afternoon carriage ride, for he could not smile and be displeased at the same time.

She felt half regretful and half relieved when they drove

up to her family's house once again. They had not spoken of much else except of the weather on the way back, and for this Cassandra was thankful. She had experimented a little by teasing him, to see how he would respond to it, and she felt she had done it quite successfully. But she had also blundered and was just as glad they had started talking of the weather, for she did not want to blunder again. The weather, at least, was a safe subject.

When the carriage stopped, Lord Blytheland handed his reins to his tiger and stepped down to help her from her seat. This time, his eyes were cool as blue eyes were supposed to be, though his smile seemed just as wide as before. She wished, suddenly, that he looked warmly upon her as he had before the carriage ride, and despondency rose in her. It was, no doubt, because she had been so gauche during their carriage ride that he looked so coolly at her now. She was not at all sure now he'd wish to see her again. Why should he? But how she wished he would!

"Shall I see you at the Marchmont's ball, tomorrow?" Cassandra blurted. Lord Blytheland's brows rose, and her face grew warm. "That is I—never mind—I should not have—" She swallowed and looked away, then summoned up a smile. "I am very foolish, am I not? I never know what to say to people. Please excuse me." She stepped down from the carriage and gave him as cheery a smile as she could. "Thank you very much for a most delightful ride, my lord. Our conversation was quite delightful, and the weather was delight . . ." Her voice faltered. She gazed down at her hands clasped tight together, then turned quickly to the door of the house.

"Miss Hathaway."

Cassandra stopped, her hand on the doorknob.

"I shall be at Lady Marchmont's ball."

She turned to look at him and found he had followed her up the steps. This time she could not help the hope and joy that rose in her heart and made her smile. "I am glad," she said.

Lord Blytheland stared at her for one moment, his expression serious. "Will you save a dance for me?" he asked. There was an intent air about him, as if he were holding his breath.

It was a ridiculous thing to be so happy over such a small thing as a dance, Cassandra thought. But she *was* happy, and she felt sure she looked like an idiot, grinning so widely as she was. "Oh yes!" she said, then firmly reined in her feelings. "Yes, thank you, my lord."

The marquess took her hand and kissed it. "I shall definitely look forward to it, then." He gave a brief smile, bowed, and went down the steps to his carriage again. Cassandra watched him as he touched his hat to her in another bow and drove off.

Cassandra turned and stared at the door of the house as she went up the stairs. She missed the doorknob at first when trying to open it, then shook her head at herself for being in such a daze. How silly she was!

She sighed and went up to her room to change her dress. Silly indeed. There was no depending upon a man's interest, really. No man had been all that interested in her before, and there was no reason why Lord Blytheland should, either.

But he has paid more attention to you than any other man, whispered a little voice that crept into her mind.

Cassandra pressed her lips together and took the little voice to task. Well, there! she told herself firmly. She was becoming foolish over a thing that was wholly insignificant. So what of Lord Blytheland's attentions? That he had paid her more attention than any other man was an insignificant thing. He could very well stop at any time, as did the others. Besides, he had only been with her one or two times.

It could be three or four or five . . . said the little voice.

And what was the use of "could be" in such matters? she argued. One was best served by placing one's reliance on what was and what *should* be.

A clock tolled the hour and Cassandra hurried up the rest of the stairs. It was almost time for the meeting of the Society for the Rescue of Climbing Boys. She had done very well, she thought, in speaking in general terms about her charitable pursuits. Mama would be quite pleased that she had not mentioned climbing boys at all during the ride with Lord Blytheland.

She hastened into her room; she would have to change her clothes quickly. Most certainly she could not wear this spencer and dress to the meeting! She glanced down at the dress and blushed—it had become disarrayed even more than before. Heavens! She would give the spencer away to Psyche, for whom it would be a little large and certainly not as indecent. What could her mother have been thinking?

The little voice began to speak up, but Cassandra quashed it as firmly as she shut the door to her room.

Chapter 5

Miss Hathaway was definitely not the sort of woman he usually liked. Lord Blytheland smiled at his reflection in his chamber's mirror as he adjusted his neckcloth. Slowly he let down his chin upon the folds of cloth. Satisfied, he turned to his valet and put on his coat.

No, Miss Cassandra Hathaway was too blunt for him, too impetuous in her speech, and she blurted out whatever happened to be in her mind. She had little finesse, though in general her manners were good, and she was inept in company. Further, it was clear she was a bluestocking, and worse, a believer in that Wollstonecraft woman's ideas.

Like Chloe.

A hard, hot anger surged in his chest, and for one moment his hand stilled before he drew his jacket together. He took in a deep breath.

No, to be fair, not like Chloe. He let out his breath and frowned slightly. Chloe had had a great deal of charm, and a sparkling wit. She would never inadvertently insult anyone. He remembered suddenly a smiling remark his wife had once uttered, and how he had thought her clever for giving a set-down to an encroaching guest with such finesse. She had done this often, he realized.

Miss Hathaway was not like this. There was something about her. . . . He grinned. She often seemed to have a bewildered, worried air, as if she were some small wild creature suddenly uncovered from under a sheaf of bracken.

Somehow he could not imagine her giving a deliberate set-down to anyone.

Which was why, despite all her awkwardness, her gaucherie, and her definite bluestocking interests, he'd asked her for a dance at the Marchmonts' ball. Blytheland pulled on his greatcoat—the Marchmonts' house was a good half hour from town, and the night was cool—then sighed as he took his hat from his valet. He had attempted to depress her pretensions, and when she had looked at him with her wide, hurt eyes, he had felt like a cad.

Chloe had never been like that. She had made fine play with her eyes, had coaxed and cajoled, she had tossed her fiery hair or smiled and reasoned with one in such a way that her desires seemed altogether sensible. He would not be so trapped again.

Yet, he was not imperceptive, either. It was clear to him that Miss Hathaway was not at all like Chloe in nature. Miss Hathaway did not cajole or coax and he wondered if she knew how to flirt with her eyes. When she looked at him, it was as if she searched for something beneath his words, down to his very heart.

Perhaps her interest in radical ideas was not deep and perhaps she could be persuaded away from them. And who would do the persuading? The thought made him pause one moment before ascending the steps to his coach.

"Thinking of setting up a nursery?" Eldon had said. Blytheland leaned back onto the squabs of the carriage and carefully let the thought settle into his mind. He was six-and-twenty years old, the only heir of his father, the Duke of Beaumont. Though his father had not pressured him into a second marriage, Blytheland was quite aware of his obligation to continue the line.

It had been two years . . . two years since Chloe had lain with another man and died of the result. An anger still burned in him from time to time, and sometimes he felt an odd ache of emptiness. No one could fill Chloe's place, for she had played a role he thought he had loved and now knew he hated.

But was he not older now, and wiser? And he was not so much of a fool as to think that all women were like Chloe. Was not his own mother a devoted wife? And his sisters were certainly faithful also, and no scandal had ever touched them.

He smiled and felt the tension fall away from his shoulders. Eldon may have been teasing, but he was quite right. It was time to think of marrying a suitable young lady of good morals and good birth. Indeed it did not matter if he loved the lady or not, it was an heir he needed and a respectable, honest young woman who would neither play him nor the title false. He would go about it in a reasonable manner this time and would select his new wife with careful reason, and pay strict attention to all that he required in a wife.

Indeed, his preoccupation with Miss Hathaway—and he admitted his thoughts had been a little too filled with her image of late—was a clear indication of one thing: it was time he was married again. He needed to continue the Templeton line after all. Marriage would certainly help assuage whatever passions he'd been experiencing lately, and he was growing tired of flitting from one brief liaison to another.

The coach rumbled to a halt in front of the Marchmonts' house, and the image of Miss Hathaway rose in his mind. Blytheland smiled to himself. Oh, she was eligible, for her breeding was good, however socially inept she was, but he could do better than Cassandra Hathaway, a baronet's daughter of moderate fortune. He was heir to a dukedom, and owed the title a lady worthy of it. One who was elegant and beautiful, preferably, and certainly one who had much better address than Miss Hathaway.

The Marchmonts' ball would be just the place to start his search. There should be many eligible ladies attending, because the Marchmonts were of good *ton* and had many connections with the best families in England. There should be no question that he had no more interest—perhaps even less—in Miss Hathaway than in any other young lady. Once he looked over the unwedded female portion of the guests, he could have his mother handle the rest . . . or perhaps not. His mother tended to have strong opinions about who was suitable and who was not, and she had objected mightily to his choice of Chloe. He grimaced. Well, she was right in that case. Perhaps it would be good to have her handle the whole, winnow out the objectionable ones, so to speak, so he could pick the one he liked best. Yes, he would do that.

He smiled as he descended the coach and stepped up to the Marchmonts' door. All he needed was a young lady of good family, comely enough for him to wish to bed, intelligent enough not to bore him, appreciative enough of music so as not to deplore his interest in it, and her family wealthy enough not to be a drain on his estate and the future of his family. Once more the image of Cassandra Hathaway rose in front of him, but he pushed it firmly aside. She was one possible candidate only, and perhaps he'd dance only the one dance he had requested of her. There would be many other eligible ladies at the ball. With such opportunities, how difficult could it be to find a wife, after all?

Bright candlelight shimmered through the windows of the Marchmonts' house. Cassandra's hands clutched her ivory-handled fan tightly. For the first time since she'd come to London with her family, she felt agitated about going to a ball. To be sure, her first one had made her a little nervous, but she'd found since then that though she was not popular as were some other ladies, she always danced at least a few dances, talked with at least a few people, and generally enjoyed the music. It became an expected thing, a weekly routine.

But this time *he* would be there—Lord Blytheland. Please, dear God, she prayed silently, keep me from acting like a ninny. Cassandra sighed as she descended the coach with her mother and father. Heaven knows she had not been herself since meeting the marquess. Stammering and blushing like a girl of thirteen instead of a lady of three-and-twenty! Indeed, worse, for even Psyche did not falter and stumble over her speech when in his presence. *Really, Cassandra,* she mentally scolded herself, *Lord Blytheland is just a man—not any different from, say, your father or your brother!*

Oh, but he was *different!* whispered what she believed was her baser side. She could not deny that. How could he not be? He looked nothing like her father, and as for any comparison of character with her younger brother—! Ridiculous! How kind the marquess was to call on her and listen to her play the sonata. Cassandra bit her lip. She should not have played the "Appassionata"; she knew her mother preferred her to play more feminine music—a ballad, or a dainty divertimento. But she'd found the music for Herr Beethoven's work at the bookseller's and could not resist playing such a moving piece for the marquess. Not that she wanted him to be moved, of course! It was merely that she thought Lord Blytheland might appreciate the sonata's beauty and power as she did, since he was such a talented musician. It seemed he thought the music unlady-like as well, but he so kindly praised her on it, and even asked to play a duet with her at a future date. Perhaps he did appreciate it. She hoped so.

As Cassandra and her parents entered the Marchmonts' ballroom, she could not help looking about her for the marquess. She did not see him. Her shoulders went up in a small, involuntary shrug, warding off disappointment. Well, it was as she thought. He was merely being kind when he had asked for a dance. Whatever the case, she would enjoy the ball. She had dressed with care in a royal blue round gown with a silver-net overdress—a trifle more low-cut than she was accustomed, but which her mother said looked very becoming on her. What did it matter that Lord Blytheland was not here to see her? She was not, after all, an ornament to be displayed.

They sat to one side of the room, close to the refreshments. "Dashed thirsty work, this dancing," Sir John said, although Cassandra did not know how her father could say this since he would dance only with her and her mother, and perhaps one other lady—if forced. She noticed that he found a seat next to an old acquaintance, and was soon deep in a discussion of Greek plays. Cassandra smiled and allowed herself to relax, watching the people begin to gather for the first set of the dance.

"Miss Hathaway, would you grant me the honor of this dance?"

The marquess's soft voice startled her, and she jerked her head around to look at him.

She'd thought Lord Blytheland handsome before, but she had rated him low. He was dressed in a blue coat so dark as to seem black, his knee breeches were of the palest yellow, his shirt points were high, and a sapphire pin glistened within the folds of his neckcloth. The close-fitting coat displayed his wide shoulders to perfection, and the breeches clung to his long and well-muscled legs. His gold embroidered cream waistcoat declared him one of the dandy set, and on any other man the effect would have been overdone. Instead, it set off Lord Blytheland's tall and elegant form, and he looked magnificent.

Cassandra felt herself blushing, but she was determined not to be missish. Drawing in a deep breath to calm herself, she put her hand in his outstretched one and said, "I would be delighted to dance with you, Lord Blytheland."

She smiled at him, for she had succeeded in controlling her voice so that it did not shake or stutter—but then she was glad she'd said her piece before she looked into his face. He was gazing at her intently, and a smile slowly warmed his expression. It reached his eyes and there something seemed to glow as if a stronger emotion than kindness existed for her.

She must be imagining it! Looking hurriedly away, Cassandra concentrated on getting to the dance set before her. It was a simple country dance, and there would be little chance for them to talk. She sighed with relief.

"A sad crush, is it not? Lady Marchmont should be happy." The marquess tapped a guest's shoulder, smiled, and passed through a small gap in the crowd.

"Yes, although why anyone should be happy that their guests cannot move an inch except on the dance floor, I do not know," Cassandra replied. He laughed. She glanced at him again. He was still smiling, but the emotion she thought she saw in his eyes was gone.

"Nor do I. But it seems to be every hostess's ambition."

"Ambition is not a virtue, my lord. It is very like to greed."

"Just so."

Cassandra cast a suspicious look at him. "Are you laughing at me, sir?"

The marquess put on an innocent look. "I? My dear Miss Hathaway, why should I laugh at you?"

A chuckle bubbled up behind her lips, and she failed to suppress it. "But you are! Odious man! Indeed, I do believe you meant to give me a set-down!"

"Not at all," replied Blytheland. "Were I to give you one, you would definitely know it."

"Now *that* is a set-down, if ever I heard one."

The marquess laughed again. She smiled but looked at him thoughtfully, and though he grinned down at her she wondered how blistering his set-downs could be. He could be quite unpleasant about it, she felt. There was that intensity about him, despite his meticulous clothing and easy address. It seemed to come out only when he played his music, but she imagined it must always be there, beneath the calm.

"Oh, Lord Blytheland! Is that you?" cried a female voice. Cassandra turned to look and stared. The lady coming toward them must have been the most—"decorated" was the only word Cassandra could think of—person she had ever seen. Her voluptuous form was draped in jewels and necklaces that covered a bosom barely contained within her bodice. Cassandra looked at the marquess. A fleeting, irritated expression seemed to cross his face, then a cool smile took its place. He bowed politely.

"*Is* it me, Mrs. Bradstead? I thought it was my twin." His smile turned more cool than before.

Mrs. Bradstead seemed not to notice. "Naughty man!" she said, lightly tapping her fan on his arm. "I know you do not have a twin, so you *cannot* hoax *me*! Now, tell me, where *have* you been? It has been an age since I saw you last!"

"An age, ma'am? I thought I saw you just a few days ago."

Her fan traced a line down his lapel. "It seemed an age to me," she said, her voice caressing.

Blytheland's finger halted the fan's progress, and he pushed it away from him. "And here I thought time passed slowly only for the young—or young in mind." He smiled charmingly at Mrs. Bradstead.

The woman looked nonplussed, as if she could not think of a reply. She looked at Cassandra. "And who is your charming—young—companion, my lord?"

The marquess's smile grew wider. "Miss Cassandra Hathaway, ma'am. Miss Hathaway, Mrs. Aurelia Bradstead."

Cassandra curtsied, feeling a little sorry for Mrs. Bradstead. The woman was clearly not good at understanding allusions or metaphor. Lord Blytheland must see this; he should not tease her so! But then, Cassandra had already experienced his teasing earlier; he was not much different in this respect from her brother. *She* could tolerate it, but it was clear this poor lady could not. Perhaps she should turn the conversation, to spare Mrs. Bradstead discomfort.

"I am pleased to meet you, Mrs. Bradstead. I hope you do not mind, but I cannot help but admire your beautiful necklaces. You do have such a lovely display of them, do you not?" Cassandra smiled kindly at her.

"Why, why, I—I have never—!" Mrs. Bradstead sputtered.

Cassandra nodded and smiled comfortingly. "You need not explain. I know how it is! When one is fond of a certain thing one tends to wear it to excess, does one not? I myself was surprised one day to find that most of my dresses are in varying shades of blue—and how tedious that could be! But there it is! One cannot help wearing what one favors."

Mrs. Bradstead shot her one burning look, then stalked away as fast as the crowded room would allow. Cassandra suddenly felt uncertain. It seemed Mrs. Bradstead had taken offense at something she had said; but how could that be? She had only complimented her on her selection of jewelry.

She glanced at Lord Blytheland, hoping he was not displeased at her. She was surprised to find a wide grin on his face. "I . . . I did not mean to offend your friend, my lord," she said tentatively.

"It does not matter," the marquess replied. He looked down at her, and it seemed that a mischievous light danced in his eyes. Was he laughing at her? Cassandra put up her chin defensively.

"If you must know, I thought you were teasing her, so I tried to turn the conversation." She gazed at him sternly.

"And very successfully, too, Miss Hathaway."

"*I* cannot see that. Why, she acted as if I offended her terribly."

"Of course you were successful. You turned the conversation so well that *she* turned and left."

"So I *did* offend her!" Cassandra looked down at her clenched hands, then gazed at Lord Blytheland earnestly. "I must go after her and apologize!" She turned to go.

She felt a firm hand on her arm. "No, don't," he said. "If you must know, I was trying to give her a set-down myself."

"That was not well done of you, my lord," Cassandra replied gravely.

"Was it? She is an encroaching creature, and malicious. I did not know it when I first—met her. It is just as well she left us." The look he gave her was as cool as the one he had given Mrs. Bradstead.

Cassandra's heart sank. She had offended *him,* now. But it was not wrong to speak the truth. She gave him a firm look. "And *that* set-down was meant for *me,* was it not?"

"Yes, but it was not very effective, was it?"

"No," Cassandra replied baldly. "I spoke nothing but the truth, after all."

Lord Blytheland's eyes lightened, and he laughed. "I see it was not at all effective."

She looked at him uncertainly. How unpredictable he was, to be sure!

They came to where the dance set had formed, but their conversation with Mrs. Bradstead had delayed them and the dance had already started. "Alas, we are too late. Would you mind taking a stroll along the terrace instead, Miss Hathaway?"

A little disappointed that she was not to dance with him, Cassandra nodded. Feeling a little diffident, she cast a glance at her mother across the room.

Apparently catching her look, Lord Blytheland said, "I will ask your parents for permission, of course." Cassandra nodded and watched him maneuver through the crowd, then bow before her mother and father. She saw them talk, and then saw her mother look in her direction. Lady Hathaway merely smiled at her, and Cassandra felt more at ease.

The marquess gave one more bow before he turned back toward Cassandra. He was carrying something, and as he came closer she could see it was her shawl. How thoughtful of him! A glowing warmth crept into her heart, and Cassandra smiled at him. She had not thought that she might be chilled in the night air, but he had.

As they stepped through the threshold onto the terrace, Cassandra felt suddenly uncertain. She thought there might be others on the terrace as well, but she could see only the vague shapes of a low stone wall and shrubbery beyond that, for the curtains kept much of the candlelight from escaping the ballroom. She did not see any people, but there must have been, for she thought she heard the murmur of voices some distance away. Well, it was not, certainly, as if they were totally alone.

The night air was cool and a light breeze brushed the curls around her face. Something else intimately brushed her neck and shoulder, but it was not a breeze, for it was warmer. Her heart beat faster. She looked up to find the marquess smiling down at her, and then her small spark of alarm faded, for she felt him drape her delicate woolen shawl across her shoulders. Really, Cassandra! she scolded herself. As if Lord Blytheland would do anything improper! She let out her breath in a long sigh.

"I thank you, my lord. This *is* pleasant, is it not? I am glad you suggested it." She looked up at the stars sparkling like tiny candles in the sky and gave a little chuckle. "When I was a girl, I used to think each star was an angel that played an instrument, and that someday I would hear a symphony if I listened hard enough."

"Ah, but they are angels, don't you know."

His voice was closer to her than she expected, and she quickly glanced at him to see him gazing reflectively at her. I will *not* be missish, she told herself, and looked steadily out at the night.

"It is best on a clear night like this; you need only concentrate, and listen," the marquess said softly. She could feel his breath upon her ear as he spoke, and then felt his fingers brush against her shoulder. He lifted a curl that lay against her neck and let it drop. She looked up at him, wondering what he was thinking, but felt she dare not ask.

"I—I am afraid the noise of the guests from the ballroom drowns them out."

"Pretend the guests are not there." He put his fingers under her chin, lifting it so that she looked him in the eye. He was gazing at her with a serious, considering expression. Cassandra held her breath. Was he . . . was he going to kiss her? And if so, would she let him?

She closed her eyes briefly, and felt a touch upon her mouth—but it was not a kiss. His fingers still held her chin, but his thumb slowly, gently outlined the contours of her lips. It seemed he watched his thumb's movement, then looked at her as if searching for something. He sighed.

"You should not go out walking alone with me on terraces."

"There . . . there are others walking out here as well." Cassandra felt breathless and oddly dissatisfied, though she should be glad, indeed, that he did not do something so improper as to kiss her.

A wide grin spread across his face. "Others who have invisibility amongst their talents, of course."

"I thought I heard some voices . . ." Cassandra could feel a blush rising in her cheeks.

"Perhaps. However, they are not anywhere in sight. We are quite private here."

"Are we?" But she knew it was so, even as she spoke. They stood just past the windowed doors that let out to the terrace, near the low stone wall that curved into the mansion itself. The curtains obscured the light from the ballroom, and only dimly illuminated Blytheland's countenance. She was glad she was in shadow, for then the marquess could not see her blushes—and then realized the reason she was in shadow was because she stood in a corner, and he blocked her way out.

From within the ballroom the orchestra struck up, and Cassandra knew that another dance set had begun. The music had a hypnotic beat, and she felt her own heart beat faster to its rhythm. Blytheland's hand came up, and she could feel his thumb trace circles along the line of her jaw, in rhythm to the music. She closed her eyes.

"Will you kiss me, Cassandra?" His voice was low and soft.

"I—I have not given you permission to use my—my Christian name, sir."

"Then give it to me now."

"I—"

"Please."

A deep sigh escaped her, and perhaps there was a yes in it somewhere. Cassandra did not have time to consider which question she might have answered, for the marquess's lips came down upon hers, swiftly, firmly, gently. She did not know what to do at first, for she had never been kissed—at least not as Lord Blytheland kissed her. There was something insistent beneath the softness of his caress, and she was half afraid of it, for she felt it was related to that intensity she'd glimpsed within his eyes before. But it seemed as if some natural force within her knew the right response and cared not for any fears she might have: a small gasp opened her mouth and she leaned forward, matching his intensity with passion.

"My God," she heard him murmur as he parted from her only a hairbreadth and for a heartbeat's time.

The music from the ballroom swirled through the open windows and around them, and made Cassandra's perceptions rise to an acute sensitivity. Blytheland's fingers moved from her cheek to her neck and left a scintillating trail, like champagne trickling across her skin. She shivered and pressed closer to him, savoring his warmth in the cool night. His lips shifted from her lips to her cheek, and then down to her throat.

Then he stilled, and stopped, and moved away. Bewildered, Cassandra gazed at his solemn face, but he looked toward the open doors. Voices, louder than she'd heard before.

Reality doused her like ice water across the face, and she drew in a swift breath. Oh, merciful heavens, someone was coming! What *had* she been doing? How could she be so stupid? It was obvious what she'd been doing. She hoped that it would not be obvious to anyone who might see her. She blushed hotly at the thought.

"I think we need to walk, Miss Hathaway," the marquess said.

"Y-yes, of course."

He bent and picked up her shawl, which had fallen to the ground, shook it, and put it around her shoulders. She pulled it tightly around her.

"Thank you."

Blytheland shot a surprised look at her.

"I *meant* for my *shawl!*"

"Of course." A small smile crossed his lips. He tucked her hand upon his arm, and they moved out from the shadows.

Cassandra was glad they strolled about the terrace. The night breeze had picked up and had become chill, and cooled her too-warm cheeks. Another couple did indeed come upon them, but they barely acknowledged Cassandra's and Blytheland's presence, for the couple were too absorbed looking into each other's eyes. Cassandra looked away, embarrassed. Is that how she had looked at Lord Blytheland? She groaned mentally. She was only thankful the couple barely noticed her.

Before they entered the ballroom, the marquess stopped and turned to her gravely. "I have little excuse to have . . . done what I did. I only hope you will forgive me any unpleasantness I might have inflicted on you."

"It wasn't," Cassandra blurted.

"Excuse me?"

"Unpleasant. It wasn't—Oh heavens! What am I saying?" She pressed her hand to her cheek, trying to suppress another blush.

"The ever-truthful Miss Hathaway." Blytheland chuckled. They stepped into the ballroom, and Cassandra saw that a set was just forming. "Perhaps we should dance this time—if you are agreeable?"

Nodding, she laid her shawl across a vacant chair and prepared herself for the dance. She was relieved the music started quickly, for then any high color in her cheeks could easily be attributed to the exertions of the dance. The marquess was no more than polite and as kind as he had been earlier before their . . . kiss. She was glad of that—glad that his behavior was no more or less than normal now—for it allowed her to gain her composure again. When he brought her back to her parents, he bowed over her hand and with a last smile merged into the ballroom crowd.

But Cassandra was not to sit quietly by her mother and father at all, as she was used to after a dance. Immediately upon the heels of Blytheland's departure, three young men came up to her parents, claiming some acquaintance through friends or relations. Lady Hathaway, beaming, introduced them all to her daughter.

"May I have the honor of this dance, Miss Hathaway?" a stocky, dark-haired gentleman asked. Sir Ellery Heysmith, Cassandra remembered.

"Oh, no, Miss Hathaway," Mr. Rowland cut in, grinning at Sir Ellery. "You must know that my friend Heysmith here is the merest caper merchant. He'll stomp your feet to splinters. You'd be much better off with me as your dance partner."

His friend gave him a wry grin. "And you, Rolly, are a

rattle, and would deafen her by the end of the dance with all your tittle-tattle."

"Here's your answer, then, ma'am," said Lord Eldon, smiling at her. "It is I with whom you must dance. Between a caper merchant, a rattle, and myself—is there any question?" He gave an elegant bow, and his friends rolled their eyes in disgust at him.

Cassandra broke out laughing. "Oh, heavens! What am I to do if I am to be fair? Let us see . . . ah! I have it. I shall choose alphabetically: Lord Eldon first, Sir Ellery second, and Mr. Rowland third."

Mr. Rowland put on a dejected look, and put his hand over his heart. "Alas, put off by an accident of birth!"

Cassandra laughed again, and Lord Eldon grinned. "Sorry, old friend. Better luck next time!"

She enjoyed a vigorous dance with him. Suddenly, it seemed she found an astonishing number of other gentlemen who had at least a passing acquaintance with some relative or friend of her parents; between them all there was not one dance in which she did not participate.

Later at home, when Cassandra finally reached her bed in the wee hours of the morning, her feet ached, and she was exhausted. Never had she had so many dance partners in her life! Her thoughts settled briefly on why she was so suddenly popular, but floated away from sheer fatigue.

"At least," she murmured to herself before slipping into sleep, "I did *not* think of Lord Blytheland's kisses all the while. Not while I was dancing . . ."

Lord Blytheland, however, did think of kisses. He could not avoid it. They were there before him—her pink and delectable lips—every time he closed his eyes to sleep. He could even feel them, soft and sweet, then opening and moving upon his with all the passion he'd imagined when she had played the piano but a few weeks ago. He groaned aloud and rolled over, pressing his face into his pillow.

After a moment, he drove his fist into its goose-down depths. The mattress beneath him only made it worse. It reminded him of the press of her form against him—firm yet supple and warm.

He sat up in his bed and pressed the heels of his hands upon his eyes. Good God, he must have been mad. How *could* he have taken Cassandra out on the terrace and made what amounted to passionate love to her? He had only meant to dance one dance with her—which he did, for all the good it did him. Thank God he was able to collect himself afterward and retain the cool exterior he so carefully cultivated. He sighed. What the devil possessed him to take her out somewhere so damned private it was as good as a bedroom?

She was lovely, but he had been around beautiful women before, both experienced and innocent. But he'd never allowed himself to imply, either by word or gesture, that he was anything more than interested in a light flirtation with any dewy-eyed damsel. Indeed, he had always kept himself to more mature and experienced women who liked their independence and would most likely not marry him if he asked—which he never did, of course, just in case. But Cassand—no, Miss Hathaway—now. He had been within an inch of letting his lips follow the smooth curve of her shoulder down to her soft and delightful—

With another groan, Blytheland fell back upon his bed and pulled his now badly mauled pillow over his face, half wishing he'd suffocate so he could be put out of his misery. Never had he meant to succumb to Miss Hathaway's charms—of face and form only, for she lacked the skills of refined flirtation he usually found so enjoyable, and was so blunt as to be—almost—vulgar.

That was it. Vulgar. Blytheland sighed with relief, removed the pillow from atop him, and settled himself down to sleep. He smiled in relief. Lord, the look on Aurelia's face when Miss Hathaway "complimented" her on her jewels! He regretted that he had had a brief liaison with Aurelia two years ago; it was a passion of the moment, but she had obviously wanted something more. She still schemed to get him—between diversions with other men—and he was glad he was out of the liaison. Certainly Miss Hathaway had put an end to any attempt on Aurelia's part to regain her old status. Cassandra had sent her to *point-nonplus* in less than a minute.

And there her upbringing was revealed—Miss Hathaway apparently did not understand that it was vulgar to comment unfavorably about one's person. A small, niggling voice reminded him that Miss Hathaway no doubt truly thought her comments were complimentary, but he dismissed it.

There now. If he concentrated on it enough, he was sure he could convince himself that she was, in some manner, too unrefined for his taste. Indeed, had he not met and danced with a number of other ladies at the ball? Many of them were far more refined than Miss Hathaway, and a few were more beautiful and higher born as well.

Relief flowed into him. Miss Hathaway was nothing much above the ordinary, not in looks nor in refinement. He had begun his search for a wife and had seen women far superior to her in birth and fortune. Now that he had seen some of what the *ton* had to offer in prospective brides, it should be easy to keep these ladies in mind; Miss Hathaway's assets paled in comparison, and whatever attraction he might feel for her would be easy to resist.

Blytheland settled himself into his pillows and closed his eyes at last. He sighed. Yes, he could resist Miss Hathaway now that he'd seen what the marriage mart had to offer. In fact, he would call upon her tomorrow, just to prove it to himself.

Harry watched Cassandra and Lord Blytheland leave the Marchmonts' ball. He smiled, satisfied. He was certain the marquess would propose at any time now, and it would be as if his mistake had never happened. Well, he hadn't *precisely* made a mistake at the time, for it was not his fault that the man had moved at the last moment and fallen in love with the wrong woman the first time. Harry moved away from the Marchmonts' house and flew toward London, to the street where the Hathaway family lived.

Psyche was quite wrong; she'd soon see that his decision to shoot Lord Blytheland was the right one. Did he not kiss Cassandra—and very passionately, too—for more than five minutes? In this day and age, it was considered a significant thing, and the rules seemed to be that a man could not signal his desires in such a way without submitting an offer of marriage eventually.

Harry spied the house at last and descended to the open window of Psyche's room. She was a kindly child and left it open for him at night so that he could come out of cold weather if he wished. Quietly, he moved to the side of her bed where she was sleeping, and pushed away a small red curl from her forehead. He did not know why he had come to her rescue those years ago when she was lost in the woods . . . perhaps there was something that reminded him of his own Psyche long ago, and who was lost to him.

He had taken on the form of a boy, not much older than herself, for he thought it would be less frightening to her to see another child in the dark, than any other shape he could take. He grimaced. The problem with that was one tended to take on the characteristics of whatever form one assumed, and the longer he used mortal form and the longer he stayed away from the realm of the gods, the more mortal he felt and acted. And it was necessary, for he knew his own Psyche was somewhere on earth, and he would take whatever form he needed to find her.

He grinned suddenly. It was, meanwhile, immensely entertaining to be a young adolescent boy, and even more so to linger around the Hathaway family and see how their fortunes went. He had grown quite fond of Psyche Hathaway—all of the Hathaways, for that matter—no doubt because of her namesake, and also because he never knew quite what she would say next. He gazed out the windows at the lights of London . . . the *ton* was still out and about. His grin grew wider. It was also very entertaining to see what came of his target practice here in and about London. He moved away from Psyche and went to the window.

Harry pulled an arrow from his quiver and twirled it around between his fingers. He chuckled quietly. The night was still young for the high and mighty, and it would be very amusing to see how far they could fall.

Chapter 6

"You must be in excellent spirits, my dear," Sir John said, looking at his wife over his spectacles. "You have been humming a tune for the last quarter of an hour."

"Have I? Well, it is not at all surprising if I am." Lady Hathaway put down her embroidery. She was making a pretty counterpane with pink hearts and blue flowers, just the thing for a newlywed's chambers. *She* could see the significance of Lord Blytheland's walk with Cassandra two weeks ago at the Marchmont ball. She sighed happily. "Oh, husband, I do think Lord Blytheland will declare himself soon! Only think! He has gone to every function at which Cassandra has appeared, and has danced at least once with her at each one. And at Lady Harley's, he even danced twice with her!"

"Well, well, our Cassandra a marchioness. But . . . perhaps he is overly fond of dancing?"

Lady Hathaway sat up stiffly in her chair. "It is *not* dancing he is fond of—" She broke off, for she caught the twinkle in her husband's eye. She let out an exasperated breath. "Oh, John, you are such a provoking man!"

He grinned at her. "But you rise so easily to bait, my dear." He sobered and looked at her keenly. "Are you sure his affections are engaged?"

His wife looked affronted. "Of course I am! The man almost haunts our house! If he is not calling on her to practice music, he is taking her out in his curricle, or inviting us to the theater. Last night Hetty Chatwick actually asked me if we had any interesting announcements to make in the near future—so I know Blytheland's attentions have come to people's notice. Well, of course I said that we certainly did not, but I am afraid I could not help feeling a little conscious."

Sir John rolled his eyes and pushed his fingers through his thick, graying hair, messing it terribly. "Amelia, now all of London will believe it is a promised thing. Hetty Chatwick! Good Lord, what a gossip! You must know now that the supposed betrothal of Blytheland and our daughter will be all over town by tomorrow."

"But I denied it!"

"Yes, and 'feeling a little conscious,' you no doubt looked it!"

"Not at all! Indeed, I looked most stern and forbade her to speak of it."

"Of course that will make her say nothing of the subject at all," Sir John replied, his voice ironic.

Lady Hathaway could not reply. She glanced at her husband resentfully and worked with great concentration on her needlework. She well knew that Mrs. Chatwick would spread it about that Cassandra was as good as promised to the marquess. But how could she help it? Any good mother would want an eligible connection for her children, and she did not exaggerate when she said Blytheland practically haunted the house. Well, so did other gentlemen, now that it seemed Cassandra had become so popular of late.

And there! That was another thing. It was clear to her that the marquess brought Cassandra into fashion. He was a much sought-after man, and any lady to whom he paid attention became just as sought-after. And if—although she could not think it at all likely—*if* Blytheland should *not* declare himself to Cassandra, why then her daughter need only choose one of her other admirers. But of course, *that* would not be the case, for the marquess must be in love with her.

To be sure, it had been only two months since he had been first introduced to Cassandra. But then Lady Hathaway had known of affections that had been animated to the point of a marriage proposal in less than a month's time. The little courtesies, the minute-too-long holding of her hand, the way Blytheland looked at her daughter—*those* had not escaped her notice. Then, too, there were the kisses on the hand— not unknown coming from her own, Lady Hathaway's, contemporaries, but unusual from the younger generation.

The door opened and Sir John and Lady Hathaway looked up.

"Mama, Papa." Cassandra smiled at them, but there was a tense air about her.

"Is there something you wished to see us about, my dear?" Sir John asked. He gestured to a chair near his, and his daughter sat down upon it, arranging her skirts neatly about her.

"I . . . I do not want to seem vain, but perhaps you have noticed that I have more . . . gentlemen callers than before." She glanced uncertainly at her mother.

Lady Hathaway smiled encouragingly. "Well, of course. And a most fortunate girl you are, Cassandra! Now, you see what comes of listening to me, and holding your peace in polite company."

"But that is just it, Mama! I speak as I always have—oh, it is not as if I have not tried to heed your words and hold my tongue, but I know I have not been very successful. And then, too, when I go about to these social functions—more than I ever have before—I find an increasing number of people who say the most cutting things about others! I cannot stay silent, Mama, truly I cannot!"

"Well, well, you must have improved somewhat, for you do have a good number of admirers," Lady Hathaway said.

"No. I think something else has changed. I say what I think, and it seems everyone believes I have uttered a witticism! I cannot understand it!" Cassandra rose from her chair, her hands clasping tightly together.

Sir John chuckled. "Ah, my dear, you have become fashionable. Once you are claimed a diamond of the first water—by those who would know and whose words have weight with the frivolous—you may say anything you like, and it will be considered manna from heaven."

"John, really!" cried his wife, scandalized.

Cassandra turned troubled eyes to her mother. "Mama, is this true?"

"Well, it is more likely—in general—that people will view one in a more favorable light than if one were *not* fashionable . . ."

"Oh, how—how detestable! As if—as if I could want them to listen to me for such a reason, and not because I spoke the truth!"

"Oh, for heaven's sake, Cassandra! Try not to be such a ninny!" cried her mother impatiently. "Be glad they listen to you now at all, for you must know they never did before!" Immediately she wished the words back, for her daughter paled and looked stricken. Lady Hathaway opened her mouth to say a few consoling words, but then closed it firmly. No. For all that she was sad for Cassandra's disillusionment, the girl simply had to accommodate herself to the ways of society and human nature. Better she bear a setdown from her mother who loves her, Lady Hathaway thought, than end up living a lonely spinster's life, shunned by those who could make her life so much more comfortable.

"I am afraid your mother is right, Cassandra," Sir John said, glancing sternly at his wife, nevertheless. "Consider which is preferable: the truth ignored, or the truth at least accepted, though lightly?"

Lady Hathaway cast a surprised look at her husband for his support. It was a different approach than she would have taken herself, but perhaps it would work.

"The truth accepted, of course," Cassandra replied reluctantly.

"Very good," her father said and smiled approvingly.

"Then, too, my dear, you must know that it is Lord Blytheland who has so kindly brought you into fashion," Lady Hathaway interjected. "You cannot wish to be so ungrateful as to repel his efforts on your behalf."

A glow effused Cassandra's face, and her eyes shone. "Oh, no, no! Of course I could not! I am sure he meant well by it, even though it is not what I could like. He is so very kind, is he not, Mama?"

My lady was not quite certain how to reply to this, for Lord Blytheland was not as kind to everyone, from what she had heard of him. She looked up at her husband and found him watching her. "I am sure, my dear, that his attentions to you have been all that is amiable and pleasing," Lady Hathaway said. She threw a challenging look at him. There! He could not say that she said anything not remarked upon by anyone else.

Sir John merely smiled, turned to his daughter, and gave his wife another shock by saying, "Your mother is quite right, and I am pleased, Cassandra, that you understand his actions were meant for your benefit, and that you are properly grateful."

Lady Hathaway stared at her husband. Could it be that he approved of Blytheland? Of course, any man would be a fool to pass over such an eligible prospect for his daughter! But Sir John was not just any man. He had little respect for titles or wealth, and he associated with any manner of people who she had to admit were of great intelligence, but some of whom were decidedly odd. She dared let hope rise in her heart: her husband favorable to the match, Blytheland sure to propose soon, and her daughter . . . She sighed. Now if only Cassandra would be so inclined as to go along with it all! But there was no depending on that. Although . . .

Lady Hathaway gazed at her daughter's face and saw a

dreamy smile hovering about her lips. Could it be . . . ? She had not really watched her daughter's behavior in the marquess's presence; she well knew that Cassandra had more than enough modesty to keep her from doing anything scandalous. She had concentrated on *his* manners instead, watching for any signs of a *tendre* for the girl.

"You *have* found Lord Blytheland's attentions . . . pleasant, have you not, Cassandra?" she said tentatively.

"Oh, yes!" And then to her surprise, Cassandra's face turned beet red. "Th-that is to say, his attentions have been very—He has been most—Not that he has been—" She stopped, looked with confused eyes at her parents, and rushed out the library door.

"Well, well! I do believe our daughter finds Lord Blytheland's attentions most pleasant indeed." Sir John chuckled.

"For heaven's sake, John, have you no sense of propriety?" cried Lady Hathaway. "For all we know he might have—have *importuned* her in an improper manner!"

"Kissed her, do you mean, Amelia?"

"John!"

"Oh, come now, my dear. I think you remember a few kisses before we were married . . . ?" He sat next to her on the sofa, slipped his arm around her ample waist, and kissed her ear.

It was Lady Hathaway's turn to blush, now. She slapped lightly at his hand, although a small smile lingered about her mouth. "*That* is neither here nor there! I must go to her and find out the extent of Blytheland's, ah, attentions."

"My dear wife, you would do best to leave it alone. The marquess is a gentleman. Though he is clearly fond of the ladies, I have not heard of any profoundly libertine tendencies about him. I have no doubt he behaved as any gentleman might around our daughter."

"That is precisely what I am afraid of!" Lady Hathaway said. She caught Sir John's quizzical look and sighed. "Oh, I do not know! Before Cassandra's coming into fashion, any gentleman could be counted to keep their distance. Now I do not know what to think! I wish Blytheland *had* kissed her!"

He smiled. "Never mind, my dear. No doubt he has. Why else should our daughter look so conscious?"

Lady Hathaway looked at her husband, aghast. "John! Do you mean to sit there, sure that Blytheland has kissed Cassandra, and do nothing?"

"No. Not at all. I plan to wait, and see how things come about."

"But that is as good as doing nothing at all!" cried his lady, despairing.

"And what do you wish me to do? Challenge him to a duel unless he marries Cassandra?" Sir John took off his spectacles and polished them thoughtfully with the end of his neckcloth. "Nonsense, Amelia. The truth will be revealed of itself, you know. What falls out will be for the best."

"Well, that is precisely what I fear! That it *will* all fall out!" said Lady Hathaway testily.

"Have faith, my dear," Sir John said. "All will be well."

His lady sighed. Her husband was the dearest man, but not at all practical. She herself would have to see what could be done. "Yes, John," she said, resigned.

Cassandra sat on her bed, pressing her hands to her face. "Oh, how could I be so stupid?" she cried. "I should have told them he kissed me—but I couldn't."

She rose, wet a cloth with the water that was left at the washstand, and pressed the cloth to her cheeks. She felt warm and knew she was blushing just thinking of kisses. It would be much better to resolve to herself that she would not allow it—if, that is, Lord Blytheland tried it again. Which he would not, of course, because he was after all a gentleman, and not an adolescent like her brother, Kenneth, who kissed maids indiscriminately.

A knock sounded on her door. "Come in!"

"Cassandra . . ." Lady Hathaway entered, taking what seemed to be tentative steps into the chamber. Cassandra looked at her mother in surprise. She looked at once hesitant and concerned—and oddly, a little guilty.

"Is—is there something the matter, Mama?"

"Oh, no, no. That is to say—Actually, Cassandra, I was wondering if you had anything to say to *me*."

"I? I cannot think what you might mean." Cassandra went to a stool by the fire and sat down upon it, staring into the flames.

"Come now, my dear, this is unlike you! Why it was obvious to your father and me that something overset you." Her mother's voice sounded so very comfortable and warm, as it always had whenever Cassandra had been in a scrape or needed to confide in her.

"I . . ."

"Is it Lord Blytheland? Has he . . . importuned you in any distasteful manner?"

Cassandra jumped up from her seat, feeling her face grow hot again. "Oh, no, Mama! How can you think it? He has always been very much the gentleman."

Lady Hathaway smiled comfortingly at her. "Then what is it? You cannot be blushing as red as a beet root and there be nothing the matter!"

"He—I—we kissed. At the Marchmonts' ball." There was silence for one moment, and Cassandra swallowed nervously.

"How deligh—Ah! And you found it disgusting and shameful, did you?"

"Oh, no, no! It was the most won—It was most pleasant, Mama! What I mean is—" Cassandra could hear her own voice quaver, and she detested herself for it. "Am I sunk in depravity for liking it so? I know I should not have allowed it."

"Oh, heavens, girl!" Lady Hathaway laughed. "Certainly

it was not proper of you—or him—to have done it. But you were not seen, were you?"

"I am sure we were not."

"Good. Your reputation would have been in tatters if you were! Although it would not have been a terrible thing if you *had* been seen, for he would have offered for you and—"

"No! Mama, I could not marry him if that were so!" Cassandra paced agitatedly in front of the fireplace, then stopped, clasping her hands tightly together.

"Why, I thought you were not . . . averse to his company, Cassandra!"

"Averse—! No, never! I—I—"

"Are you *fond* of him, then?"

"Fond! No. That is, yes, but—I have not thought—Oh, Mama, I do not *know*!" cried Cassandra, sinking down upon the footstool again next to her mother. "I have known him but two months! How can I know, truly?"

Lady Hathaway smiled and patted her on the shoulder. "Well, well, you are right. It is only past the middle of the Season, and there is plenty of time to come to know each other better."

"Yes, of course, Mama," Cassandra said, still feeling confused. Mama had told her long ago about not submitting to a gentleman's attempts at an embrace, but now she seemed positively merry about the prospect. Lady Hathaway had maintained a delighted smile throughout their conversation. She could not understand it. Perhaps . . . perhaps kisses were not so reprehensible as she had believed?

"You are looking concerned," her mother said. Cassandra looked up at her with a grateful smile at her quick perception. "Is it that you are worried about kissing?"

Cassandra nodded.

"Well, it was only one kiss, after all! It is not as if it never happens. I will even confess your father and I shared a few before we were married. Not that my mother would have approved, mind you!" Lady Hathaway smiled reminiscently and looked almost young.

Cassandra stared at Lady Hathaway. She tried envisioning her mother's plump form and father's lean one in the same embrace as she and the marquess had shared and failed miserably. But it must have been so, if her mother said it. Well, it was obvious she had refined too much on the matter, and she felt relieved.

"Oh, Mama! I am so glad you came to talk to me about it. I have felt so confused!"

"Of course, my dear. Am I not your mother? You are a good girl, and I know you try your best to behave with propriety." With one more affectionate pat on Cassandra's shoulder, Lady Hathaway rose from her chair and left the room.

Married. Cassandra had not thought of it—or at least, not dared think of it in connection with Lord Blytheland. Of course, she knew the purpose of having a Season in London was to find an amiable husband, and she knew her parents were kind enough to let her follow her own heart. But never, never would she allow the marquess to propose to her under such circumstances in which he would feel forced to do so! If he ever did propose, that is. Certainly she could not expect that he would. He could look far, far higher than herself for a wife.

Or . . . could she? Could he possibly want to marry her? Cassandra shook her head fiercely. No. If so, he would not have so kindly brought her to fashion, would he? For then he would have rivals for her favor. She dismissed the thought that his kiss would have meant anything. After all, kisses did not mean to gentlemen what they did to ladies. Why, she need only think of her brother Kenneth to know that! She had caught him kissing a parlor maid once, and then a week later she found him with a chambermaid. Of course her brother could not seriously intend to marry a servant, and certainly Lord Blytheland did not think she, Cassandra, was a servant, but it just showed how little men treasured kisses or embraces.

Well, then! She would just keep that in mind and make sure they were never caught in any sort of embrace—not that they *would* kiss again, of course! With that firm resolve, she readied herself for the duet she would have with the marquess.

Lady Hathaway leaned against the chamber door she had just closed, and shut her eyes. "Thank you, God," she murmured under her breath. Lord Blytheland *had* kissed Cassandra! He would not have done it if he had not been enamored of her. Never, never had she heard that the marquess trifled with the affections of a young unmarried lady. And, miracle of miracles, Cassandra was not so much of a bluestocking that she found his embrace objectionable. Further, Lady Hathaway was certain her husband would not object—for whatever eccentric reason—to the match.

Ah, what a success it would be! And Lady Chartley thought *she* had done well marrying her girl to an earl's son. Well, perhaps she had, at that, for the chit was but a sallow little thing! Cassandra, now! *She* would not only be a marchioness, but eventually a duchess! Lady Hathaway's heart felt full to bursting with joy, and her step was light as she walked down the stairs to the parlor.

"So . . . I understand you might be looking for a marchioness, Blythe, old man?" Lord Eldon leaned against the marquess's wardrobe and negligently twirled his quizzing glass on its ribbon. He watched as his friend carefully wound his neckcloth around his neck while the valet hovered anxiously next to him.

"Who told you that?" Blytheland pulled one end of the cloth through a loop he had made with the other end.

"You haven't been to White's lately, I see. It's in all the town's betting books."

"What are the odds?"

"Ten to one you'll be in the parson's mousetrap before the end of the Season."

"Good odds for you—if you are betting *against*."

"Should I be?"

Blytheland, holding a twist of neckcloth firmly to his neck, turned to look at his friend. "Why not?"

"Well, I might lose, Blythe-my-old." Eldon grinned at him. "Seems to me you've been seen much more than once at Hathaway's house."

"Miss Hathaway is a superb pianist. It is rare that I can play against a performer who is more than competent."

"Oh, and let's see—you danced with her twice at the Amberleys' ball, you escorted her to supper at the Bramhursts' rout, and I think I saw you at the theater with her last week," Lord Eldon continued, ticking off each item on his fingers. "And then of course there was that stunning beginning where you disappeared with her on the Marchmonts' terrace—" He held up his hand at the marquess's icy look. "Oh, never fear! It wasn't long enough for scandal, just enough to raise eyebrows."

"I never listen to gossips, frankly."

"Neither do I. But admit it, my old, you've been flitting around that Hathaway chit like a moth to a flame."

"I am not likely to be burnt, believe me!"

Eldon contemplated his friend. The marquess was still concentrating on tying his neckcloth, his movements were still smooth and careful, but there was a tenseness in his answers. He wondered how far he should push Blytheland. He was not exaggerating when he intimated that talk was rife about his friend's seeming infatuation with the lovely bluestocking. Better have it out, he decided. He almost grimaced at the thought. They'd almost had it out when Blytheland was first courting Chloe—his friend had a temper, certainly. But dash it all, for all that it was clear his friend wouldn't listen to him, he'd had to say something back then . . . as he

had to now. Miss Hathaway was nothing like Chloe, and
Blythe was a marriage-minded sort, even though he tried to
deny it. La Hathaway would be perfect for him, if Blytheland would only see it. And if he didn't, he would certainly
hate to see the poor girl hurt, for she was clearly caught.
Eldon grinned to himself. Well, he never thought he had the
romantic in him, but he always did have an eye for a
matched pair.

However, Blytheland was too inclined to keep things to
himself, and next thing you knew he'd blister you up one
side and down the other for saying something perfectly innocent. He could have a nasty temper, Blytheland could, if
he didn't air it once in a while. He'd have to watch his step.
Eldon sighed.

"Well, I didn't think you were one to change your ways.
Why should you? Once burnt, twice shy, after all."

Blytheland gave him a cold, sharp glance—definitely
threatening. Eldon mentally retreated and decided to take
another tack.

"And Lord knows you could have your pick of the *demi-
mondaine*. I hear even Harriette Wilson has cast her eyes
your way."

The marquess gave him a pained look. "Really, El, I
thought you did not listen to gossip. Harriette Wilson. Good
God. I hope I have better taste than that."

Lord Eldon nodded. "That's what I thought. Anyway, it's
just as well you don't have an interest in La Hathaway.
Rather thought I'd have a touch at her myself."

"What!" Blytheland's hand jerked, and he slewed his
head around to stare at his friend. "You?"

"Milor'! Your cravat!" cried the valet, his hands clutch-
ing his hair in artistic agony.

"Damnation! Fichet, get me another, *vite*!" The marquess
stripped off what used to be an impeccably starched length
of cloth and threw it on the floor. He barely seemed to no-

tice his servant's heartfelt groan at this desecration, or the man's muttered imprecations on the vagaries of the English.

Lord Eldon peered at the ruined neckcloth through his quizzing glass. "My, my. I haven't seen you do that since the time you heard Lady Montmorency was increasing—how long ago was that? Before you married Chloe, I think. Luckily it turned out to be Montmorency's brat, all right and tight. Platter-faced little thing—looks just like its father, no mistake. Never did poach on another man's territory after that, did you, Blythe?"

Blytheland threw him a fulminating glare. "Never mind about Montmorency! What the devil does he—I can't believe it. You, El? Setting up your nursery? You are younger than I am—five-and-twenty—if that!"

"Didn't stop my brother."

"That is different. *You* have never been one for chasing petticoats."

Lord Eldon grinned. "Not as much as you, at any rate. Thing is, I'm the eldest. Must do my duty and all that. You might think about it yourself, one of these days." He gave his quizzing glass one more twirl, then neatly pocketed it.

"But why Miss Hathaway?"

"Why not? Lovely girl, good figure, dresses well, good manners. Should do me proud. I don't care much for music, but just as long as it isn't some damned caterwauling I'll listen. By the way, I must thank you for bringing her to my notice. Truly enchanting." He kissed his fingers to the air in salute.

"But damn it, she's a bluestocking!"

"Bothers you, does it?" My, but old Blythe was getting red under his collar, Eldon thought gleefully.

"Yes! No! That's not the point. I've never seen *you* exchanging quotes from Sophocles with anyone! And I'll wager you've never done so with Cass—Miss Hathaway. That would be doing it a bit too brown, my friend."

"True." Cassandra, was it? Well, well. Lord Eldon was

hard put not to smile. "But the world of conversation is large. There are other things of which to speak—her charities, for instance."

"Charities?"

"Terrible situation, my old. There are starving folk all around us. She quite convinced me to contribute to the aid of these poor creatures."

"You?"

"Blytheland, you pain me. Of course, *me*. I may be a Pink of the *ton,* but I am not without heart. And never tell me she hasn't spoken of her charities to *you*."

The marquess looked uncomfortable.

"Ah, I see she has. Laid out any blunt for it?"

"Yes, and I promised to ask my father to speak at the House on it."

Lord Eldon laughed. "Persuasive creature, isn't she? But there you are. We shall rub along quite well together, don't you think? She with her causes, I with the money to fund them."

"You are getting as vulgar as she is," Blytheland retorted.

"I? Vulgar? should call you out, my old, if I didn't know how good you are with the pistols." Eldon moved himself from the wardrobe and sank into a large chair next to the fireplace. "But tell me. How is Miss Hathaway vulgar?"

"I should not have said vulgar," the marquess amended. "She is, certainly, indiscreet."

"Better and better," Eldon leered.

"I did *not* mean to imply she was a light skirt, damn you, El! She's more pure than—than that damnably ill-tied thing you have around your neck! *I* should call *you* out, if I knew you had the smallest ability to drag yourself out of bed before eleven."

His friend looked complacently at his own snowy white neckcloth reflected in the mirror and smiled. "Pure as an angel, I should think. Well, now. Indiscreet?"

"She can't control her tongue. She says whatever comes

to her mind. Lord, the number of times I have seen her give a set-down to some stiff-rumped hypocrite! And sometimes she is not even aware she is doing it!"

"I should be amused, I think."

"Amused!" The marquess grimaced into the mirror. "Well, it is amusing," he admitted. "It is also why I brought her into fashion. I thought it would be entertaining if I did so. That's all there is to it, and so you may tell your betting cronies." Fichet entered with another, freshly pressed, neck-cloth. He warily handed it to his master.

"Hmm . . . And not because you are enamored of her?"

"I have known far more beautiful women than Miss Hath-away."

Lord Eldon noticed that his friend did not actually answer his question. He smiled to himself, then rose from the chair. "It's just as well, old Blythe. I just didn't want to step on your toes, you know." He put on his hat at a precise angle and took up his cane. "Think La Hathaway might come to see herself as a baroness? Perhaps I should go see her soon."

"I'd prefer you go to the devil, Eldon," said the marquess through clenched teeth.

"Better than being blue-deviled, my old!" His friend laughed, and left the room.

Blytheland cursed and ruined another neckcloth.

But Eldon's words came back to the marquess, niggling at him, for they were not content to settle in the far corner of Blytheland's mind, where he had consigned them. He glanced at Miss Hathaway, who was at the pianoforte flex-ing her fingers in readiness for the recital. Thoughts of Cassandra and marriage, of the natural consequences of marriage—the marriage bed, for instance—leapt upon him like a cat upon a mouse and played with his emotions un-mercifully and with a killing instinct. They pounced on him when he happened to be near her and looked at the lips he had kissed, and when she played the pianoforte, he thought of how her fingers caressed the keys into soft sound and how they might caress his—

Blytheland took a deep breath and set his violin upon his chest and tried not to look at Cassandra as she began to play the sonata. There were plenty of things to focus upon in Lord and Lady Langdon's house, for it was well lighted and decorated with finely executed paintings, so he need not look at Miss Hathaway at all during the performance. He needed to pay strict attention to the music, for they were before Lady Langdon and her guests, and all eyes were upon them.

It was a piece of music both of them knew well and had practiced before either of them had met, and so it needed only two practice sessions to see if they could play together. There had been an initial awkwardness at first, but they had gone through it well enough, and quickly. He was not sure he could have gone through a third session; he'd been distracted enough during the first, almost as much as he had been distracted when Cassandra first played her pianoforte for him.

He'd look at her only once to signal the beginning of each movement and not look at her while they played. He would concentrate on the music, and that was all.

Silence descended on the guests, he took a deep breath, and nodded to Miss Hathaway. He watched her fingers touch the keys, then he closed his eyes and drew his bow across his violin.

It was a mistake. He should have known not to have selected this Beethoven sonata. If the presto beat made him take in a breath, the first notes in the minor key took it away from him. He had intended to select a difficult piece so that there would be a higher chance of Cassandra stumbling in her performance. He would be able to focus on his own performance then. But she did not stumble now, not as she had done when they had practiced before. She had obviously practiced more, afterward.

And now, now he was lost, for she played it perfectly. The music from the pianoforte twined around his own and pressed itself against him until Blytheland almost gasped and drew his bow across his violin with greater force in defense. But it was as if she would have none of it: her music wrestled with him. Passion gave way to crying sweetness, so tangible and sharp it sat on his tongue and he nearly groaned when he drew in his breath, for it was the taste of lovemaking.

Blytheland opened his eyes and stared at Cassandra. It did not help. Her whole concentration was on the music, and she did not look at him. It did not matter—no, it was worse, for she looked like a woman sunk in pleasure: her cheeks flushed, her eyes heavy-lidded, her breath coming quickly from between her lips. He could imagine it, making love to her, almost feel it.

The music, the music! Think of the music! he told himself, but that did not help either, for the music pulled at him and caressed him like a lover's hand—Cassandra's hands. He looked down at the keyboard, how her slender, delicate fingers stroked the keys and lured the notes from the instrument, so that he wanted to weep with the sweetness of it. But he could not. His violin wept instead and wailed the anguish within him.

The sound caught at Cassandra, and she lifted her eyes and stared at him. The room did not exist—the guests, the house. There were only the notes that pierced her heart, only the way Lord Blytheland looked at her, just as he had when he kissed her at the Marchmonts' ball. Her breath halted in her throat, and she remembered how his lips had moved across hers, how his fingers had traced a scintillating path down her throat, just as his fingers now moved upon the violin and drew out sweet music.

She pulled her gaze away from him, concentrating on the sonata, but she knew he was still staring at her—she could feel it. Cassandra looked at him again; he did not smile, but there was a fiery warmth in his eyes, and his gaze shifted downward to her mouth. She could feel her lips heat as if he had kissed them. She almost missed a note and brought her attention back to the pianoforte. But the music conspired against her, for she could not help looking at Lord Blytheland again when his music moved with hers, and she felt drawn to something she was afraid could not be real.

Joy and fear caught her, and she pounded it into the keyboard, trying desperately to focus on the notes she remembered. But the violin's notes curled around and about her, and touched her in hidden places, seducing her. She had known of emotions that welled up within her when she played or heard a fine piece of music; she did not know music could make her feel these other things. Did he know? She was half afraid of the answer and almost glad the sonata was nearly over. Almost over; it was safe, then, to give in to the music, for it would be done soon. The violin said so— the high, sweet notes whispered in her ears: come, love, listen. Her eyes filled with tears at the sound, and her heart came open as she touched the last chords of the sonata.

Cassandra sighed and felt a drop of wetness upon her hand, and she lifted her hand to wipe at her wet cheeks. She looked up at Lord Blytheland who extended a handkerchief to her.

She smiled and dabbed her eyes with it. "So silly of me! I have never wept before like this. I do not know what came over me."

He said nothing, but only looked at her, a disturbed expression in his eyes. He turned to the guests, then bowed.

The guests! Oh, heavens. Cassandra grew conscious of their silence, and turned also. She felt her hand grasped, and looked up at Lord Blytheland as he pulled her from her seat at the pianoforte.

"Curtsy," he hissed.

Hastily she did. She dared look at the guests, and she could not help blushing. What had she done? She could not help seeing the clearly speculative looks on many of their faces, or sly, knowing expressions. The memory of her feelings during the performance came to her, and she blushed and despised herself for blushing. She hoped that the guests would think she was blushing at their applause, but she had learned enough now—especially with the way they looked at her—that they probably did not. Whatever she might have felt, she did not want anyone else to know. It was a stupid thing to hope, for however many men had seemed to be attracted to her, nothing had ever come of it. Each time she had hoped, and each time she had died a little, inside.

Lord Blytheland turned to her and smiled a stiff smile and bowed low over her hand. "Don't," she whispered.

He looked at her with brows raised, but she only pulled her hand away and smiled tentatively in return. She gave another curtsy to the guests and returned to her seat next to her parents. Her mother smiled and nodded at her, and her father looked at her with searching eyes.

She smiled again, briefly. "How glad I am the performance is over!" she said as cheerfully as possible. "I become quite anxious performing in front of so many people." It was not quite a lie, for though she had lost all nervousness while playing—heavens, she had felt everything except nervousness!—she had felt it at the beginning. But she noticed the speculative looks from the people around her fade, and she was glad of it.

A new set of musicians were tuning their instruments, and the guests looked toward them in readiness for the next piece. Cassandra breathed a sigh of relief and looked cautiously about her for Lord Blytheland. He was nowhere in the room that she could see. Perhaps he had left already . . . although he usually liked to stay for all of a musicale in the past, she had noticed. She sighed again. If he was as conscious of the looks they had received from the guests, she would not be surprised if he had left.

*   *   *

Lord Blytheland had indeed been conscious of the speculative looks from the guests at Lady Langdon's musicale, and more. He needed refreshment, as he always did after a performance, and had gone to the punch bowl at one end of the room. The musicians were tuning up for the next piece of music, and the guests' eyes were drawn to that corner of the room, and so he doubted he was much noticed as he quickly took a cup of punch and downed it behind a large fern on a pedestal. Certainly he had not been noticed by the ladies who came to stand next to the punch bowl with their backs to him.

"Did you *see* the way he looked at her? Hetty Chatwick said that they were good as betrothed," said one of them.

"*I* cannot see what anyone might see in Miss Hathaway—she is a bluestocking, you know!" the other tittered. "But *she* is a sorry case as anyone can see, for I do believe she has fallen completely in love with him, if looks are any indication." the lady nibbled at a small sandwich, then giggled. "I vow, she seemed almost to pant after him like a dog after a bone! So vulgarly obvious. I feel quite sorry for her. Lord Blytheland can look higher for a wife than she."

The first lady laughed. "Who, like you, Amanda? You may not be a baronet's daughter, but you are not much higher than that."

Lord Blytheland clenched his teeth. He did not like being discussed like a bull to be bought by farmers.

"A viscount's daughter is much more eligible than anything Miss Hathaway can lay claim to," Susan said complacently.

He could stand it no longer and emerged from behind the fern. "For your information, ladies, nothing would compel me to consider either of you as a prospective wife." He bowed curtly and turned on his heel, catching enough of their red and chagrined expressions to feel a savage satisfaction.

But as he went down to his coach and left Lady Langdon's house for his own, he knew he had erred greatly in paying so much attention to Miss Hathaway. If it had indeed been bruited about that they were as good as betrothed—and he would not have put it past Lady Hathaway to have hinted it to her acquaintances—then he was sorely mistaken in how much time he had spent in Miss Hathaway's company. He grimaced. Eldon had been right, and he had been wrong to ignore his friend's warning. For all that Eldon liked to tease and had a damnable way of poking his nose where it shouldn't be, he was a good friend and knew all the gossip around about town. He should have listened to him.

Did Miss Hathaway expect anything from him? He did not know. She had never hinted at it . . . only perhaps wished for his company, for she had never yet refused an invitation to ride with him in his phaeton. But he could not distinguish this from—

He took a deep breath as his coach came to the door of his house, and it only slightly cleared the ache in his chest. If he were a true gentleman, he would at least offer for her. Her birth was respectable, and he supposed so must her dowry be, if her family could afford to stay in a house in the best part of London. She was not like Chloe, he knew that now. She was too blunt, too ignorant of many of the *ton's* rules to pretend and hide behind a facade.

An odd twisting pulled at his gut, and he knew he was afraid. He sneered at himself. It was a stupid thing to feel, for marriages for reasons of inheritance were made all the time, and he need not consider a possible marriage to Miss Hathaway to be anything more than that. And if he was worried that she might ever play him false, he could watch her carefully until she bore him his heir.

He opened the door of his coach with a restless movement and descended. Ah, who was he trying to deceive? He was in love with Miss Hathaway, and he was ten times the fool for it. He did not know what had caused him to fall in love with her—the music, or she herself. Perhaps both. He pulled up his shoulders as if against the cold, although his house was warm enough when he entered it. He thought of how Chloe had fooled him and knew he would not be fooled again.

Of course, if he was careful, he could prevent it. If a woman knew his affections were engaged, she'd take advantage of it. It'd be best if he presented his proposal to Miss Hathaway in a formal manner and said nothing of his love for her. He'd convince her that it was for her own good, for the alternative was more embarrassing whispers, and he was certain she'd not want that. A feeling of relief came over him, and he smiled a little. and of course she'd see the advantage a good position in society could give her. There was much he could offer her, and he'd be rid of his stupid impulses in return. It was really a perfect proposal all around.

He would see what she thought of it tomorrow, and then he'd approach her father about it—no need to do the thing formally if she was opposed to marrying him, after all. They could announce it at the alfresco luncheon to which he'd invited her and her family, as well as his own family and his friends.

A feeling of relief went through him, and his shoulders relaxed. Well, there it was. All he had to do was propose to Miss Hathaway, marry her, and he could stop thinking about making love to her because she'd be in his bed soon enough. That should make his life a great deal more comfortable, he was sure.

Chapter 7

"Only think! Lord Blytheland even offered—he insisted!—that I attend the alfresco luncheon with Mama, Papa, and Cassandra next week. Do you not think he truly is a very kind gentleman?" Psyche bounced upon the sofa seat in happiness.

"Oh, I suppose he is—when he wants to be." Harry sat upon the drawing-room windowsill, his wings pressed against the windows. He shifted uncomfortably, then turned and opened them. He stretched his wings in a contented manner. "There. That's better." He turned to Psyche with a smug smile. "So you see, he is the right husband for her, and she is perfect for him."

"I cannot feel comfortable about it, though. You said he is in love with Cassandra, and he has always been kind to me—though he need not pay me attention, as Mama has said, for I am not yet out. But you have *made* him love her, you see. What if your arrows stop working, and he stops loving her? Then they will be miserable."

Harry looked offended. "My arrows don't stop working."

"How do you know?" Psyche said instantly. "Have you ever been around long enough to find out?"

A brief uncomfortable expression flashed across Harry's countenance, but a slow, crooked grin replaced it. He pulled an arrow from his quiver, twirling it deftly around between his fingers. "I could always shoot some more."

Psyche recognized the grin and grew alarmed. "Don't

you *dare*! You leave Lord Blytheland alone, and Cassandra, too! They are well on their way to marriage, Mama has told me, and need no help from you."

" 'The course of true love never did run smooth,' " quoted Harry. "Besides, if you think the effect of my arrows may fade after a while, then the logical solution would be to apply them again."

Psyche gnawed her lip. What a troublesome thing it was to fall in love! But it was a thing adults did, and she supposed she must do so, too, someday. "Well, Cassandra's love will be true—*if* you leave them alone. No doubt even if the arrows lost their effect, Lord Blytheland will still come to love her, for she is the best sister imaginable, you know. Everything will come out for the best, I think, just by themselves."

"I doubt it. There are too many loose ends left untied."

"And you are the one to tie them up? I *doubt* it."

Harry sighed impatiently. "I wonder when you will understand, Psyche, that I know more about these things than you do? I am much older than you, and have more experience."

"Oh, really? You don't look more than two or three years older than I. Not much experience there, I should think! And when have you fallen in love, pray tell?"

Harry looked taken aback. "Fallen in love? It is not at all necessary that I fall in love to know about it. I need only observe."

"There! That proves it. I admit I have never fallen in love either, but I have read much upon the subject. So I know at least a little!"

"Read what?" Harry flew over to the sofa and rummaged behind the pillows. He brought out a small volume. "This?"

"Harry, give it to me at once!" He tossed it in her lap, then sat next to her. Psyche hugged the book to her chest, then looked at its cover fondly. "Well, yes, it was what I was talking of. It is full of the trials one goes through for love."

"The Tomb of the Accursed," Harry read, peering at the book. "That does not sound like anything to do with love."

"Oh, but it does! Only listen: 'Corimunde! Keep true to your virtue and our love! Do not veer from the true course of our affections!' And then *she* says, 'Though I starve in my dank and gloomy chamber, though my heart and limbs be rend from my body by the evil Orcanto, though demons seize my blood-hued dreams—my soul, my soul, O Gerard, is yours for eternity!' " Psyche recited in thrilling accents, closing her eyes in utter bliss.

There was a long silence. She opened her eyes and looked at her friend. "Well? Was that not truly moving?"

One corner of Harry's lips moved upward, but the rest of his mouth twisted in a pursed sort of way. It was as if he had eaten something sour and was politely trying to pretend he had not. Psyche frowned.

"You must have felt something! What did you think of it?"

"Well . . . I thought it sounded rather gruesome, actually."

"Gruesome!" Psyche felt crestfallen. It was her most favorite book. She had hoped Harry would appreciate it, too. "It *does* end happily, though. Gerard and Corimunde are married after going through horrid trials and adventures, and after Orcanto has a halberd driven through his vitals and dies horribly."

Harry's wings shuddered. "If that is your vision of true love, then I wonder that you care to have your sister and Blytheland married at all." He looked over the biscuits on the table next to Psyche, selected one, then ate it in a contemplative manner, as if wondering if he should have another.

Psyche laughed merrily. "No, you goose! Of course, Cassandra and the marquess are not characters in a book, but you must admit they do not have to go through the troubles that Corimunde and Gerard must! *That,* I am sure, does not happen every day. Now it is not reasonable to think that if Corimunde and Gerard can keep their love through horrible events, that Cassandra and Lord Blytheland can come to find love far more easily when they do not have to defeat villains like Orcanto? *Without* your help?"

"No," Harry replied. He picked up her book and leafed through it. He rolled his eyes and shut the book again, then selected another biscuit.

Psyche let out an exasperated breath. "You are the most odious boy! How can you say so?"

"Corimunde and Gerard are made-up people. Blytheland and Cassandra are not, and mortals need more help than made-up people. That is because characters in books are ideals, and mortals are far from that."

Sometimes Psyche thought it quite unfair that Harry did not have someone keeping an eye on *his* hubris. "What has that to say to anything? Lord Blytheland and Cassandra still have far fewer trials than Corimunde and Gerard. They will do well, I know."

"*If* I help them!"

"*If* you *don't*!" Psyche retorted. "Now promise me you will not shoot any more arrows at Lord Blytheland or any at my sister."

Harry looked at her with an impudent smile and said nothing.

"Harry!"

He made a face at her. "Very well. I will compromise: I will only shoot an arrow if you wish it." He sighed. "I have shot any number of arrows into Lord Blytheland already, enough to make anyone mad with love, but he is a stubborn case. Besides, I am tired of it anyway."

"Promise?" Psyche looked at him warily.

Harry sighed again. "I promise."

The door suddenly opened and Cassandra walked in,

holding the hand of a little boy. Psyche cast a warning look at Harry. He had an innocent expression on his face, which she did not quite trust, but she had to be satisfied with it for now.

"Psyche, where is Mama and Papa?" Cassandra looked a little harried, but turned to smile at the boy—quite dirty and ragged, Psyche noticed, so it must be one of Cassandra's climbing boys. "Tim, you must sit here—or, no, perhaps not there. Mama did not like the soot on the damask cushions the last time. Well, here by the fireplace." The boy shrank away from the fire, and Cassandra grimaced. "Oh, dear! No, no, I will not ask you to climb it . . . see, I will even give you something to eat. That is all I wish from you, do you see?" She went over to the dish of biscuits next to Psyche and gave him one. The boy snatched it and stuffed it in his mouth, then cautiously sat down on the floor by the fire, watching Cassandra and Psyche carefully.

Cassandra turned to her sister. "Have you seen Mama, Psyche?"

"Yes." Psyche nodded. "She went out only a quarter of an hour ago to Aunt Mary's house, and you know they will talk for hours. And Papa is at one of his scholarly meetings."

"Oh, heavens! I don't think I can wait until they come back, for it is getting late, and I wish to start out before dark." Cassandra wrung her hands a little and looked worried.

"Are you going to take the boy home?" Psyche asked. "And may I come with you?"

Cassandra smiled. "No, not this time. I barely have enough of my pin money left to bring myself home again. And I know Mama does not like it when I keep the boys here overnight."

Psyche nodded. The last boy had wailed loudly throughout the night, and the one before that had broken an imported Chinese vase and a porcelain figurine and had stolen

Papa's pocket watch. "I shall tell them you have gone, then—I suppose you are taking the traveling coach?"

"Yes, and a footman, an undergroom, *and* a maid, so Mama need not be worried that I will be unprotected."

"Mama will not like it, even so, Cassandra," Psyche said.

Cassandra sighed. "What else am I to do? The last time I let the servants transport one of my boys, he ran off and another chimney sweep caught him! None of them have run away from me, you see."

Psyche looked at the boy sitting on the floor and believed it. Tim gazed at her sister as if she were a goddess, following her every move with his eyes. All of the boys had been this way, and always minded her. A pang of sympathy went through Psyche. She supposed it was because they had no parents to care for them, as she was cared for.

"Well, I will tell Papa first, and I know he will approve of what you have done, and then Mama cannot say anything about it," Psyche said.

Cassandra grinned. "That should work very well—thank you, love!" She went to her sister and hugged her. "You are the best of sisters." She looked uncomfortable, then said, "But be careful of whom else you tell, please! I cannot like it, but I did promise Mama not to speak of my activities to anyone except those who are family, or close friends."

"I won't, then," Psyche said. "Although I don't understand why anyone would disapprove."

Her sister smiled at her. "Some don't, I have found, but I suppose Mama is right in that we should be cautious." She rang for a servant, then turned to Tim. "Now do be a good boy and stay here. I will be right back, and you may have all the biscuits you want until I return."

The boy nodded and looked so bereft and frightened at Cassandra's departure that Psyche felt sorry for him and brought the whole plate of biscuits to him. He gave one wary look at her and seized the plate, stuffing the food into his mouth and into whatever available pockets he had.

But Psyche was glad that Cassandra came back quickly, though, for once the biscuits were stowed away inside and upon Tim's person, he began to stow away other small items in the drawing room, and Psyche was hard put to keep him from doing it. Harry was no help at all! She gave him a meaningful look, but he merely sat on the sofa watching her take one thing after another from Tim, and shaking with silent laughter.

"No, Tim! Put that back, if you please!" Cassandra said as she entered the room and firmly took a small porcelain shepherdess from the boy's hand. "And the rest of the things you have taken!" Cassandra held her hand out to him. "I have some clothes for you—we will go into the kitchen and you will put them on—and then we will go to the nice place in the country. With horses, Tim!"

The boy's eyes widened, and he hastily took five items from his pockets, then followed her out the room. Psyche sighed, eyeing the crumbs on the floor. Cassandra was a very good sort of young lady, and the best of sisters, but sometimes her goodness was very untidy and inconvenient.

Lord Blytheland had ruined four neckcloths before he was satisfied with the result this morning. He admitted to himself that he was nervous; one did not go about proposing marriage to young ladies every day after all. It was not that he thought Miss Hathaway would refuse him, of course, for he'd present to her the problems of being an object of gossip, and she'd not want any of that. Further, there were all the advantages of being a titled lady of wealth and substance. That, no doubt, would have some weight with her. These were solid, practical things, and was she not an intelligent lady of good reason? But he still hesitated before he raised the knocker on the Hathaways' door and firmly knocked.

"Is Miss Hathaway in?" he asked the butler, giving him his hat and cane.

The butler bowed. "I believe so, my lord. This way, if you please, my lord." He took the card Lord Blytheland offered him, and led the way upstairs. Blytheland could feel his hands becoming a little damp as the door opened to admit him. He rapidly thought over the words he would say, stepped into the room, and took a deep breath.

"Miss Hathaway, I—" He stopped and looked at the girl in front of him. "Miss Psyche! I hoped your sister was here."

"Oh! I am so sorry," Psyche said, her voice contrite. "Was I wrong in not telling our butler not to admit you? I thought perhaps I should tell you myself. I would not want to be rude, you see, in having only a butler tell you that Cassandra is not here."

"Ah." Blytheland felt a little deflated. He had worked himself up to the point, and it was disappointing to have his efforts go to waste. He smiled at Psyche nevertheless. "I will be perfectly content to say pretty things to you while I am here, since your sister is not here."

Psyche shook her head and laughed. "You need not, you know. I know one needs to have blond or black hair to have pretty things said to them, so I know you would only be funning. But Cassandra will return soon. We are all going to your luncheon, after all. She is only going to see to one of her children and should be back tomorrow—" She pressed her lips together, suddenly remembering that she had promised not to speak of Cassandra's climbing boys. But it must be permissible to tell him, since he was becoming quite a close friend? And if he was as close to marrying Cassandra as Harry said, he could certainly be considered almost family.

"Children?" The marquess went suddenly still and his face seemed to pale.

Psyche began to feel uneasy, for an expression of anger had flickered in his eyes before his face became smooth and polite. "I—I'm sorry. I thought perhaps she had spoken

to you of them, because I have heard you are as good as—
That is, you are a frequent caller to our house, and have
been very amiable. I am not supposed to speak of the boys,
because Mama says not everyone approves of such things."

"No, they would not." His voice seemed a little strained.

"You mustn't think she is very unusual for it," Psyche
said earnestly. "I have heard other ladies do it, too. Mama
says it is an eccentric thing to do." She sighed. "But I suppose we are all a little eccentric, and too softhearted to see
any of the children cast off." She peered at him, wary.
"You are not angry, are you?"

Lord Blytheland stared at her for a long moment, and
Psyche felt a little afraid at the darkness that crossed his
face. But then it cleared, and he smiled a little. "No, no, I
am not angry at you." He stood up, and his movements
seemed stiff. "I have another call to make . . . I hope you
will excuse me?"

Psyche nodded and watched her sister's suitor leave the
room. She had a dreadful feeling that she had said something she shouldn't have and hoped it wasn't too awful. But
she was not at all sure of that.

Lord Blytheland strode back to his house, not bothering
to get back into his coach to drive home and telling his
groom to return it for him. He was not at all certain he
could keep his hands steady on the reins, not after the blow
he'd received.

The pattern was there, was it not? Miss Hathaway, deep
down, was no better than his wife had been. Was she not an
intellectual? Was she not a follower of Mrs. Wollstonecraft? And did he not hear Miss Hathaway's own sister say that she had gone to tend her children?

Bile rose in his throat, and he swallowed. He had been
astounded that a young girl would even be allowed to know
such things, or would talk of it with such ease. Not with
total ease! That was clear, for she had stumbled over her

words and looked guilty, as if she had let out a secret she was not supposed to know, much less speak of. He had been mistaken in the Hathaway family . . . he had thought they might be respectable enough, since Sir John was an acquaintance of the duke, his father. But his own father had unusual interests, and his associations were not always of good *ton*. He had assumed—wrongly, for Miss Psyche herself admitted that her family was eccentric—that the association gave the family some cachet, some respectability. It was clear this was not entirely true.

Or, perhaps, in the way of ambitious people—and Lady Hathaway was certainly ambitious—they sought to cover up any indiscretions that might mark their family as undesirable. But to push off an unvirtuous woman as Miss Cassandra Hathaway upon the *ton* was beyond ambitious, it was supremely foolish. They had neither the connections nor the wealth to pull it off. It did explain, however, why the lovely Miss Hathaway was not yet betrothed despite her adequate fortune, and why the Hathaways had left their home to come to London to snare a husband for her.

A hot anger filled Lord Blytheland, and the street seemed to burn in front of him. He walked faster. He'd been a fool—again. He'd been caught—again. God, when would he stop being such a idiot, led by his passions and his obvious lust? For that was what it was, certainly. He should have slaked his lust on some woman long before this, so that he could have chosen his bride with more sense and reason.

He could ruin them. He could let it be known the kind of woman Miss Cassandra Hathaway was, and they'd never show their faces in London again. A small part of him reminded him of his passions again, and he took a deep breath. No, he could not do that. Miss Psyche, at least, was an innocent, for all that she was being raised in such a family. She'd be ruined, too, by association, and that would be unjust.

Then, too, he'd already invited them to the luncheon. He supposed that he could send a note telling them not to come. But again the memory of Miss Psyche's innocent gaze made him think again. He knew what it was to be betrayed, and he was not going to be one to betray a promise of a treat to a child like Miss Psyche. But certainly, he could forgo their company—and that of Miss Hathaway's—after that.

He remembered Cassandra's bluntness, and he frowned. She was different that way. The truth was, he was fool enough not to want to believe Cassandra was like Chloe. Perhaps he had misconstrued Miss Psyche's words, perhaps there was some other explanation for them. Anger warred with reason, and memories of Chloe mixed with that of Cassandra. Perhaps he would give her another chance . . . but he had done this with Chloe, too.

He found himself at his house before he knew it, and walked into the house and up the stairs. He had left his violin in his chambers; he would play it again, and he could get all his anger and passions out of himself and into the music. Then he could think clearly once again.

Blytheland took his violin from the case and slashed his bow across the strings, and the violin wailed in despair and anger. He played the music he knew over and over again, it seemed for hours. But when he was done, the house sounded empty and still, and he knew it was not enough for him.

The late May sun shone brightly and warm upon the group of ladies and gentlemen as they rode in their various conveniences to Marquess of Blytheland's alfresco luncheon. It was not a large group, small enough to make it convivial, but with enough variety in its members to make for interesting conversation. Psyche had been overjoyed when Lord Blytheland had included all of her family in his invitation—except Kenneth, of course, for he was at Cambridge.

How wonderful to be out in the sunshine after a week of being cribbed indoors! Psyche leaned out against the coach's side, staring out at the countryside. She could see the marquess's curricle far ahead of them, and could barely make out his and Cassandra's forms there. They were nearing what must have been one of Blytheland's country houses just outside of London, for they turned off the main road through black iron gates onto a smaller road.

"Do stop leaning out the side of the coach, Psyche, and maintain a ladylike demeanor!" Lady Hathaway said, but it was said without any real reproof in her voice. Psyche nevertheless sat back in her seat.

"Now, I hope you understand, child, that you are to keep out of people's notice," continued her mother.

"Yes, Mama."

"And I do not want you to wander off where you might get lost!"

"Yes, Mama."

"I understand there are other young people about your age, but you are to comport yourself as a mature young lady. Do you understand?"

"Yes, Mama."

Lady Hathaway patted her daughter's hand, satisfied. "You are a good child, Psyche. I hope you will show it today."

"Yes, Mama." Psyche looked up to where the coachman was and nearly burst out laughing. Harry was sitting next to the coachman, behind her mother, shaking his finger at her in a mock-admonishing way. Really, she wished Harry would not do that. It made her want to giggle, and was disrespectful of Mama. But she was glad Harry was coming to the luncheon, nevertheless. It was her first grown-up event, and though she felt excited about it, she was also quite glad there would be someone else she knew. *Would* she be able to do all that she ought?

Looking at Harry, she noted that he had brought his bow and a quiver full of arrows. She felt a little nervous, but remembered his promise. Harry always kept his promises and never lied to her, so she knew she should not worry that he would shoot Blytheland or Cassandra. The thing was, he never promised he wouldn't shoot anyone else. She would definitely have to keep her eye on him. Oh, but the day was too beautiful for worries! Psyche sighed. Perhaps it would not hurt to let Harry have a little bit of fun with his arrows—as long as it was not with her sister or her beau. It seemed to be Harry's nature to matchmake.

The coach slowed, and Psyche found that they were at the doors of the marquess's country house. It was possibly twice the size of her own home in the country, and her father was not an impoverished man by any means. She watched Cassandra descending the steps of the curricle in front of them, then Lord Blytheland escorting her to the house.

Cassandra felt uneasy. The marquess had been very attentive to her, even when driving his curricle. It must have been a difficult thing to maintain an amusing conversation with her while directing the horses, but he did it with an ease that belied the fast pace or the powerful action of the horses. And yet, there was something still and cool about him. No, not cool; that was only a veneer. She gazed at him when he brought his attention to his horses and tried to discern what it was that made him seem so distant, and . . . tense was the best word for it. But she could not elicit much more than common pleasantries from him, and she was no wiser than when they had started out.

When they reached the marquess's house, the ladies and gentlemen retired to their separate rooms to refresh themselves before the luncheon. Cassandra could not help marveling at the fine carpentry of the rooms, the bright brocade tapestries, the fine Aubusson rugs that cushioned her footsteps. It was just, *just* a little intimidating. Her own family had far and above enough funds to provide large dowries for herself and Psyche, as well as maintain a comfortable abode both in town and in the country. But this! This was opulence—in no way vulgar, but the sheer elegance and fine workmanship of the house spoke of a far more than comfortable income, indeed.

Quite, quite above your touch, my girl, said a small voice in her mind. Oh, it was not that she did not come from a respectable and old family, to be sure! It was just that looking at this house brought all the inequalities of their stations to the fore. Her father was by heredity a baronet; the marquess would someday become a duke. Lord Blytheland, of a surety could, and most probably would, look higher than a mere Miss Hathaway.

Cassandra sighed and picked up a wet cloth to freshen her face. She wished she knew what his intentions were. A light flirtation? Something more serious? She did not know if she should let herself—Well, she would think it: let herself love him.

Oh, it would be an easy thing to do. He need only gaze at her warmly, press his lips to her hand, and smile his smile upon her once or twice more. He had paid her more attention than any man had before; she was quite afraid that he would go away like so many others. She had fancied at the beginning of the Season, that she had formed a *tendre* for one or two gentlemen. But they had left for other more lovely young ladies, and it had all come to naught. So she put a guard on her heart, knowing that she was not the most attractive lady in London, and understanding that she would be fortunate, indeed, to find someone who would regard her with affection.

But now, here was the marquess, who escorted her to his home, who danced with her, and took her to the theater.

And with him came his friends—Lord Eldon, Mr. Rowland, and Sir Ellery. They, too, paid her a great deal of attention, although she believed they did so merely for the sake of fashion. Lord Eldon was very much a Pink of the *ton*, a bit more dandified than Lord Blytheland. The marquess, though he took a great deal of care about his clothes, leaned more toward the Corinthians in his preferences, she had discovered.

Cassandra put down the cloth and carefully combed back stray hairs from her face. Perhaps . . . perhaps if Lord Blytheland was merely interested in a flirtation, she could look to Lord Eldon. *He* seemed more and more attentive of late. A little ache seemed to settle in her heart at the thought of looking elsewhere, but she had to be practical, and could not risk being hurt again. She was tired of hoping. Certainly the baron was closer to her station in life than the marquess. And yet, her heart sank when she thought of it.

Nonsense! Lord Eldon was all that is amiable and gentlemanly, she told herself firmly. How could she know if she could feel for him the same—if not more—than what she felt for the marquess? Her mind wandered over the sensations she felt when near Lord Blytheland, and then she thought of Lord Eldon. Well, they were *not* the same. She felt a regard, and a friendship toward the baron. As for Lord Blytheland she, well, she did not know what to make of her reactions to him at all. She despised the way she acted so insipidly around him, blushing and stuttering like an idiot. How could he like her at all? Cassandra sighed, and wished she could comport herself with more assurance and maturity.

Perhaps she should favor Lord Eldon; she had no difficulty acting in an intelligent manner around him. But then, her *experiences* with these two men were quite, quite different. The marquess, for one, had kissed her. Lord Eldon had not. Perhaps if she tried to kiss Lord Eldon also, she would know if she was destined to act like a ninny around men who kissed her. Cassandra felt her face growing warm at the thought, and she put the cloth again to her cheeks.

It would be an experiment, she told herself, and done quite scientifically. If she kissed Lord Eldon and felt the same as she did with the marquess, then she would know whether she would act just as stupidly around men who kissed her. After all, it was something men did with their wives, and how awkward it would be to be such an idiot around one's husband. And besides, Mama did not say kissing was a bad thing, after all, just as long as she didn't do it *often*, and if no one saw.

Cassandra felt much better. There now! She would do her little experiment, and then she could decide what she felt, and if she should encourage Lord Eldon's attentions. Papa was right. One needed only to think things through logically, and one would find the answers. On that thought, she lifted her chin in a resolute manner and left the chamber.

When Cassandra went down to the hall, she saw most of the company were there. Lord Eldon, who was talking to the petite blonde Miss Hamilton, glanced up briefly at her entrance and smiled. There was Sir Jeremy Swift and his lady, and Lady Swift's daughter Georgia Canning (whom she remembered vaguely from her brief stay at the Bath boarding school) and her betrothed, Lord Ashcombe. A few other gentlemen and ladies were also there, but she did not know their names. She looked around the room and caught her father's eye, and he beckoned to her. She smiled at him and her mother as she approached. Psyche, she noticed, was standing quietly behind Lady Hathaway, looking intently at everything in the room. She glanced at Cassandra, gave her a quizzical look, and then continued her perusal of the room. Cassandra almost shook her head. Sometimes she was not sure she understood her young sister.

"Now there," Sir John said, pointing his chin at Lord

Ashcombe, "is a well-informed young man. Educated at Oxford, graduated with honors. He knows Arabic! I must see if I can bring him and Blytheland's father together to work on a translation of the *De Res Medicos*." He sighed. "Wouldn't mind someone like him for a son-in-law."

"Papa! You cannot think that a gentleman's education can be the only consideration for a husband!"

"It would certainly be convenient, though," replied Sir John, looking wistfully at Lord Ashcombe.

Lady Hathaway tapped him on the arm with her fan. "My dear, it is too late, as you can see! Miss Canning and Lord Ashcombe are betrothed and clearly enamored of each other. And your daughter is right. There is more than just education to be thought of in a marriage."

Cassandra looked over at the young couple. If one did not know that the two were betrothed, one could guess it from their demeanor. She watched as Lord Ashcombe tucked his fiancée's hand gently in the crook of his arm, how Miss Canning looked up at him with a tender smile, and how he returned it with a regard that was more than warm. Cassandra felt a small ache in her heart and wondered if anyone would someday look at her in that way.

The door opened once more, and she looked up to see Lord Blytheland enter the parlor. His gaze immediately went to hers, and then turned to the rest of the company. There was little expression in his eyes except for a cool civility.

"If the ladies and gentlemen are ready, we can all proceed to the lake. The servants should have set up our luncheon there by the time we arrive."

There was a general murmur of assent, and everyone went out into the sunlight once again.

"Oh, dear!" exclaimed Psyche, "I wonder if we should have brought umbrellas?" She was looking toward the west, and Cassandra followed her gaze. A thin line of clouds obscured the horizon, although in front of the cloud bank the sky was a brilliant blue.

Cassandra smiled at her sister comfortingly. "I believe we shall be quite comfortable; we have only a breeze blowing from the east, you see, so I doubt we will have any rain at all."

It was not very far to the lake. They walked past the gardens and the maze, which the marquess invited the guests to try later if they liked. The house and gardens were on a small rise, and down the hill and further, for a few yards away the servants had set out the luncheon by the lake.

It took a great deal of self-restraint for Psyche not to run as she wished to down to the luncheon. The day was beautiful and the field was just the sort on which to run until one was breathless. She eyed the other people closer to her age, but they were few and she did not feel inclined to converse with them. One girl looked quite standoffish, and even sneered in her direction. A tall, thin boy walking not far from her own family had eyes for nothing but the luncheon. Not very likely people to talk to, thought Psyche.

Blytheland's servants had set out various tables for the guests, and makeshift sideboards groaning with food. It was a snatch-pastry's dream—not that she, Psyche, was a snatch-pastry. Harry certainly was, however. She watched enviously as he flew swiftly toward what looked to be a sumptuous spread of edible delights. How she wished she could fly, unseen, wherever she wanted! She had never seen him eat much before, and she had often wondered if he ate only for show—or in earnest. Well, she did now know it was in earnest: though he picked at this dish or that, he picked much. There were lobster patties and hams, bread and cakes and tarts. Wine was served as well, although she was only allowed lemonade. Harry, she noted enviously, helped himself to the wine.

Hoping that her parents would not notice her immediate escape, Psyche inched herself toward the luncheon. She noticed the tall, thin boy—older than Harry, she thought—was already at the table and had picked up a dish. Well, Mama could *not* say she had made unseemly haste to the food. That boy was here before her after all, and she had walked *very* slowly to the table.

She glanced shyly up at the boy. He smiled kindly at her.

"Hallo! Do try the jam tarts. They really are superb," he said, his voice a little muffled from a bite he'd just taken. "My name is Garthwaite. Bertram Garthwaite. Oh, and the lobster patties are first rate!" He put two more on his plate.

"Are they? I do like them, they're my favorite," Psyche replied. "I am Psyche Hathaway." She looked at his burgeoning plate. "Goodness, but you must be hungry!"

"I am," he replied frankly. "I've just come down from Cambridge on holiday. Never get enough to eat there, let me tell you! And what they have is pretty poor fare, to boot."

"Cambridge! Do you know my brother Kenneth Hathaway?"

"Mmmm . . . Oh, yes. Doesn't run with my set—he's a year ahead of me—but I've met him. He's a great gun, up for any lark. I imagine he'll come home to you any day now."

Psyche felt some consternation. No one had received word that Kenneth was coming home. She hoped that he was not in trouble again. "Is . . . is he in a scrape, do you think?"

Bertram looked nonplussed. "Well—That is to say—I've heard he does have the most deuced good luck—it might not be as bad as all that."

"Oh, dear." Psyche bit her lip. "Well, I will not worry about it. It is something Papa will need to deal with, after all."

"That's the ticket." He nodded approvingly. "No need to worry about something you can't influence."

She looked across the table and saw that Harry was looking at Bertram intently. She grew alarmed and made what she hoped was a dismissing motion with her hand at Harry. Mr. Garthwaite seemed a good sort of young man, and she didn't want Harry to shoot him with any of his arrows. She wriggled her eyebrows at her friend, hoping that he would take it as a warning to stay away from Mr. Garthwaite as well.

Harry rolled his eyes, then shrugged his shoulders. He reached over and cut off a cluster of grapes from a bowl, and started eating the grapes.

"I say, did you see that?"

Psyche glanced up to see Bertram staring at the grape bowl.

"See what?"

"Those grapes. There was a cluster of them I had my eyes on and then they disappeared!"

She threw Harry a reproachful look and turned to Bertram again. "Are you sure? I did not see them."

He shook his head. "Must be hunger pangs. They are affecting my vision. I must tell Father I need more of an allowance for food." He nodded in a bemused fashion at Psyche and went off with his plate to the edge of the lake.

"Oh, Harry! If you refuse to show yourself to anyone else but me, I do wish you would be more discreet!" she scolded him. She was glad no one else had come to the buffet table yet, so that she could talk to her friend without whispering.

"You needn't worry, Psyche. He did not see me, and only thought the grapes were his imagination."

"Well, that is true, but do be careful! And why were you staring at him so?"

"Oh, you know, just seeing if he was worth bothering with."

"Bothering with?"

Harry popped another grape into his mouth. "Yes. There wasn't anyone around who I thought might be suitable for him. And he's young yet—only eighteen. No need to hurry; he's not wild like your brother. Or stubborn like your sister and the marquess."

"Remember your promise, Harry!"

Harry sighed. "I remember!"

"Besides, Cassandra and Lord Blytheland are doing very well by themselves. You must have seen them in his curricle!" Psyche picked up a lobster patty that the amiable Mr. Garthwaite had recommended.

"Yes. But Lord Blytheland is angry about something, and I think your sister is planning something with Lord Eldon, instead."

"What? How can you say so?" Psyche's lobster patty stopped halfway to her mouth.

"*I* have kept watch on them, if *you* have not. She keeps casting glances at Lord Eldon instead of the marquess. And Lord Blytheland doesn't look happy. But then, he tends to be rather moody, so that may not mean a great deal."

"No. You must be mistaken!" She put her food down upon her plate again and gazed at Harry skeptically. "Besides, how can you tell just by looking at her? She could just be trying to catch his attention."

"Oh, she is catching his attention all right and tight," Harry replied. "And I know because I am very good at reading faces. I learned it from my cousin Hermes."

"Cousin? I did not know you had a cousin," Psyche said, intrigued. Harry only rarely spoke of his friends or relations.

He smiled. "You never asked. Besides, I thought your father would have told you all about me and my family."

"Now that is nothing but a faradiddle and you know it, Harry! Papa telling me of you, indeed! Why you said my father did not believe you existed, and that you were all from my imagination!"

"He does."

Psyche shook her head impatiently at him. "Oh, do stop roasting me, Harry! Now let us get back to Cassandra."

"Yes, do let's," Harry said. "I'll wager you your jam tart that your sister will stroll across the grass with Lord Eldon instead of the marquess. You'll see what comes of my not shooting my arrows."

"Done!" replied Psyche, and she walked quickly back to where her parents were sitting.

She gazed at her sister. Cassandra seemed a little abstracted, the same look she always wore when she would try to puzzle out a problem. She sat on the other side of their parents, but Psyche sat herself down where she could surreptitiously observe her.

She watched as Cassandra glanced at Lord Eldon, not once, not twice, but three times. The third time, he responded with a smile and came over to her.

Psyche bit her lip. Oh dear, she thought. Harry has just won my jam tart. She looked at her friend, then silently held the tart out to him.

Harry looked at the tart but did not take it. He could not. He felt something odd—he'd call it remorse, if he were a mortal. He remembered feeling it once, literally ages ago, when the gods' presence was felt more strongly than it was now, but not since that time. Perhaps he felt it because he had no friend in the world of the mortals, except for this young girl. He did not know, and it annoyed him. "What do you wish me to do?" he asked, and then wished he hadn't said it. It was almost an admission that he had made another mistake.

Psyche sighed and smiled at him, clearly relieved. "Don't shoot any arrows at Cassandra. I would feel horrid if she became all silly like the Mademoiselle Lavoisin and the Comte de la Fer. Could you . . . could you make Lord Blytheland the way he was before you shot any of your arrows at him?"

"It won't work if I do, Psyche."

She pressed her lips together and lifted her chin stubbornly. "They have met already, and have got to know each other. I don't think they need any more help with your arrows."

Harry stared at her for a few more moments, wondering why he bothered with her or the Hathaway family . . . but the thought of leaving them made him feel even more odd than that remorselike thing he'd felt earlier.

"Oh, very well!" he said. He made a face at her, feeling childishly better for doing it—well, was he not in boyform, after all?—but Psyche merely smiled at him gratefully.

"Thank you! You are a true friend, Harry! You'll see, they'll come about properly!" She looked away from him toward where her sister had sat, but Cassandra was gone.

"Don't worry," Harry said. "Lord Blytheland's gone with them, it seems. I'll find them." He selected an arrow from his quiver, a different one than he'd used before, and rose into the air. He sighed. Perhaps Psyche was right . . . but he doubted it. He was the god of love, after all, and no mortal knew more of love than he did, especially not a young girl.

Chapter 8

Miss Hathaway, Lord Eldon noted, kept glancing at him, and he could not help wondering why. He had never received so much attention from her before.

"I think I need to walk a little—I feel a little stiff from travel still," Miss Hathaway said. She put down her fork on the plate the servant had given her. She had hardly touched the food, although she had taken a little lemonade and then wine. Lord Eldon caught another glance from her. He could see also Blytheland turning toward them at her words, but she did not look toward the marquess at all. Lord Eldon felt a stirring of curiosity. Something in the wind? he wondered.

"I would be most happy to oblige, Miss Hathaway," he said, and smiled at her. He rose and offered his hand. She returned an uncertain smile and put her hand in his. Lord Eldon risked a glance at his friend and almost burst out laughing. Blytheland's expression was a mix of surprise and irritation. So much for his insistence that she was only "a superb pianist," to him, eh? He could tell his friend was madly in love with Miss Hathaway, and she would be perfect for him. He had disliked Chloe from the start, and he often thought she still had her claws in Blythe even though she was gone. Well, there was nothing like a bit of rivalry to get a man to realize what he might be losing.

Eldon turned to the lady at his side. "And where would you like to stroll, ma'am?"

She glanced at him, again uncertainly. "I . . . I think perhaps the gardens, by the maze. It seems very pretty there, and I would like to see the flowers."

"It would be my pleasure."

They walked up the rise to where the gardens formed the entrance to the maze. They conversed about the weather and Miss Hathaway exclaimed over the flowers. Lord Eldon noted with amusement that it was the most desultory and unenlightening conversation he had ever had with her. Something must be bothering her, he thought, and it must have to do with my dear old friend. How amusing. Miss Hathaway must have more than a passing fancy for Blythe, he was sure of it. But why did she choose *him*, Eldon, to escort her to the garden?

He watched her as she spoke of more inconsequential things and noted a rising blush in her cheeks. A mischievous urge rose in him. He would so much like to see how much pinker Miss Hathaway could blush.

"I see you must be a little overheated, ma'am. Perhaps you would like to sit for a little while?" He was rewarded by seeing her turn two shades more pink than before.

"Yes, yes please. Perhaps over there on that bench, where it is private." A guilty look appeared in her eyes, and her cheeks turned positively red.

Private? thought Lord Eldon. Well, well. Now what?

They sat, and Miss Hathaway arranged her skirts around her neatly, and then fiddled with them some more. They were somewhat in shadow, for part of the hedge and ivy that covered the maze overhung the marble bench on which they sat. Eldon removed his hat, looked at her downcast gaze, and waited, suppressing a wide grin. Poor Miss Hathaway! She was no doubt getting up the courage to say something, but what?

She looked up earnestly at him. "Lord Eldon, will you kiss me?" she said, all in a rush.

"Eh?"

"Kiss me. For—for experimental purposes, you see."

Lord Eldon paused before he spoke, trying to put strong control over his overwhelming urge to laugh. Oh, Lord! Was that what this was all about? And why in the world did she feel she had to do this? He thought of Blytheland and wondered if he had kissed her—probably. He certainly had the chance to do so at the Marchmont ball!

"For experimental purposes?" he managed to reply after a short struggle with another upsurge of laughter.

"Oh, please don't be offended, my lord! I like you very well, and I was wondering if, if your kiss would be like— That is, what your kiss would be like."

"Oh, is that it? Well, I would be most happy to oblige, Miss Hathaway. For experimental purposes, of course."

"Would you?"

"Yes."

"Oh." She stared at him for a moment and then put on a resolute expression. She closed her eyes and presented her face.

Lord Eldon gazed at her for a long moment. Oh, he shouldn't. He really shouldn't. But his deeply ingrained mischievousness could not let this priceless moment pass by. Especially when he noted from the corner of his eye his dear old friend Blythe coming up the path. He bent over Miss Hathaway and kissed her firmly on the lips.

They parted, and she looked up at him, clearly puzzled. "That was pleasant, Lord Eldon, but . . . Did it feel pleasant to you?"

"Most pleasant, Miss Hathaway," he replied. He had to admit to feeling a bit warmer than usual. La Hathaway was, after all, a most delectable young lady.

"What the *devil* is the meaning of all this?" The marquess stood before them, his hands balled tightly into fists, fury writ clear in his eyes.

Miss Hathaway rose hastily and pressed her hands to her

mouth. Lord Eldon stood as well, but more slowly, and carefully brushed the dust from his coattails.

"What did it look like, Blythe-my-old?" Eldon replied provocatively.

"It looked damn well like you were kissing Miss Hathaway! I *don't* take well to having any of my female guests molested!"

"Molested? Strong words, old man." He turned to the lady by his side. "Was I molesting you, ma'am?"

"Oh, no! I—I asked him to kiss me, you see," Miss Hathaway replied.

"You what!?" Blytheland's voice rose.

"It was for—for an experiment. I asked him to kiss me."

Poor Miss Hathaway! She looked more and more distressed. Lord Eldon sighed regretfully. He really should put a stop to this.

"Look here, Blytheland. It was all very innocent. In fact, I knew you were coming up the hill and I couldn't help tweaking at you a little. Being a bit of a dog in the manger, don't you think? You never said you had any claim on her—denied it, in fact. And I did tell you I thought I might try for her affections myself, since you didn't say I shouldn't."

"You said you'd have a *touch* at her! By God, Eldon that was a damn sight more than a touch! I should call you out for this!"

"No!" cried Cassandra.

Both men ignored her.

"Nonsense, my old. You know I wouldn't oblige; I detest arising before eleven o'clock. Besides, I know you wouldn't shoot me—I wouldn't shoot you! We've been friends too long, and it would cause a devil of a scandal for Miss Hathaway here."

The marquess turned a blazing look on Miss Hathaway. "Scandal! If she were sunk in it, it would be all that she deserves!"

"Now, just a moment, Blythe!" Eldon said sternly. "If I were so inclined, I would call *you* out for *that*. You heard her. She has no more notion about kisses than an infant. If anything, your argument should be with me."

"No, no! It was all my fault!" Cassandra cried. "I asked him to—truly, I did! It was an experiment!"

Blytheland turned to her and grasped her by the shoulders. "You little idiot! Anyone could have seen you here! *I* certainly did!"

"Idiot! I am *not* an idiot!"

"It was certainly stupid of you to kiss Eldon here in full view of the lake!"

Lord Eldon wondered if it would be discreet or cowardly if he left the two of them to join the rest of the company at the lake. It was clearly a lover's quarrel and a third party would definitely be *de trop*. He gazed at the marquess and Miss Hathaway, both of whom looked furiously into each other's eyes.

"Ahem. If you two don't mind, I thought I might go back to the lake . . . ?" Eldon said tentatively. "I still feel a trifle sharp-set. Thought I might see if there was any of the luncheon left over."

"It was not in full view of the lake! You can see clearly for yourself how we were hidden!"

"Oh? And if so, then why did I notice it?"

They were clearly not interested in his presence at all. Lord Eldon decided that leaving would probably be discreet more than not. And perhaps getting whatever problem was between them aired would be for the better. He picked up his hat, set it neatly on his head, and after an elegant bow in the couple's direction, sauntered back down to the remains of the luncheon.

Lord Blytheland still grasped Cassandra by her shoulders. "I have never known anyone so indiscreet as you, Miss Cassandra Hathaway! By God, if you are not sending people to *point-non-plus* in the most embarrassing way with your blunt comments, you are letting yourself be kissed by all and sundry—and in full view of God knows who! Or perhaps you don't particularly care who sees you."

"I only try to speak the truth, my lord," Cassandra replied furiously. "And as for truth—I do not know how you dare to say I let myself be kissed by 'all and sundry'! You have been the only other one who has kissed me. I asked Lord Eldon to do so only for an experiment."

"An experiment!" The marquess sneered. He stared at her, rage boiling up inside of him, almost choking him. He had wanted to give her another chance, and she took it—showing her true colors. She lifted her chin—Chloe used to do the same thing when she wished to have her own way. How similar were they? He did not truly know, and God, he wished he did.

"You need not sneer, you horrid man! I believed we were private, and—"

"Private! That you should want to be private with—" He released her shoulders, but took her wrist in a tight grip instead. He needed to know, and he would find out, or he would go mad not knowing. A thought flashed through his mind that perhaps he was mad now, for never had he been seized with such anger, such agony, not even with Chloe. But he could not stop, not now. He pulled her toward the maze's entrance, and walked swiftly around one corner and another—right, left, and right again. "Private. You're so deuced indiscreet you don't know the meaning of the word!"

"What are you doing? Where are you taking me?"

"Some place *private,* of course," Blytheland replied through clenched teeth. His steps were swift, and he could hear Cassandra almost running behind him. He turned right again, then left, another left, and two rights, and the enclosing hedges opened up to the center of the maze. A delicate Grecian gazebo stood in the middle of the small garden clearing, but Blytheland strode past it to the hedge behind it. He pushed aside some branches and heavy over-hanging ivy, and revealed an old oaken door. He moved the handle, and the door creaked open. Pulling Cassandra through the door, he shut it firmly behind them.

He had not come here in a long time, not since Chloe died. He watched Cassandra look around her in an angry, bewildered way at the riot of blooms and flowering trees around her, and the sparkling fountain that cascaded dia-mondlike drops of water into a mosaic pool. She turned and stared angrily at Blytheland instead. "And where is this, pray?"

"This, my dear Cassandra, is the heart of the maze. It is a place so damned private that no one would see us to-gether. No one would see *anything* we might do here. What a wonderful way to avoid scandal, yes?" He pulled her to him and lifted her chin so that she stared into his eyes. She was still angry. He felt a queer relief at it—per-haps he was wrong about her. He hoped she felt as furious as he did . . . but he needed to know, dear God, he needed to know. "Tell me, my dear. Why did you kiss Eldon?"

"I told you, it was an experiment! I wanted to find out how his kiss might compare with yours, and that was all!" She stamped her foot. It would have landed on his toe, but he moved it in time. "And I did not give you permission to use my Christian name!"

Anger seized him again. "Oh, my. I think the blunt and truthful Miss Hathaway has told a lie! I definitely remem-ber a ball, out on the terrace—"

Her face flamed red in memory, then paled again in clear fury. "I did not say yes to your using my name!"

"Then what did you say yes to? Kissing me? Do you al-ways say yes to requests like that—or was that an experi-ment, too?"

"No! Yes! Oh, you odious—!" She stamped her foot again.

"Odious, am I? Are my kisses odious to you, too? Well, how does *this* compare with Eldon's?"

His lips took hers swiftly, hard against her mouth at first, but he let out a deep sigh and moved upon her lips more softly. How could he not? He drew away briefly, staring at her delicately formed lips. They were full and open, and he remembered them the way they were when she had played the piano at the musicale. It would be a sin not to savor them slowly, feeling every little indentation and curve against his own. Her green eyes were wide and startled as they looked into his. He felt he could drown in them. Blytheland gently brought his lips to hers again.

They were as soft as he'd remembered them from the Marchmonts' ball. He tasted the sweet sherry she'd had at luncheon, and breathed in the scent of violets that emanated from her. She opened her mouth on a sighing moan, and suddenly the passion was there—as he had imagined it, as he'd experienced it before. Now her lips moved upon his, her arms came around his neck, and she pressed herself close to him. He deepened his kiss in response and moved his hands to her waist.

He needed to feel her closer. . . . He bent his knees slightly and tried to feel for one of the benches or chairs he knew were in the garden. But then Cassandra leaned forward even more, and they tumbled down upon the grass. She landed half on top of him, and the marquess pulled her fully to him so that she was, indeed, much closer.

"Ah, God, how I've wanted you, Cassandra," Blytheland murmured against her lips.

"Yes . . ."

"Paul. My name is Paul." He rolled to his side, taking her with him and brought his hand up to her breast.

"Ohh, Paul . . ." she sighed, and pressed her lips against his again.

He must have lost his mind—love and fear had robbed him of all reason. He kissed her cheek, her lips, her throat.

She responded with even more passion than he'd thought possible, arching against his hands and his body. Heat moved through him and he shifted his lips from her mouth, trailing kisses on her cheek, her neck, and down to the soft skin his hand had uncovered.

Cassandra shivered as she felt his—Paul's—lips move upon her throat and lower, and lower until—

A drop of water splashed upon her cheek. Then another on her forehead, one on her nose, and another on her eyelid. She opened her eyes. The thin clouds that had appeared at the beginning of their luncheon had gathered to a large thunderous mass. It was raining, and raining in earnest.

Warm kisses coursed across the top of her breasts, trailing downward. She struggled to rise.

"Stop! Oh, please stop!" Cassandra pushed the marquess away from her and sat up. To her horror, her dress gaped open, and one cross-end of it flapped in the wind that had suddenly sprung up. Oh, heavens, how could she have allowed it?

Hastily she closed her dress and looked at the marquess. He, too, sat up. He had a bewildered expression on his face and seemed oblivious to the rain now pouring steadily upon his head. He held out his hand tentatively toward her.

"Cassandra—"

"How *dare* you!" she cried.

"But I—"

"You *dare* accuse Lord Eldon of molesting me when you—*you* went far further than a mere kiss!"

Blytheland's eyes snapped angrily. "Well, I didn't hear *you* protesting!"

"*That* is neither here nor there! What we are discussing are *your* base assumptions about Lord Eldon's actions and my intent. *He* did not force me to the middle of this maze, or force his attentions upon me!" A stab of guilt passed through Cassandra's mind, but she dismissed it.

"Oh, so I forced my attentions on you, did I? Did you scream? My, my, I must be getting deaf in my old age," he replied, his voice ironic. "If you recall, I stopped when you told me to—quite some time after we began."

"Ohhh, you odious—! How *could* I say anything when you—you had your lips over mine?" Cassandra rose swiftly to her feet. Blytheland did as well.

The marquess looked pointedly at her bodice. "I recall instances when my lips were not on yours at all." A slow smile grew on his face.

Cassandra's hands itched to slap that expression from his face. She closed her hands against the sensation and formed two tight fists instead. Oh! How *could* he? She had thought him a true gentleman, but his actions proved her wrong. Why, he was no better than her younger brother Kenneth, who kissed maidservants! And the marquess had no excuse, for he was well over Kenneth's immature nineteen years of age! Well, *she* was no lowly chambermaid! But as she looked at him, his face grew dark and contemptuous.

"Besides, how do I know you don't do this—as well as kiss—other men as well? Your sister told me of your children, after all."

"Children?" Cassandra stared at him, bewildered. "What do my climbing boys have to do with this?"

The contemptuous look vanished, and the marquess seemed to pale. "Climbing boys? Your sister said she had been warned not to speak of it . . . I thought—"

"You thought—you thought—" Cassandra gasped, her breath almost taken away with grief and anger. "I never— how could you ever think I am that kind of—" She clenched her fists tighter, trying to hold back the tears that threatened to burst from her. "You thought I was—And to think I came to love you, while all the time you—" Her voice caught in a sob.

A sudden fluttering sound, a burst of wind pushed the

hair from her face, and a quick twanging hiss of a bow-shot seemed to sear her ear. But Cassandra paid no attention to it, or to the rain that fell hard and fast upon her. She stared at Lord Blytheland, at his clearly confused and handsome face, and for one small moment hatred flared, then turned into white-hot anger. Humiliation and shame warred fiercely with it in her heart, and she could feel her face flame hotly. Anger won.

Her fist flew out. With a right curve that would have gained the approval of Gentleman Jackson himself, it landed directly on the marquess's right eye. Blytheland fell—arms flailing—right into the mosaic-lined pool.

Cassandra stared at him, horrified at what she'd done, her hands clenched tightly against her lips. Lord Blytheland sat in the pool with a stunned look on his face, his eye slowly turning color. A lily pad floated gently across his middle. Rain dripped upon his head, and a tiny stream of fountain water coursed down his forehead and trickled off the end of his aristocratic nose.

Oh, heavens! Never, never had she even thought of violence against another person, much less done it. She had been raised to act like a lady by loving parents, and never had a hand been raised against her as a child, for her parents did not believe in corporal punishment. She abhorred violence, but now she had hit someone—Lord Blytheland. She had thought she had more control over herself than that, even when she had been at her angriest, however she might justifiably be angry. What was wrong with her? Ever since she had met the marquess, she had acted in a manner that she despised: blushing and stuttering like the merest schoolgirl, allowing her passions—yes, she admitted to herself, passions—to rule her instead of her mind, and now this! She turned away and covered her eyes in shame, confusion, and anger now at herself.

"Miss Hathaway, if I may ask a favor of you . . . ?"

Cassandra turned back to him. He was still sitting in the

pool, but was holding a hand out to her. He smiled at her charmingly, and if she did not know better she would have thought that smile on his face was positively merry. Was he mad? She had just hit him, with good reason, it was true, but one did not grin happily upon receiving a flush hit.

"If you would be so kind, ma'am, I believe I need some help from this pond."

"Of course!" It was the least she could do, after inflicting violence upon him, and it would show she had gained control over herself again. She went to him and grasped his hand.

A hard tug pulled her into the pool with a splash. The initial shock of cold water made her gasp, and she choked, spluttering water from her mouth. She fell against the marquess's hard body, and looked up to find her face inches from his. His expression had definitely lightened, and the darkness she had seen in him had fled. He stared speculatively at her face, and then grinned, almost boyishly. "What's sauce for the gander . . ." He bent his head to kiss her.

"No!" Cassandra pushed herself away from him and rolled to find herself sitting next to him in the pond. She struggled to stand up, but fell onto her hands and knees. She had almost been hypnotized by his look, but she pulled forth all the will she had left within her and made herself move. "No. You will not. Not again!"

Her dress dragged against her limbs as she crawled out of the pond. It was ruined; there was no doubt in her mind about that. Cassandra could feel strands of her hair straggling over her face, and though she had managed to tie the wet ends of the dress ribbons together, they had become tangled in her haste and she knew she would have to cut them off when she changed clothes. She must look dreadful.

The rain fell in sheets, and thunder roared in the distance. The marquess rose from the pond, sodden, his hair plastered to his head. His pantaloons adhered to his legs like a second skin. It made no difference; somehow he looked just as elegant as always. It was maddening.

Cassandra pushed a lock of hair from her eyes. "You . . . *horrid* . . . man! I thought you were a gentleman. I thought—I thought you *cared* just a little." She felt tears start to her eyes, but she bit her lip to keep them from flowing. "But you never did. You thought me no better than a—a whore." She forced her voice to be sarcastic.

Blytheland's face turned stormy at her first words, but the look faded, and his expression became confused. "I— Cassandra, I did not mean—I shouldn't have—That is, I thought . . ." He stopped, seeming at a loss for words.

His loss was her gain. Cassandra gathered herself together and said in a dignified tone, "I would appreciate it, Lord Blytheland, if you would escort me out of this maze."

"Of course." The marquess's voice was subdued. He offered his arm to her, but she looked pointedly at it and did her best to sneer. She had never sneered at anyone before, but it seemed she succeeded, for Blytheland's face grew stony and he turned from her.

"Very well, ma'am. Follow me."

Careful to stay close enough not to lose him, Cassandra followed. She was glad she had quelled the impulse to leave by herself, for she knew she would have become quite lost. They turned this way and that, and after a few minutes finally walked into the garden. The other guests were long gone; down the hill she could see the last of the servants carrying away the remains of the luncheon in a sack upon his back.

Cassandra wanted to leave Blytheland as quickly as she could. She almost ran and stumbled in her attempt to hurry. A hand caught her elbow before she fell, and she looked up into the marquess's face.

"Unhand me, sir," she said, and stared steadily at him. Anger flared clearly in his eyes, and she almost thought she saw despair—but it was gone, and she knew she must be mistaken. He pressed his lips together, causing them to whiten.

"Very well, ma'am." His voice was terse and strained, and he let go of her arm instantly.

Walking quickly, Cassandra headed toward the marquess's house and was soon at the doorstep. She could not help looking back at him.

He had not moved from the garden. He stood there, hands clenched at his sides, but for all his clearly angry stance, he looked curiously bereft. Cassandra bit her lip and shook her head. No. She must not let her emotions overcome her reason. He had not said one tender word to her, but had insulted her, and clearly saw her as someone too far beneath him to consider for anything more than a— Cassandra swallowed down a feeling dangerously close to grief. He was a marquess, and someday to be a duke. He could look higher than a Miss Hathaway for a wife. He was not in love with her at all, but had thought her a fallen woman. She was a fool even to have thought he had cared for her.

Taking a deep breath, she opened the door and went up the stairs to the room allotted to her. She ignored the slap-slap of her dress against her legs and the wet trail she was sure followed in her wake. Once in her room, she rang for the maid and carefully took off her dress, even untangling the mess of ribbons at the sides of it with slow, controlled movements.

The maid arrived, exclaimed at the ruin of her dress, and wrapped Cassandra in a warm quilt.

"Please, I would like to rest for a while. Could you make sure I am not disturbed? I believe I have the headache," Cassandra murmured.

"Of course, miss. Shall I get you a tisane?" the maid replied.

"No. No, rest is all I require."

"Very well, miss. When shall I wake you?"

"Before dinner, or if my mother asks for me." The maid left.

Cassandra lay down on the bed and pulled the quilt over her head. Then she cried and raged and cried again, for she knew she still loved Lord Blytheland, against all reason, against all hope. And she had not one idea how to stop it.

Chapter 9

If Lord Blytheland had despised himself for a fool before, he knew he was a hundred times that now. He looked in his chamber's mirror and saw his eye was turning purple. Cassandra had been right to hit him, though he did not expect such a flush hit from a lady. She had said that he had acted worse than his friend Eldon. It was true. He had no right to accuse Eldon of importuning her with a simple kiss, when he had done far worse.

He closed his eyes, and her image rose before him—her eyes full of anger and confusion at his unjust accusation of his friend. And then later, in the center of the maze . . . Mixed in her anger and confusion, he could see disappointment. She had been disappointed in him. The thought made him want to writhe in embarrassment. She had, obviously, believed him a gentleman. Except for those kisses at the Marchmonts' ball (for which he had apologized), he had treated her with all the respect and consideration he would normally give to any lady. Even more than that: he had invited her family to his house as visitors, to the alfresco luncheon and to rest for the night before they returned home. He had never given that sort of attention to any woman. She must know it and her hopes had no doubt been raised. He had insulted her and disappointed her and he deserved the black eye he had received.

Blytheland went to a chair by the window and sank into it, pushing his fingers through his hair. What the devil had prompted him to act in such a totally uncontrolled manner? He could not blame her if she thought him mad, for he had acted like he'd come straight from Bedlam. Was there something about Miss Hathaway that caused it? He'd never acted this way around any other woman. Countless times he'd caught himself staring at her: the way her midnight hair framed her face, the laughter in her green eyes, the elegant line of cheek and throat and bosom, the earnest expression that creased her brow whenever she talked of her charities. She was intelligent, too, and had a sense of humor. All these, other women he had known possessed in part. But the sum of them existed in Cassandra, and he found the whole irresistible.

No, he could not blame her. He had been seized with a madness and had acted like an idiot. Was there a way to retrieve her good opinion of him? He had accused her of a terrible thing . . . and did not know if she would forgive him. Certainly, he could not expect it. He closed his eyes tightly and winced, for his eye ached, and it reminded him all over again of why she had hit him.

But she had said she loved him. Perhaps, perhaps there was some hope.

It was that which must have taken the madness from him: the anguished look in her eyes, and her cry that she had loved him. He had felt it suddenly, as if he had been shot through the heart, and the pain of it cleared the hot mist from his eyes. He saw in that instant how stupidly he had acted, without reason or consideration. For all his anguish at Chloe's betrayal, he had not been as consumed with—yes, he admitted it—jealousy as he had when he thought Cassandra cared for Eldon, and not for him. Well, the scales had fallen from his eyes and he saw everything clearly now, and what he saw of himself he did not like.

But there was nothing for it: he had to apologize and perhaps if she could forgive him, he might have a chance at proposing marriage to her. He glanced in the mirror at his

bruised eye and grimaced. He had little right to hope, however. If she refused to ever speak to him again, it was all
that he deserved.

A knock sounded on the door, and Fichet entered, carrying a large piece of raw meat.

"If it please you milor', I 'ave brought ze beef steak," the
valet announced. His eyes went to the marquess's messed
hair, and a pained and sorrowful expression crossed his
face.

Blytheland raised an eyebrow. "I thank you, Fichet, but I
do not desire beef for dinner, much less raw beef."

"No, no, milor'! It is not for ze meal, but for ze eye. I
'ave noticed it when you came from *le jardin.* It is to put
upon ze bruise, *n'est ce pas?*" The man looked at the beef
critically. "It is of a very fine cut milor'—not of ze best, but
it will make little ze blackness of ze eye."

"*Je ne veux pas*—and *no.* I do not want a bloody piece of
meat anywhere near my eye. It will do quite well all by itself."

A look of profound understanding grew upon Fichet's
countenance. "Ah! *C'est l'amour!* Why did I not think of
it?" the valet murmured, and nodded to himself. "It is ze
thing that will make a man mad—even to ze destruction of
his coiffure and eye."

"Nonsense." Blytheland shrugged impatiently and turned
from him.

"But see, milor'! Your hair! Your eye! They are in a con-
dition deplorable, *hein?* But because it is la Mademoiselle
Hathaway blacks ze eye, *la voilà!* You do not take care of
these things."

"What did you say?" The marquess swiveled his head
abruptly toward his servant.

"Milor' you do *not* turn the head so fast! It will ruin the
cravat!"

"The devil take the cravat! What did you say about Miss
Hathaway?"

The valet threw up his hands. "English! *Le Diable* will not take the cravat; it is around the neck of milor' le Marquis, and ruined because you jiggle ze head around. Not even *le Diable* would take ze ruined cravat."

Blytheland's glance at Fichet was stormy. "Enough of cravats! How did you know that Miss Hathaway . . . blacked my eye?"

Fichet shrugged. "It was for all to see—if zey looked out ze *chambre* of milor', as I did. I see ze maze, you, and Mademoiselle Hathaway. When you leave, the dress of Mademoiselle is wet, as is milor's coat zat is now in a state ze most execrable. It make me to think. 'Ow is ze clothes so wet, but ze rain just begin?" The valet tapped his head wisely. "But of course! Zere is a pond. Ze beautiful mademoiselle, ze most distinguished marquis—it is a course *naturelle*." The valet put his hand over his heart, and closed his eyes. "*La voilà!* Zey have *l'amour* so violent zey fall into ze pond!" He sighed soulfully.

The marquess ground his teeth. "We did not make love in the pond, Fichet!"

His servant only smiled, bowed, and looked at him skeptically.

"Besides, if—*if* we were so enamored of each other, how is it that I received a blackened eye?"

"Ze English have no finesse, even you, milor' sometimes," Fichet replied placidly. "*La pauvre petite* was frightened of ze violence of ze passions, *hein*? *Eh bien!* She strikes ze eye. With ze Frenchman, it would 'ave been different."

"Oh, really?" Blytheland snarled.

"But of course," the valet said, clearly unmoved by his employer's mood. He lifted the piece of meat expectantly. "Now, milor', ze beef . . . ?"

A grimace of a smile formed on the marquess's lips. "Of course. Do let me take it from you, Fichet." He took the meat between his fingers, went to the window, opened it, and threw it out.

"Milor' Marquis! The beef!" The valet looked offended.

"I do not *want* the beef. In fact, I am beginning to *detest* beef," Blytheland said between his teeth.

"But ze bruise! What are you to do of it?"

"I, Fichet, am going to ask for Miss Hathaway's hand in marriage."

"But zat 'as nothing to do with ze eye!"

The marquess sighed. "It has everything to do with it."

Cassandra awoke with a slight headache. She rose from the bed, and went to the mirror. She looked very much like she felt: her face was pale, her eyes puffy, and there were dark streaks under her eyes. Covering her eyes, she groaned. She simply could not appear like this at supper.

A knock sounded on the door. "Yes? Who is it?" She desperately hoped that it was not her mother.

"It is I, Mary, ma'am. You asked that I wake you in time for dinner."

"Yes, yes of course. Please come in." Cassandra sighed with relief.

The maid looked at her curiously. "Excuse me, miss, but is there aught I can do for you?"

I must really look dreadful, thought Cassandra. "No— yes. If you would be so kind, will you bring some cold water and a cloth for me? I have a bit of the headache."

"Of course, ma'am."

Cassandra sighed and sat down on the bed, looking absently at her hands. She opened and closed them, holding them out flat and then curling them into fists. She closed her eyes and bit her lip, feeling her face grow warm. How *could* she have lost control over herself and hit the marquess? Oh, but she had been so angry! He had been so unfair, so, so accusatory and insulting! As if she had done something horribly wrong. Well, perhaps she should have chosen a more secluded spot for kissing Lord Eldon, but no one else saw! And then when they were in the maze . . .

Feeling her face grow hot, she pressed her hands to her face. What in the world did he think he had been doing? Well, that was clear—he thought her nothing but a light skirt. *What in the world did you think you were doing*, murmured a nasty little voice in her head. It is not my fault! she mentally cried back to that voice. I did not know he was going to do—all that! *But you must have known it was not proper . . . and you did not stop him until you were almost undressed, replied the horrid little voice.*

Cassandra groaned. She felt foreign to herself, she who prided herself on her learning and her logic. Pride was a sin, indeed, for now she had her reward: all she had was confusion and could not see or think clearly at all. He did not make sense to her, and worse, she did not make sense to herself either.

Cassandra sighed and made herself sit up straight. That was the crux of it, was it not? He was not what she thought him. She'd thought him a gentleman, someone considerate of others' sensibilities. Someone who was kind and gentle. It was true that he had kissed her at the Marchmonts' ball, but it bore only a tangential resemblance to what she'd experienced in the maze. At the Marchmonts' the kiss had been gentle and absorbing. But this one! It had been hard— well, at first—and, and overwhelming. She reviewed her past encounters with the marquess and nodded her head. Yes. She had thought once that perhaps there was more to his surface calm, and she had been right. She had been deceived by his manners and outward consideration. Really, it would be better for her to keep her distance from him.

But you love him, and now you are afraid, the irritating voice said, and a responding cry of despair almost wrenched its way past her throat. But Cassandra shook her head and firmly banished that horrid little voice to a deep, dark chamber in her mind. She was afraid of nothing.

Mary returned with the cloth and water and started laying out Cassandra's dress for the evening. Cassandra pressed the cold cloth to her eyes. She simply must go down tonight. She could not stay upstairs, or else her parents—indeed the guests—would think that something was amiss. She could very well plead the headache, since it was true. But her headache was not nearly close to bad at all, and there was no excuse for cowardice.

When Cassandra put on her dress, she looked in the mirror and sighed. Her eyes were no longer puffy, but the light green satin did little to enhance her pale face and seemed to emphasize the shadows beneath her eyes. She pinched her cheeks, but that only brought two high spots of color to them. She sighed again and shrugged. It did not matter. It really did not matter. Hitting Lord Blytheland was perhaps remotely excusable, considering his horrible opinion of her, but she could hardly expect anything more than civility now. What had been between them—what she had thought was between them—was over.

The marquess paced his study and nervously put a finger between his neck and neckcloth. He really should not have tied it so tightly. But it was too late to remedy that right now. Sir John had sent up his note that he would meet with him shortly. Two raps on the door preceded the butler's entrance.

"Sir John Hathaway, my lord." The butler bowed and ushered Cassandra's father into the room.

Sir John gave him a sharp, assessing glance. "You wished to speak with me, Lord Blytheland?"

"Of course. That is, yes. Er, would you like to be seated? And refreshment. Brandy. Would you like some brandy?" The marquess groaned mentally. God, but he must sound inane. How does one set about asking a man for his daughter's hand in marriage?

"Why, thank you, my lord. Brandy would be excellent."

Blytheland was not certain, but he thought he saw amusement in Sir John's eyes. He looked at the older man again, but the expression was gone. He poured a glass for him and then after a short pause poured a small one for himself. The marquess drank it almost without tasting it, feeling the brandy's heat flow down his throat. He did not feel all that much better, however.

"You must be wondering why I requested your presence here today," Blytheland said.

Sir John merely smiled and gazed at him with interest.

"You must have noticed that my attentions to your daughter, Miss Hathaway, have been most marked of late. Indeed, I must confess that I have not always acted as a gentleman ought in her presence."

Sir John's eyebrows rose. "Kissed her, did you?"

"Er, yes." Bytheland could feel his face heating, but damn it, he could not bring himself to tell the man he had done more than that. Surely it was not necessary.

"Thought so."

Lord Blytheland looked a question at him.

"From the way she reacted when she mentioned the Marchmonts' ball, you see. It seemed she was not . . . unmoved." Sir John gave a slight smile.

"Then perhaps she would not be adverse to my suit for her hand in marriage," said the marquess, all in a rush. He felt his face grow warmer. "That is, with your permission, sir."

Sir John waved a careless hand. "Of course, of course."

"Thank you."

Silence ensued. Lord Blytheland cleared his throat. What *did* one do next? He did not remember it being this difficult with Chloe. Becoming engaged was a damnably awkward thing.

"However," Sir John said suddenly, "there *is* the question whether she will accept you." He looked pointedly at

Blytheland's blackened eye. "I assume it was Cassandra who blacked your eye?"

"Whyever do you assume so, sir?" Blytheland replied, hedging wildly. He almost groaned aloud. Damn, did *everyone* know?

"Logic and reason will someday answer the questions of the universe, my lord. To apply the mind's ordered faculties to such matters as your blackened eye is but a trivial exercise." Sir John pulled off his spectacles and paced the room, eyes concentrating mightily on the floor.

"Is it?" the marquess replied, his voice full of ice. He had not until this time thought his eye a trivial matter.

"Of course," Sir John said, apparently oblivious to the marquess's change of tone. "The bruise is of a shape similar to that of a lady's fist—should a lady know how to make a proper fist, that is. I recall, once, my son Kenneth showing Cassandra a few techniques of the art of pugilism—which she despises, by the way. There is the possibility she recalled it from somewhere in the recesses of her mind. Then there was my daughter's absence from the luncheon, and then yours. Lord Eldon returned before you, but since he is your friend and his expression was untroubled and merry and his appetite unaffected, I believe he was not the one who hit you. Prior to your absence, your eye was unmarked. Some hours after we returned to the house, you appeared with the bruise. You mentioned to your guests earlier that you stumbled and collided with a piece of rococo molding in the library. A maid tells my wife that Cassandra is indisposed with a headache."

The baronet paused in his pacing and cocked an eyebrow at Blytheland. "My daughter," he continued, "almost never has headaches. And rococo molding does not protrude to such a distance from the paneling that it would blacken anyone's eye. The most probable conclusion?" He paused.

"You behold me in breathless anticipation," Blytheland said, and could not help his sarcastic tone of voice.

A small smile touched Sir John's mouth. "The conclusion cannot be anything but that Cassandra hit your eye." He gazed critically at the marquess's bruise. "And a rather flush hit, if I may say so myself. I have heard that a slice of beef over the eye will reduce the swelling."

"I do *not* want beef, I thank you, sir," Blytheland replied through clenched teeth.

"Ah, well. But I warn you, my lord, Cassandra is not your ordinary young miss. The things that attract most young ladies do not hold much weight with my daughter. She may not accept you."

Blytheland smiled cynically. "Oh, I concede she is certainly not ordinary. But she cannot be so far different from her peers that a title and all the luxuries of life hold no sway with her."

Sir John gave him a quizzical look. "Ah, but, my dear Lord Blytheland, Cassandra has few peers."

"Of course."

"You think I am a overly fond father, I see." Sir John gave a wry smile that was also kind. "Well, I perceive I cannot convince you. You must find out for yourself whether my daughter will accept you or not. I understand she has risen from her rest. Perhaps she will see you now." He put his spectacles back on his nose, bowed, and gave his leave.

Blytheland stared at the door Sir John had just closed. Perhaps he should go to her now—or, no, did he not have some business with his bailiff—? On the other hand, there was no need to hold Miss Hathaway in suspense. Perhaps she was expecting some declaration or apology from him. It was the honorable thing to do, after all. Yes. Yes, he would ask for her, and declare himself immediately. He sighed. "If it were done when 'tis done, then 'twere well it were done quickly," he murmured to himself. Then remembering the context of that quote from Macbeth, he grimaced. He wished he did not feel he was going to an execution instead of proposing marriage.

Cassandra started nervously when she heard the parlor door open. She stared out the window at the landscape before her, but the gray clouds dulled the trees' and flowers' colors and did nothing to lighten her mood. She shivered, feeling just as cold and colorless as the view.

Her father had said that Lord Blytheland wanted to speak with her, and she could not help thinking that his desire to see her was quite unnecessary. What would he say? Would he apologize? Would he reproach her for striking him?

"Miss Hathaway."

She turned, slowly raised her head to look at him, and could not suppress a small gasp. A broad purple-and-yellow spot colored the area just below the marquess's right eyebrow, the side of his nose looked red, and a dark streak under the eye emphasized it all. The rest of him was, as usual, impeccable. But the eye ruined the effect; it was a blight on an otherwise pure landscape, a marring spot on a perfectly executed painting.

"Oh! Your eye! Does . . . does it hurt much?"

"Er, no, not much." The marquess looked quite uncomfortable, and Cassandra thought he must be in more pain than he admitted.

"I . . . I have heard that a slice of cold beef over the eye will lessen the pain and hasten the healing," she said tentatively.

"I do *not* want any beef!" he snapped.

"Well, you must excuse me, but I thought it *might* help!" Cassandra turned from him and stared angrily out the window again. Really! He was the crossest thing imaginable. She was only trying to help, after all!

"It would have been better if you hadn't been so free with your fist—or your kisses—in the first place!"

Cassandra turned swiftly to face him. "You need not

throw my actions in my face! I well know I should not have used violence against you—but you must admit, my lord, that I was under extreme provocation!"

"And what provoked you to try your little 'experiment,' " pray?" There was a hint of anger in his voice. Anger boiled up within her in response, heating her face.

"Do not start again! I explained it before, and I need not justify my actions to you. What right do you have to dictate to me?" She glared at him. He gave her an icy look in return, but it did nothing to cool her temper.

"Right? I have all the rights of a future husband!"

"What?" Cassandra felt her breath catch in her throat. She stared at Lord Blytheland, uncomprehending.

An uncomfortable look passed across his face, but he lifted his chin and said firmly, "What I meant to say is, will you marry me, Cassandra?"

She clenched her hands. "How *dare* you make mock of me!"

"No, I am not! You must marry me."

"Must? I think I might have a *little* say in this, my lord!"

The marquess impatiently paced the floor in front of her. "Not really. We were seen. My valet saw us go into and out of the maze. I think that is all who might have seen us, but I cannot be sure. Not only that, but your father deduced that we were alone together for quite a long time. I have no choice but to ask that you be my wife."

Cassandra's heart beat madly, but whether it was in grief or anger, she did not know. She had dreamed once, a week after they first met, that he had asked her to marry him. She had dismissed it as a notion beyond probability. Now he asked her to marry him in truth, and she felt it was a nightmare. It was all for propriety's sake—a necessary and bloodless thing that she knew many people lived with quite comfortably, but she knew she could not. She had hoped one day when she received a marriage proposal, that it would be from a man who loved her. But Lord Blytheland had said nothing of love, nothing of respect or esteem.

She looked up at him, putting all the control she could over her emotions. "You have no choice, do you? Ah, but I do. And I say no. No, Lord Blytheland, I will not marry you."

His lips pressed together briefly, as if he clenched his teeth. "And why not?" he asked.

Cassandra drew in a deep breath. "Because, my lord, I know from your words and actions that you neither esteem nor respect me." Or love, she thought. A stab of pain went through her heart at her own words, but she repressed it. "I, at least, can choose with whom I wish to marry and live for the rest of my life. And I choose not to marry someone who has not even one care for me." She turned away from him and looked out the windows, not seeing at all what was before her.

"I . . . care," said the marquess. His voice sounded closer to her.

Don't turn back to him! Cassandra told herself sternly. You cannot give in to him. She shook her head. "No. You care only for your consequence, and your honor, perhaps. I am sorry, my lord, but no. That sort of care is not enough."

"Then if you must hear it, I love you."

Cassandra gasped, then shook her head. No, impossible. His voice had been low and harsh, as if he'd been forced to confess it against his will. How could he love her and accuse her of base things, thinking she was a woman of no virtue? It made no sense! *And your feelings make perfect sense, do they?* said the nasty little voice inside of her. She firmly quashed the voice—it was the uncontrolled and unreasonable side of her, and she felt if she listened to it, she would break apart inside. No, it was best to think clearly, and logic told her he did not love her, but wished only to have his way. Cassandra took a deep breath and once more felt in control of herself. She turned to him once again. His expression was confused and lost.

"No, Lord Blytheland, I think you do not know what love is. My answer is most definitely no." She moved from him toward the door and opened it with what she felt was remarkable calm. "Good day, my lord."

"But wait—!"

The door closed behind her.

Chapter 10

"You did what?" Lady Hathaway's voice rose to a shriek on the last word.

"I refused him," Cassandra said calmly. She carefully put the last pair of earrings into her jewelry box and handed the box to her maid.

Lady Hathaway sat abruptly upon a chair and stared at Cassandra and wondered if a cockatrice was hiding beneath her daughter's apparently unmoved countenance. Certainly she felt as if she'd turned into stone, for Cassandra's words had stopped her heart and she felt numb. She became aware of the maid's interested gaze and waved her hand at her in dismissal. The maid left, her steps clearly reluctant. Lady Hathaway took a deep breath.

"Now, let me see if I heard correctly. Paul Templeton, Marquess of Blytheland, heir to the Duke of Beaumont— Lord Blytheland, who is a young, highly eligible, handsome, talented man of great fortune—proposed marriage to you, and you refused his suit." She held up her hand as Cassandra opened her mouth to speak. "No, no! Say nothing, at least for a few minutes . . . I wish to savor the fantasy that I did not hear the words, that I have reached my dotage at last and have lost all my senses and faculties of mind."

There was an obedient silence as Lady Hathaway closed her eyes and indulged in this hopeless flight of fancy . . . hopeless, indeed, for she opened her eyes and saw her daughter before her, lips firmly closed and eyes downcast.

She could not believe it. Oh, she could believe that all the material benefits of marriage to the marquess would not have weight with Cassandra. But she had been so certain that her daughter's affections had been engaged, and the girl certainly had not objected when the man had kissed her at the Marchmonts' ball! Why, she had even admitted to finding his kisses pleasant!

What had gone wrong? The man had positively haunted the house and Lady Hathaway had been certain he'd propose—and she'd been right! Anyone could see he was clearly enamored of Cassandra; it was the talk of the town, if the gossips were to be believed. *They* had been right, too, for he *had* proposed.

And had been refused. Her daughter Cassandra had refused him. Had she gone mad?

"Come, look at me, Cassandra."

The girl raised her head and stepped forward, and Lady Hathaway could see at last the shadows beneath her daughter's eyes, her pale skin, and her eyes dark with grief. Something was terribly wrong, and Cassandra was clearly miserable. Her heart melted. Silently, Lady Hathaway held her arms out to her. With a sob, Cassandra ran forward and flung her arms around her mother's neck. She wept noisily, as she had not done since she was a child, and Lady Hathaway stroked her hair.

"Hush, hush, child," she murmured. "That's it, love, a little crying will make you feel better."

Her words seemed to make Cassandra cry harder, but it was always thus, thought Lady Hathaway, even when she was a little girl. Cassandra had always been logical, her father's daughter, and tried so hard to emulate his intellectual demeanor. But Lady Hathaway knew she was also like herself, with a deep well of womanly passions, and for all Cassandra's training and studiousness those feelings would surface, will she, nil she. Those emotions always exploded from her, like the steam from a boiling pot too tightly closed, and Cassandra was always better for some venting. Lady Hathaway patted her daughter's back, rocking a little, as she used to do when Cassandra was a child.

At last Cassandra's sobs subsided, and after a few hiccups, she raised her head and smiled weakly at her mother. She searched about her for a handkerchief, then took the one Lady Hathaway gave her and dabbed her eyes.

"Thank you, Mama. How stupid of me! I cannot understand what overcame me. Why, I—"

"Enough, Cassandra! I nursed you myself when you were a babe, unfashionable though it was in some circles, and I remember every tear and smile you gave me since then. I am your mother! Would I not know when you are hurt to your very heart?"

Cassandra's smile wavered, and she shook her head. "Oh, don't—I fear you will make me cry again, Mama."

Lady Hathaway smiled and squeezed her daughter's hand. "Well, I think you have done quite a lot of that already. Perhaps a better idea would be to tell me what transpired between you and Lord Blytheland."

She listened in silence as Cassandra haltingly told her of her "experiment" and how Lord Blytheland had seen it. Lady Hathaway suspected from her daughter's hesitant speech that she did not tell her everything . . . but she would deal with that later. She suppressed the despairing sigh that threatened to burst from her. Heavens! She had not known Cassandra was so naive—she had thought her intelligence would make it easy for her to understand society's ways. Then, too, she'd thought a little naïveté would be an attractive thing in a young lady, but this was more than a little! It was her own fault for not insisting that Cassandra stay in the select boarding school she'd sent her to, but had allowed her husband to teach her instead. And she should have expected that her daughter would turn out so, for she herself had learned discretion and proper conduct at the young ladies' academy to which she had gone when she was a girl.

Clearly Cassandra had misconstrued her instructions and had taken her acceptance of Lord Blytheland's kisses in general terms.

It was clear to Lady Hathaway why Lord Blytheland had lost his temper—he was jealous, and possibly mad with love. Such madness was a rare thing, but she had seen it happen and she was sure it was thus with Lord Blytheland, for he had never been known to act in such a way before, not even in rumor. But it was not time for her to reveal this to Cassandra quite yet. For as she listened to her daughter, there was no hint the girl would admit to loving him, or that her grief and pain came from love, and not from mere insult. She was certain, however, that Cassandra did love him, and was most probably aware of it.

But as Lady Hathaway listened, a burning anger grew in her as well. For however Cassandra had acted, he had behaved in far less than a gentlemanly manner when he took her into the maze, kissed her, and accused her of a lack of virtue. It mattered not whether he was mad with love or was jealous; he should have had better control over his passions than that. And to suspect Cassandra's climbing boys to be her own! If it were not so insulting, she would have laughed. She suspected that someone had referred to the charity in vague terms . . . possibly Psyche, for that literal-minded child had been warned not to mention climbing boys, and only the family referred to the charity as "Cassandra's children." She would definitely have to talk to Psyche soon.

She patted Cassandra's hand and squeezed it in a comforting manner, and her daughter smiled in return.

"Well, we shall be leaving this house soon, and Lord Blytheland need not bother you again. He has proposed—as he should have done, after practically compromising your virtue!—and you have refused. I am sorely disappointed in him—he had seemed so gentlemanly as well as eligible! But that is the end of it, and we need not acknowledge his invitations or his calls to us in town if you do not feel you can face him. And I would not blame you if you did not wish to see him! For all that you were indiscreet—and I will not excuse you on that head!—you did not deserve such treatment from him."

Cassandra cast a tentative look at her mother. "Could we . . . could we leave London and go home, at least for a while?"

"No, that would be admitting you were at fault, should word of this ever come out to the *ton,* as it will, eventually. However painful it is, we must return, and put a good face on it. Besides, *you* were the one to refuse his proposal, therefore there must be something wrong with *him,* not you. If we left London, it would be thought quite otherwise."

Cassandra nodded and was silent, clearly taking in this advice with deep consideration. Lady Hathaway gazed at her, and felt that something had changed, that Cassandra would perhaps show a different face to society than she once had. Lady Hathaway knew a moment of regret and sighed, for she felt torn. Part of her wished that the blunt, outspoken Cassandra had stayed, for it was how she had been since a child, and to see it modified or changed was to see her daughter as a little girl no more. But Cassandra was a woman grown, and to try to keep her from being one was foolishness.

"Besides, you have grown quite popular, have you not? There is no reason why you should not enjoy the entertainments during the rest of the Season. There are other eligible gentlemen in London, too, when you are able to think of proposals again—Lord Eldon, after all, did not refuse to kiss you, after all! But there is time enough to think of that later," Lady Hathaway said hastily at Cassandra's despairing expression. "It is best to think of balls and dresses and other frivolous things."

Cassandra raised her brows. "But frivolous things—"

"No, I do not want any of your homilies about frivolity," Lady Hathaway said. "There is such a thing as balance in

one's life, and I think you have had enough of seriousness
and disappointments for now, am I not right?"

There was silence, then Cassandra pressed her lips together and nodded. She looked at Lady Hathaway and
smiled gratefully. "You are the best of mothers! I know you
must be disappointed, for you seemed to like Lord Blytheland over any other gentleman . . . and he is the only one
who has proposed, after all. He could be my only—" She
swallowed, then smiled again, though it was a smile full of
pain. "The only proposal I will receive."

Lady Hathaway patted her hand. "I would not want a husband for you who did not love you as you deserve, my dear.
And I am not at all in despair! Why, Hetty Chatwick told
me last week that the Viscount Bennington was quite taken
with you when he saw you in our opera box! And did not
Mr. Rowland and Sir Ellery Heysmith both dance with you
at the Marchmonts' ball *and* at Almack's?"

She chattered on, watching Cassandra's face as she outlined new entertainments and future balls. Her expression
had lightened a little and she was clearly listening to her
mother's advice. But a dark sadness still lingered in her
eyes, and Lady Hathaway feared that her daughter's heart
might be badly broken.

"It is my fault. It is all my fault," Psyche said, and pressed
her hands to her eyes. She had heard her mother's shriek,
and had—admittedly—eavesdropped, then ran to her bedroom. She knew she would weep and did not want anyone
to see her, and it was close to the time she usually slept anyway. "I mentioned the climbing boys and I shouldn't have,
and it made Lord Blytheland angry at Cassandra, and she hit
him on his eye and now *she* is angry at him, and they will
never be happy again!"

Harry flew down from his perch on the window ledge to
the bed upon which Psyche sat and hugged her comfort-

ingly. "No, it was not your fault he was being stupid. Besides, he said it was the rococo molding."

Psyche shook her head and wiped away a tear with the back of her hand. "No, I know she must have hit him, because I saw them come out of the maze and his eye looked terrible. He hadn't walked into molding at all." She bit her lower lip to keep it from quivering but her tears still fell. "Oh, I wish I hadn't told him! I have ruined it for both of them! I am so disappointed in Lord Blytheland. I never, never thought he would be mean to Cassandra, for he has always been kind to me. How could he be so horrid to her? I don't understand! I thought you said he was in love with her, Harry!"

There was silence, and Psyche looked up at her friend. He felt tense next to her, and an odd expression, a mix of affront, surprise, and guilt was on his face. She had seen him affronted before, but she had never seen him look surprised or guilty about anything.

"Is there something the matter?" she asked.

He looked at her, and this time the guilt was clear in his eyes. He swallowed. "I think . . . I think it is my fault a little, Psyche."

"But I thought you turned him back to what he was before you shot him with your love arrows!"

"I did! But, well, I, er, got there too late," he said in a rush. He definitely looked uncomfortable now.

"Oh, Harry!" Psyche said.

"I thought there was no need . . . I thought perhaps it would work well as it was, and I suppose . . . I suppose I didn't go as fast as I should have." He rose from the sofa, went to the fireplace, and fiddled with a few of the ornaments on the mantelpiece. He put them down and walked to the window, then back to the fireplace again, his movements restless. "And . . . and I think I might have shot too many love arrows into him the first time."

"Too many arrows? Why?" Psyche felt a queer ache inside of her, as if something she held dear was quickly sliding from her grasp.

"He was stubborn! He refused to think he could love anyone, or that he could be loved! All he could think of was his stupid dead wife who could never truly love anyone and who he—Who he—" Harry clenched his fists, frowning terribly. "With whom he fell in love because he looked at the wrong woman when I shot him with one of my arrows!"

"You mean you made a mistake."

"No, I never make mistakes. It wasn't my fault he looked at the wrong woman!"

"Not your fault! Why, I would say you should have known he could have looked at the wrong woman if there were more than one about him! Oh, you and your, your *hubris*!" Psyche said hotly. "You say we mortals shouldn't have it because it offends you and your relatives, but I think it's precisely the opposite! If you hadn't been so toplofty as to think you never make a mistake—and you certainly did, don't deny it!—you would have been more careful! You wouldn't have had to shoot Lord Blytheland with too many arrows and—"

She stopped and stared at Harry. "You said too many arrows . . . what did you mean by that? What do too many arrows do?"

"I don't see why I should tell you, especially if you're going to be a witch about it all." A mulish look settled about his chin, and he stared at her angrily.

"You *shall* tell me!" Psyche cried. "It's important! I know my sister has a broken heart—she cried and cried and she *never* cries! If you don't I swear I'll not leave my window open at night, and you will have to stay outside until morning and if you catch a horrid cold it shall be all that you deserve!"

"What do I care? I don't catch colds," Harry said scornfully.

Psyche bit her lip again, for she could feel it begin to quiver and she didn't want to cry again.

"Oh—very well!" Harry said impatiently. "If I shoot too many arrows in someone they become mad. They don't always act as they ought and sometimes they become stupidly jealous. There. I hope you are satisfied."

The ache Psyche had felt earlier grew hard and hurt worse now. She stared at Harry and knew some of the ache was disappointment, for though she knew he was not perfect, a part of her always thought he was. But now his actions had made Lord Blytheland act in a mean way to Cassandra, and now Cassandra's heart was broken. And Harry could not even admit he had made a mistake!

"You horrid, beastly boy!" Psyche cried. "It was all because of you that Lord Blytheland was so odious to my sister! I *told* you, you should not have shot him! I *told* you it was a mistake! But you didn't listen, did you? You knew *so* much more than I! You *never* make a mistake, do you?"

"I suppose your blabbing about Cassandra's climbing boys to Lord Blytheland had nothing to do with it?" Harry hunched a disdainful shoulder. "If you think me so odious, I wonder you care to have me about!"

"Well, I don't!" Psyche retorted. "I hope I never see you again!"

Harry gave her one burning, angry look, and with a rush of wind and feathers he was gone.

"Harry!" Psyche whirled around, looking for him. "Harry, where are you?" No answer, no glowing light, no whisper of feathers or rattle of arrows. He was gone, truly gone. Her lip trembled in earnest now. Oh, heavens. He had been right, really—she was still partly at fault, even though most of the fault was his. But she had been so angry!

"Harry?" she whispered. Silence. She was alone now, and she wished she had not scolded him. And . . . she had told him that she never wanted to see him again. "I didn't mean

it! Please come back." She flung the window open wider
and strained to see into the night's darkness.

But still there was silence, no sound except the wind outside the chamber window.

Lord Blytheland watched the guests leave in their carriages and watched in particular one coach in which a young
lady sat. He lifted his hand and placed his fingers on the
drawing-room window. The coach now looked no larger
than the width of his thumb. If he could, he'd pluck up the
carriage and bring Cassandra Hathaway back to him again.

But he could not, of course. He picked up a glass and
swallowed a mouthful of brandy, not tasting it, and hardly
feeling the heat of it going down his throat. Grimacing, he
put the glass down on the marble-topped table beside him.
The madness that had seized him was gone now. How long
had it held him? He was not certain, and there was only confusion and despair left in its wake. He had pushed her away
with his jealous rage, he was sure.

He pressed his palms against his eyes and groaned. There
was no reason Miss Hathaway—Cassandra—should forgive
him. He had not only insulted her but his proposal of marriage had been so badly done that no self-respecting woman
would have accepted him.

But she had said she had loved him. He should not hope;
his actions should have killed any love she might have had
for him. And yet . . . and yet she had not said that she hated
him, not precisely. It was not much, perhaps, but it was
something.

It was, he realized, more than he had had from his wife or
from any of his mistresses. None of them had said words of
love to him—appreciation, perhaps, for he was fairly skilled
at lovemaking and showering those under his protection
with trinkets and other expensive gifts. But none of them
had said they loved him. He knew now he'd come to expect
it: that for all his wealth and title, there was something

wrong with him, something in him that was ultimately unlovable. Blytheland half groaned, half laughed. How ironic it was that he'd hear it at last from blunt, outspoken Cassandra, after showing how unlovable he could be. And now she'd left his life—possibly forever, if the cold, haughty looks he received from Lady Hathaway were any indication.

The door opened, and his butler bowed. "Lord Eldon to see you, my lord." Blytheland nodded, and the butler opened the door wider.

Lord Eldon raised his quizzing glass and peered at his friend, his gaze resting for a moment on Blytheland's black eye. "Now that's a wisty castor. Didn't know rococo molding protruded that far out from the wall. Architecture's a damned nuisance, if you ask me."

"It wasn't rococo molding, El," Blytheland said.

"Ah. Thought not. La Hathaway has a handy bunch of fives on her, eh?"

"Flush hit. Knocked me down flat into the pond."

Eldon's brows raised. "Remind me not to have a lover's quarrel with her. Can't hit a lady, after all, and I wouldn't have a sporting chance, then."

Blytheland laughed reluctantly, then looked steadily at his friend. "The field's clear for you, El. She's refused me. Not that I blame her. I'm a villain, a monster, the way I've treated her. She deserves much better for a husband than someone like me." He gave another bitter laugh. "You should have called me out when you had the chance. I deserved it. In fact, feel free to use my pistols now. I promise I won't return the shot."

"Happy to oblige, Blythe-my-old, but I might get blood on my hessians. Can't have that."

"No, of course not."

There was silence for a moment, then Eldon said, "Truth to tell, Blythe, I was hoping to hear wedding bells for you. Seems I miscalculated."

The marquess raised his head and stared at his friend.

Lord Eldon looked a little uncomfortable. "Thing is, you were dancing around the lady so much we all thought it was a promised thing. Betting on it at White's, too. Then you told me it wasn't in the pocket at all. Bad thing to do, friend, especially when she was so clearly top over tails in love with you from the start."

"I couldn't see it, El." Blytheland hesitated. "No, I did not want to."

"Chloe?"

"Yes."

Silence again. Eldon, apparently in deep thought, twirled his quizzing glass on the end of its ribbon.

"Well, I believe you know what I thought of Chloe," he said. "So I won't go into that. But I'll be frank: I had Miss Hathaway figured as the perfect match for you. Everyone did. Music, brains, charities, not to mention a lovely face and form—most everything you like, my old. Thought you could see that, too."

"Had a thought to play the matchmaker, did you, El?" Blytheland said mockingly.

Eldon rubbed the side of his nose and looked a little embarrassed. "You'd been moping about Chloe for, deuce take it, two, three years now? Time to stop mourning for a woman who was little better than a whore."

The marquess stood up abruptly, fists clenched. "I'll remind you not to talk about—"

"Oh, stubble it, Blytheland! What else do you call a woman who came home only to whelp another man's child?"

Lord Blytheland caught his breath. "How do you know—"

"If you'll remember, you lost your way down Pall Mall, after imbibing three bottles of White's finest the night she died. If I hadn't peeled you off the lamppost and brought you to my lodgings to sleep it off, you'd probably have blabbed the whole to the street." Lord Eldon bent a kindly eye upon his friend. "You were pretty badly off, so I daresay you might not remember it. I would have been the same with three bottles in me—in fact, I was, the last time Lightning-Be-Gone placed fifth at Ascot. Lost a deuced thousand pounds, too, and was sick as a dog the next morning.

"Thing is," he continued after Blytheland sat down again, "you're a marrying man. Thought perhaps Miss Hathaway would be the ticket to church for you. But you denied it every time, despite the way you were hovering around her like a bee to honey. So, when she asked me to participate in her, ah, experiment, I thought it'd be just the thing to make you think about what you might be losing." An embarrassed look grew on his face. "Thing was, I didn't think you'd rake Miss Hathaway over the coals, or insult her. You never did that before to a lady, not even with Chloe when you found out about her, ah, indiscretions."

"I'll thank you, El, not to interfere in my affairs in the future," Blytheland said, but he said it with no heat, no anger. He had, after all, no one but himself to blame, and Eldon was quite right. Miss Hathaway was perfect for him, and he'd been making up excuses right and left trying to tell himself she was not. "Well, it's too late now." He rubbed his hand over his face. God, he was tired thinking of it all, and the brandy was not making it any better. "I'll see you in town in a month or so."

Eldon nodded in an understanding manner. "Can't be seen in town sporting an eye like that."

Lord Blytheland hesitated and then gazed at his friend. "Would you look out for her, El? I won't be in town, but she will. She has no more notion about how to go about society than a kitten, for all her intelligence. I suppose . . . I suppose with all the attention I have been paying her, there will be gossip. Let it about that I did propose, and she refused me." He smiled wryly. "If they wish to think I am suffering a decline in the country because of her rejection of my suit, they may do so."

"No, no, not so bad as that!" Eldon protested, clearly revulsed. "But I shall see that she's partnered at every dance, at least."

"Thank you, El. You're a true friend." Blytheland poured himself another glass of brandy and drank it down.

Lord Eldon cleared his throat and looked embarrassed. "Not at all, not at all. You'd do the same for me, should the occasion rise." A look of horror crept upon his countenance. "That is—Good God. I hope not. Not that La Hathaway isn't what a man would want—That is, I wouldn't want to be in the same boat as you right now. No offense meant, Blythe-my-old," he said, looking uncomfortable.

The marquess laughed at last. "No, I know you don't." His smile twisted, and he shook his friend's hand. "Let me know how she goes on, will you?"

"Of course." Eldon turned to leave, but hesitated. "Think you might try again?"

Blytheland sighed and wearily rubbed his unbruised eye with his hand. "I do not know, El. I really don't. Sometimes I think—Well, I suppose it doesn't matter."

Lord Eldon gazed at his friend sympathetically for a moment, then took his leave and closed the door. He frowned. Blythe was in a bad way, but heaven only knew how he'd get himself out of it. He was willing to wager that Miss Hathaway was fair to being miserable, too, by the look of her face before she left. Lord, what a tangle! Well, he'd watch out for Miss Hathaway as his friend had asked, and perhaps put in a good word or two for old Blythe as well.

He'd denied that his friend would go into a decline, but he was not all that certain of it. Blytheland's bottle of brandy was already half empty, and the look on his face was worse than the one he'd had the night Chloe died. He doubted that the man would feel much better in the morning. Worse, in fact. Much worse.

Chapter 11

"And would you know when Lord Blytheland will be returning to London, Miss Hathaway? It has been three, perhaps four weeks since he has been in town, has it not?" Lady Fairway asked.

Cassandra swallowed her anger and bit back an acid retort. She smiled at Lady Fairway. "I have no idea, my lady. I am not privy to Lord Blytheland's activities." She took a sip of tea, glad that her hand did not rattle the cup on the saucer when she put it down again. Perhaps she was not always discreet, but she had learned much control this month. It was important so that she would not scream the hurt and anger she still felt every time someone poked at her for answers to Lord Blytheland's absence from London.

"But I thought you and he . . ." Lady Fairway said, her voice rising at the end in a question.

Cassandra widened her eyes innocently and raised her brows. "Lord Blytheland and I? What have we to do with—Oh! You must mean our mutual interest in music. There was some talk of doing more duets, but I do not know if it will come about. I suppose we might, but I cannot say until he returns to London. It is always a difficult thing to agree upon a piece of music that is mutually satisfactory to both players." She shrugged a little and smiled.

She saw her mother nod in approval at her from across Lady Fairway's drawing room. Her mother had given her support for her spirits and much encouragement, and she was grateful for it. This time she would listen, and try harder to understand the rules of society, however nonsensical and contrary to the philosophies she had learned. There was such a thing as practical application, after all, and one must modify one's theories to real situations instead of to the hypothetical. Even her father had agreed this was true.

Lady Fairway raised her brows and her smile was sly. She tittered. "And to think that there were rumors about your betrothal to him!"

Cassandra could feel herself blush, but she made herself laugh. "As you see, you have made me blush at the notion—it is so ridiculous! How anyone could think such a silly thing, I do not know. Why, Lord Blytheland can look higher than myself for a wife, after all. Everyone must know that."

"A silly notion, of course," Lady Fairway agreed and her smile was odiously sweet.

Cassandra bit back a heated retort, almost losing her resolution to be silent upon the subject—she could easily have mentioned he *had* proposed to her. But she was not at all certain when he would return to London, if at all this Season, and she would much rather deny he had an interest in her beyond mere flirtation. Her mother had thought it might be best to discreetly let people know of the proposal, but though Cassandra agreed to every other one of her suggestions, she could not bear thinking of his proposal, or anyone questioning her about her refusal. Her mother had reluctantly agreed; the subject would be a thing to cause speculation whatever anyone said.

"Oh, hardly silly, Lady Fairway," said a voice behind Cassandra. She turned and swallowed nervously—it was Mrs. Drummond-Burrell, one of the strictest of the patronesses of Almack's. Her cool gaze warmed a little and she nodded approvingly at Cassandra. "Miss Hathaway is clearly a modest young lady of good birth, and that is al-

ways attractive in a prospective wife. She is very accomplished as well. Who is to say that a man of Lord Blytheland's breeding and lineage would not look to marry her? I
see it as wholly possible that he might propose to her in the
future, and be considered most fortunate in his choice."

Cassandra blushed furiously now. "Oh, heavens, Mrs.
Drummond-Burrell. Truly, you are too kind. I pray you will
not say more. Really, there is nothing between us except an
interest in music."

The patroness of Almack's nodded kindly at her. "You
are a good, modest girl, Miss Hathaway." She gazed sternly
at Lady Fairway. "One does not often see such modesty in
young ladies these days, I am afraid."

This time Lady Fairway blushed, and with a hasty curtsy
and murmured excuse she left to talk with some acquaintance she had just noticed from across the room.

"Odious woman," Mrs. Drummond-Burrell remarked
calmly. She turned to Cassandra and gave her a slight
smile. "You did very well. I do hope Lord Blytheland pro-
poses to you and that you accept. He needs someone as sensible as you, Miss Hathaway. His last wife was a horrible
woman, immodest and wicked. However, you are wise not
to set your sights upon him; gentlemen are not always as
sensible as ladies where marriage is concerned. It is remarkable how many of them make the same mistakes again
and again." With a nod, she turned to talk to an acquaintance.

Lady Hathaway beamed her approval at her from across
the room, but Cassandra felt trapped. Oh, heavens! She *had*
refused the marquess. If the *ton*—and Mrs. Drummond-
Burrell—heard of her refusal and disapproved, would she
be turned away from the doors of Almack's? She almost
groaned in despair. It seemed it mattered not what she did
or how hard she tried, she could still founder in the murky
shoals of society's rules.

And what was she to do when Lord Blytheland returned?

They were bound to see each other from time to time, and it was bound to be awkward. Her mother said that all she needed to do was be civil . . . but such coldness and distance between them would be marked by everyone in the *ton.* Lady Hathaway had shaken her head. There was no escaping it; it would be noticed, and they would have to bear whatever whispers and speculations they heard with aplomb.

A brief silence suddenly stilled the drawing room, and Cassandra knew without looking toward the door that Lord Blytheland had returned. She could see glances from Lady Fairway's guests go between the door and herself; who else would engender such speculative looks? Conversation began again, slightly louder than before, as if everyone were trying to cover an awkward moment.

Awkward indeed. She looked up to see Lord Blytheland before her. The bruise was gone from his eye, only a slight yellowing close to the side of his nose. His gaze was solemn as he bowed to her.

"I trust you are well, Miss Hathaway?" His voice was soft and deep, and she wished desperately she did not feel joy rising in her upon hearing it.

"Y-yes, I am well, thank you. And you?" She could not help glancing at the eye she had hit and her face grew warm with embarrassment.

"I am better, thank you."

Cassandra swallowed and looked away. "I am glad," she murmured.

"Are you?" Was there a slight eagerness in his voice? She was not certain.

"I would not want anyone feeling less than well, my lord." There, that was nothing more than a neutral sentiment.

"Of course." The marquess's voice was cool, and when she looked at him again he did not meet her eyes but seemed to look past her shoulder. She wished she could say something witty or light, but she could think of nothing, and only gave him a brief, weak smile and looked away.

"Perhaps I could call upon you tomorrow or the next day, Miss Hathaway?"

Oh, heavens, what should she say? Cassandra glanced at her mother across the room, but she was talking to the lady by her side. She looked at him; he gazed at her again, and though his face was smooth and cool, he had a questioning look in his eyes. She did not know he would return at this time, she was not prepared for it. At the very least, she needed a day—a few days—to compose herself, to think how she might speak with him from this time on. She wet her lips nervously.

"I—I would be pleased to have you call upon me," she said as calmly as she could. "But not now . . . that is, in a few days. I shall not be home to callers in the next day or so. I have been so busy, you see, and have fallen behind on some of my duties." She hated to give such an excuse, although it was not a lie—she did need to see to some of her duties to her charities—but in truth she was a coward and did not want to face him. She looked down at her clasped hands on her lap. Oh, but she could not, could not speak to him just yet!

She could hear him taking in a deep breath before replying, "I see. Perhaps . . . perhaps in three days?"

"Yes . . . yes, that will do."

"I thank you. Your servant, Miss Hathaway." He sketched a bow and turned away.

Cassandra watched him leave, then caught her mother looking at her questioningly from across the room. She shook her head and then looked down at her lap again. Three days. She wondered what Lord Blytheland would say to her when they met again. Well, she would have enough time to compose herself and rehearse whatever words she might need to . . . what? She did not know. Her hands twisted together and a lump rose in her throat.

She looked at the clock on the mantelpiece—she would have to stay another fifteen minutes before she could go home. And she wished desperately to go home. For right at this moment, there was nothing she wanted more than to fling herself upon her bed and cry and cry until she had no tears left.

Psyche sat and stared dully out at the street in front of the house from her window. She shivered. She wished she could go home to the house in the country—there were many things to do there, not like London. Dull, boring London, with nothing to do and no . . . friends.

Even the scold she had received from her mother upon their return from Lord Blytheland's alfresco luncheon was better than this. She felt a little better about being punished, for she knew she deserved it for ruining things between Cassandra and Lord Blytheland. Well, the marquess *still* should not have acted so odiously, but he would not have if she had not misled him about Cassandra's charity.

A dull, empty ache pulsed inside of Psyche's chest, and she felt like crying again. It was not as if the scolding had helped her sister in any way. She hated how falsely cheerful Cassandra would become when in her, Psyche's, presence, and could see how her sister seemed so listless and sad when she thought no one was looking. Psyche had also heard some weeping in Cassandra's room next to hers . . . whatever Cassandra said, it looked very much as if she *did* love Lord Blytheland anyway. However bad one might argue with someone, it did not mean you hated them, after all.

Psyche sighed. And well did she know that! She wished desperately that she had not argued with Harry. It was awfully lonely without him, for he was always amusing to talk to, and always had a story to tell or would play a game of cards or chess with her. But now there was nothing to do, for she could hardly play chess with herself, and playing game after game of patience was becoming dreadfully boring.

She heard a door open and shut out in the hallway, and a rush of activity in the next room. Did Cassandra have a caller? Psyche gnawed at her lower lip and frowned. She was not allowed to see anyone who called upon them, and was more or less confined to her room for the next two weeks. But a certain rebelliousness rose in her. She had not totally been at fault for the argument between Lord Blytheland and Cassandra; it was Harry's fault, too, and the marquess's. So her confinement to her room was quite unjust. Really, it was only fair that she be allowed a little peek at who was calling at their house, and if she was careful, no one would be the wiser. Psyche quashed a little quiver of conscience. No, she had taken on punishment that should have been Harry's, too. She *deserved* to leave her room at least a little!

She waited until the voices from Cassandra's room were silent and the door opened and closed for a last time. She glanced at the ormolu clock upon the mantelpiece and waited for another five minutes. There. That should be enough time.

Carefully, Psyche opened the door to her room and looked around it out into the hallway. Nothing. She breathed a sigh of relief and tiptoed silently down the hall. The stairs went down to a small landing, and there she sat, peering between the balusters. She could hear someone pacing below . . . ah! It was Lord Blytheland. His head was bent, his hands clasped behind his back, but there was no other gentleman of their acquaintance who had such golden blond hair and impeccable clothes. He looked nervous, Psyche thought, as if he were trying to think of something to say. The door of the drawing room opened. He straightened, and his face became smooth, as if he had never paced or looked nervous at all. Psyche wondered how he could do that, for she was never able to control her features at all.

Perhaps it was something that came with age. The door closed behind him, then her mother came out, and Psyche shrank back behind the balusters again.

"I will give you fifteen minutes, my lord. That should be quite enough for anything you have to say to my daughter. I shall be in my sitting room across the hall, should either of you need me," Lady Hathaway said into the room, looking very stern, as if she would have liked to have confined Lord Blytheland to his room, too. She left the door ajar, then went across the hall to her room.

Psyche stared at the open door and fidgeted. Perhaps she would go down the stairs to listen at the door. She might as well go back to her room if she was going to let herself be bored by sitting on the landing and staring down at the hall, after all. There was a very large potted fern sitting upon a table just next to the door; if she was very careful, she could conceal herself there and listen.

She rose and tiptoed down the stairs. There was a slight space between the fern and the wall next to the drawing-room door, enough for her to slip behind and curl up beneath the table. She made herself very still, and listened.

Cassandra sat and folded her hands before her in her lap and was glad she could control their shaking. But her palms felt damp, and she took out her handkerchief and surreptitiously dried them. She did not look at Lord Blytheland, for she was afraid of what she would blurt at him if she did, especially since she had no idea what she would say to him. That was what had made her say indiscreet things, she found—not knowing what she'd say in any particular social situation. She had tried to think of potential events before she went anywhere so as to practice what she would say. It had worked well, too, for no one had walked off in an offended manner for a month now, and she had many gentlemen calling upon her the next day after dancing with her.

But for all that she had had three days in which to practice before Lord Blytheland would come calling, she could think of nothing except how she had felt in his arms, how she had kissed him as shamelessly as he had kissed her, his words to her in the maze and how she had hit him. How was one to practice proper responses to thoughts like those? And so here she was, wordless in front of him, twisting her handkerchief into knots, and feeling as if her stomach were twisting into a knot as well.

"Cassand—Miss Hathaway," Lord Blytheland said abruptly, making Cassandra start and stare at him. He had a tight look upon his face, his lips thin and frowning, his eyes tired and a little reddened, his face pale. Was he ill, perhaps? She hoped not . . . although why she should care when he had treated her so badly she did not know. She twisted her handkerchief tighter. She did care, and there was no deceiving herself about that, stupid as it was.

"Miss Hathaway," Lord Blytheland began again. "I . . . I have come to apologize." He began to pace the floor in front of her. "I should have come to town earlier, but was . . . indisposed." He grimaced, then smiled ruefully. "Frankly, I was afraid to show myself with a black eye."

"Oh!" Cassandra closed her mouth tightly to keep herself from saying more. She felt a pressure of words behind her lips, and heaven knew what she'd say if she opened them. Not now, she told herself. Not now. Listen and *think* first.

"I was a brute, I treated you badly," he said, his words coming quickly now. "There was little excuse for it except . . . except I seemed to have gone a little mad. It is not something I have done before—well, I suppose anyone might say that." He raised his hand—a slight, beseeching gesture—then dropped it to his side. "But you may ask any of my friends—Lord Eldon, Mr. Rowland, Sir Ellery."

"I suppose your friends would speak well for you," Cassandra said carefully, trying to keep her voice neutral.

Anger flickered in his eyes, then faded to resignation. "I

wish . . . I wish I knew what to say. I wish to be in your good graces again, so you will not think ill of me . . ."

Cassandra turned away, embarrassed, not really wishing to hear more, for it seemed to be more of the same thing he had been saying before. She had known people who disliked anyone to think ill of them, not because of any remorse, but out of pride, because they could not bear a tarnish on their public mask. It was beginning to seem Lord Blytheland was such a man. She had sensed the passion— no, anger—beneath the surface mask, and he had shown it, and now he wished to hide it, pretend that it would not happen again. But such anger often repeated its performance in one way or another. Did not Mrs. Wollstonecraft say it, also? And Cassandra did not want to see it again. Or be tempted to display your own temper in response, the nasty little voice said inside of her. She firmed her lips. Yes, or be tempted to display her own temper again.

"Please, Cassand—Miss Hathaway—please look at me."

Cassandra turned to him again, gazed into his eyes, and a sharp pain went through her heart. He had stopped before her, his eyes were full of despair, his face pale with strain.

"What I said before was true. I love you. I wish you to be my wife, not because of any scandal, but because I love you. I swear I'll never accuse you falsely of anything, as long as I live." He ran a shaking hand through his hair, messing it terribly, then began pacing again.

Her hand trembled as she pressed it to her lips. There were so many things she wished to say, all fighting for a place on her tongue, all full of conflicting feelings and desires. Anger, weeping, fear. And love? She thought so, but her emotions were so mixed and fiery, they boiled inside like a pot on a stove, and if she put her hand down from her mouth, she knew the feelings would spill forth, confused and heated. She had never felt so much before in her life and did not know what to think, what was right and proper. Nothing her father had taught her of various philosophies helped her, for they were full of theories and hypotheses, and none of them seemed to fit her situation now.

Lord Blytheland stopped again in front of her, gazing at her earnestly. "Please—deuce take it, I know I'm a fool for asking it, and I would not blame you if you never wish to see me again, but I must know. You said—" He hesitated, then rushed on. "You said you loved me, there in the maze. Do you still?"

Cassandra rose, stepped toward the window, and stared blindly out of it. What could she say? Her heart was too full, and she was afraid of what was in it.

"Please, Cassandra . . ."

She turned swiftly around and faced him. "I don't know. I don't know!" She clasped her hands in front of her to still their shaking. "I did, before you—Before we—" Cassandra cleared her throat of the tears rising in it. "I have not been able to think clearly since then." She gave a hesitant laugh, a little bitter, a little sad. "I used to think I was very good at discerning what people were like after I observed them for a while. But you . . . well, I suppose I should not have been so sure of my abilities. And now I am afraid."

"Not of me—I swear—"

"I do not know how you will act in the future, Lord Blytheland," Cassandra said. "If I wed you, how do I know you will not act jealously again? It will be too late, after we are wed."

He gazed at her, frustrated. "How can I prove it to you, that I know I will not do it again?"

Cassandra shook her head. "I do not know how you may prove it. I do not even know what I think or feel." She turned from him, and went to the fireplace. She leaned her head upon the mantelpiece and stared into the fire.

"If I give you time, time to think about it—" Lord Blytheland said eagerly.

"Perhaps," Cassandra said dully. She suddenly felt tired, and her mind refused to work and moved sluggishly. "I think perhaps that would be the best thing, to give me time."

"I see." Lord Blytheland said only the two words, but they were heavy with despair and pain. Something inside Cassandra cracked and flowed hot inside her, and she pressed her hands to her eyes to push down the rising tears. "I am sorry. Perhaps it is best that I leave. You may assure your parents I will not annoy you again, if that is what you wish."

Cassandra could not respond; her whole body felt leaden with the weight of confusion and unshed tears. She almost told him, crazily, that her father had gone out of town, that she would be sure to tell her mother—irrelevant things, for the important ones would not come. She heard his steps, swift, away from her, and she turned at last. But it was too late—he had left, quietly, with no more words.

She stood, mute, staring at the door. Then it opened again, and her heart hammered in hope . . . but it was only her mother, who gazed long into her eyes. Lady Hathaway said nothing, but held out her arms.

With a low moan, Cassandra ran to her and when her mother held her and drew her to the sofa, she moaned again, deep, for the tears she had held back for so long would not come now.

"Hush, child, hush, hush," Lady Hathaway murmured, patting her back gently. "It will come about, you will see. Hush, love, you will see."

She said the words again and again, rhythmically, a soft lullaby like the ones she had sung when Cassandra was a little girl, and at last the tears came, hard and hot and more full of grief than she had ever had since a child. When she was a girl, she could hope. But being a grown woman was a different thing, and hope did not come so quickly, especially when her heart and mind had become that of a stranger's, no longer familiar or sure.

* * *

Psyche crouched behind the potted fern, her fist pressed tightly to her mouth. Silent sobs shook her, for she had heard it all, the hopelessness and love in Lord Blytheland's voice and now Cassandra's weeping. She could not bear that they were so unhappy, and it had been her fault and Harry's. What was to be done now? Their hearts were broken, and it seemed nothing could be done to make it better again. Lord Blytheland was right—he had suffered a sort of madness, for Harry had shot many arrows into him, enough to make him act in a way he would never have acted otherwise. The marquess would not act so again, now that Harry had cured him of the arrows.

It seemed Lord Blytheland might go away, and she wished he would not. He must stay in London, for Cassandra did love him—why else would she cry when he left? He must not give up, he must not leave. Psyche was certain they were meant for each other—did not Harry say so? And he was usually right about that, however they might disagree about his arrows.

Psyche squeezed her eyes shut tighter, thinking of Harry. She did not want to cry loudly, as she wished to, for she knew Mama would hear. But she missed Harry so! If only he were here! She was sure that between them they could think of a way to help her sister and Lord Blytheland.

She took in a deep breath, wiped away the tears with the back of her hands, and hiccuped. She would *not* think of Harry. It would be best if she returned to her room before Mama came out of the drawing room again. Psyche was certain she had not seen her behind the fern, for it was a very large plant, with long leaves that trailed down to the floor.

The afternoon was turning into evening; Psyche could see the sky now dim through the open window of her bedroom. The tears welled up inside her again. She had left the window open, as she always did for Harry. But he was not here. She always hoped perhaps he would return, but he never did, and it was a whole month since he had left. Slowly, she went to the window and slowly closed it, dashing away a tear with her other hand. It was stupid to hope. She had sounded as though she didn't like him anymore when she had shouted at him, and who would want to be friends with a girl who did that?

Psyche crept into her bed and sat against the pillows, hugging her knees. Her stomach grumbled, but she did not really feel hungry, and did not feel like going downstairs to have her dinner or her supper. Perhaps she would ask a maid to bring up something to drink, and then she would sleep. She was not feeling very well, at least not in her heart.

But she would not let herself despair. Cassandra and Lord Blytheland needed help, and even if Harry were not here, she would think of what to do herself. She sighed, feeling very tired, and closed her eyes and leaned against the pillows of her bed. She could do very well without Harry's help, she was certain. Perhaps she would go to Lord Blytheland and explain how Cassandra truly felt about him. Yes, she would go to him tomorrow—properly accompanied by a maid, for she knew Mama would not like it if she were unaccompanied by a maid—and tell him all about it. And if he was not convinced, she could find out where Lord Eldon lived, and make him talk to his friend. Psyche yawned and settled down into the pillows more deeply. Lord Eldon was a very nice man, and because he was Lord Blytheland's friend, he would want him to be happy, too. And then she would talk to Cassandra and tell her all about Harry's arrows, and how it was all a mistake . . . perhaps Harry would come back someday, and tell her . . . himself. . . .

The room was silent, and Psyche turned over to sleep on her side away from the window, as she always did. So she did not see the slight glow just outside, or hear the light tapping upon the window.

The glow hovered about the window, moving back and forth as if trying to see within the room. There was the light tapping upon the window again, but Psyche did not move. The glow stilled, then moved away slowly. For one moment, it seemed to hesitate.

Then it was gone.

Chapter 12

The sun struck Cassandra's eyes and woke her. She kept her eyes closed, for she did not really feel like getting up just yet. Today is just another day, like any other day, she told herself. You will have breakfast, and then you will find Psyche and give her Italian lessons and lessons in geography and mathematics. Then you will do all the other things you have always done since you came to London, only you will not see Lord Blytheland, and it will not matter to you one whit, for you are fully capable of going on as you have before, without him.

Hard words, and they struck her heart like stone. She turned and pressed her face into her pillow. She would not cry. She had done enough of that, enough for a lifetime. Pushing herself from her bed, she rose and pulled the bell rope. Today she would dress and everything would be as it was the day before, and the day before that.

Though she admittedly picked at her breakfast, she ate it, and when Psyche appeared for her lessons, she went through them as she always did. Her sister seemed unusually silent—but though she had received quite a scold from Mama a month ago, and Psyche was very sensitive to scolds and was clearly still affected by it. Cassandra hugged her sister after they finished the lessons.

"Psyche, please do cheer up. I know you did not mean to mislead Lord Blytheland. You see, I do not mind it, for it showed me his true nature, and I cannot wish to wed a man of such violent temper."

Psyche gazed at her wide-eyed and shook her head. "I think you do mind it."

Cassandra looked away and began fiddling with a fold in her dress. "Oh, at first I did, but not now. It was for the best, truly." She glanced up to find her sister still staring at her, her head cocked to one side.

"Well, you may say what you like, Cassandra. But it will turn out well. Lord Blytheland does love you, I know it. Perhaps I could help—"

"Heavens, no!" Cassandra hunched a shoulder. "Please, let us not talk of him. I would prefer not to think of him—or of his feelings." Especially not his feelings. His admission he loved her struck hard every time she thought of it. He *said* it, but what did it mean? He could have very easily—

No. She would not think of him. There were better things to do today. Cassandra waved her hand at Psyche. "I will need to run a few errands soon. Do you wish to accompany me?"

Psyche hesitated. "Where are you going?"

"To the milliner's to see if my hat is finished, and then the draper's to find some ribbons to match the hat."

"No, thank you." Psyche shook her head. "I don't wish to go anywhere right now. Perhaps tomorrow."

Cassandra gazed at her sister for a long moment. "Is there something the matter?" Psyche loved to go to the shops on New Bond Street, and her refusal was unusual.

The girl looked down at her hands clutched tightly together. "I . . . I know you do not like me to speak of him, but I have not seen Harry for a long time. And I wish he were back."

She looked so forlorn Cassandra did not have the heart to remind her that Harry was imaginary. She gave her another hug. "Perhaps he will return . . . or perhaps this means you are growing up, and do not need ima—such friends anymore."

Psyche shook her head. "If growing up means I shall not have Harry for a friend anymore, I do not wish to grow up."

Cassandra gave her a comforting pat on her back. "Well, perhaps he *shall* come back, soon."

"I don't know . . ." Psyche said, dully. She shrugged and rose from her seat. "I am going to read for a while. Do tell me if you see anything amusing when you return."

"Of course," Cassandra replied. She would buy something for Psyche while she was out, a book, or perhaps find some music for her to sing, for her sister loved to sing. She would play the piece upon her piano, and she and Psyche could do a duet—

A book would be better, Cassandra decided, for she did not want to think of music or duets quite yet. She sighed and went upstairs to put on her walking dress. She wished her father would come back to London, for perhaps he could give her advice. He had gone to Cambridge because Kenneth had got himself into trouble again, for her brother detested the place and had often wished—loudly—to join the army. In this one thing, Cassandra thought her father erred. Kenneth was not stupid by any means and if he applied himself he could be quite brilliant. But he hungered for a pair of colors and wished more than anything to fight in Wellington's army against Bonaparte. She could understand her father's wish to keep his son and heir safe in England. But he could speak with someone in government—he had quite a few friends there—and purchase Kenneth a relatively safe position in the army.

As Cassandra finished dressing and tied the ribbon of her bonnet under her chin, she wished life were not so difficult or so hard to understand. Her mother said these things were part of life, what one must bear and from which one must learn, as important as learning of Goethe's ideas or Aristotle's. She had not thought of it in that way before, but she

saw practical application of one's theories was always useful. And so she would bear the pain that seemed a constant
companion, and put up with the ache in her heart that
seemed not ever to go away, and hopefully learn from
them.

Psyche waited a whole fifteen minutes after Cassandra
left before she rang the bell pull for a maid. It was Gwennie
who came to her, and Psyche was glad, because she knew
the girl would do anything she asked. She had given her all
of her pin money once when she had heard Gwennie's little
brother was ill so he could have a proper doctor, and he had
become well again. So she had no trouble at all convincing
Gwennie to accompany her on her errand to Lord Blytheland's house.

For she had determined, with or without Harry, that she
must do something about her sister's and Lord Blytheland's
broken hearts. It was, after all, partly her fault. And since
Harry was at fault, too, and he was her friend—had been
her friend—she was responsible for him, too. Making Lord
Blytheland and Cassandra understand how wrong they
were about each other and perhaps making them be friends
again would go a long way to making up for the problems
she and Harry had caused.

A brisk wind blew at her and pulled at her bonnet, but
she was glad for the breeze, for it was a warm day. It took
longer than she thought it would to get to Lord Blytheland's house. Though she remembered where it was, she
had only gone past it in a carriage, and it was hard to gauge
how long it would take to walk there. At last she was in
front of the house. Lord Blytheland's was one of the largest
on the street, and the most elegant. Psyche frowned. But
there was a traveling carriage near it. The coach had a crest
on it, too, and though Psyche did not remember exactly
what the marquess's family crest looked like, it looked very

much like it could be his. Was Lord Blytheland going away?

She stepped up to the house and knocked at the door, her maid close beside her. The door opened.

The butler did not see her at first, because she was admittedly rather short and he was very tall. But then he glanced down and frowned at her.

"Yes, miss?" he said, looking down his nose, his voice quite frigid.

Psyche pressed her lips together firmly; she would *not* be put aside from her purpose. Besides, everyone knew the best houses had butlers who were always very high in the instep. She needed only convince him she was Quality, and that her mission was serious. "Please," she said, "I must see Lord Blytheland. It is very important. My name is Miss Psyche Hathaway, and as you see I am calling upon Lord Blytheland in a very proper manner, because I have my maid with me. He knows who I am, because he played his violin while my sister Cassandra played the pianoforte, and I was there to listen. He was very kind to me, too, and let me listen along with Mama."

An odd look came over the butler's face, as if he were trying very hard to suppress some strong emotion. His lips quirked up for a moment before turning into a frown, and he cleared his throat a few times before saying, "I am afraid it is not proper for a lady to call upon a gentleman even when she is accompanied by a maid."

"Oh!" Psyche said, and frowned. "Well, I thought a lady might go anywhere with her maid, except Bond Street. Will you please tell him he must come call upon me soon? Today?"

"I, er, I am afraid he is not in at the moment."

Psyche gazed at him suspiciously. "Does that mean he is at home, but he doesn't want to see anyone?"

"No, miss, he is not present in his house at this time." The butler's lips quirked again.

She crossed her heart with her finger and looked at him sternly. "True blue and will never stain?"

The man's stern expression cracked completely and he grinned. He crossed his heart as well. "True blue, miss."

"Oh! Well . . . when will he return?"

"I believe it will be within the half hour. But I doubt you will catch him even then. He will prepare to leave town as soon as he returns."

"Heavens!" Psyche exclaimed. "What am I to do?"

The butler looked at her kindly. "I believe he went to call upon your family one last time—he mentioned he was going to Sir John Hathaway's house. Perhaps if you hurried home, you will find him there."

"Yes, yes thank you!" Psyche gave him a smile, and turned from the house as the butler bowed and closed the door. But her gaze caught the coach in front of her, and she frowned again. She could not be sure she would see Lord Blytheland at her home, for by the time she walked there, he might well be gone. And she could not depend on finding him on the way home. If she waited in Lord Blytheland's traveling coach, she definitely would not miss him, and she could explain everything to him when he stepped into it. She bit her lip and glanced at her maid. It would be awkward to have Gwennie in there, too, for she wished to discuss family matters with Lord Blytheland, and Mama always said it was important not to discuss such things in front of the servants. Well! She would just have to get rid of the maid.

The breeze blew quite strongly, and with a quick tug she untied the bonnet ribbon beneath her chin. The wind obligingly picked up and threw her hat off her head—with only a *little* help from her hand.

"Oh, no!" Psyche cried. "Gwennie, do fetch my hat! Mama will be so angry with me if I return without it!" She was very pleased when the maid ran off immediately after her bonnet. She would give the girl two whole shillings later for her trouble.

Quickly, she climbed into the coach, her heart thumping hard. Did anyone see her? She peered out the coach window carefully. She did not think so. With a sigh, she relaxed against the squabs of the seat.

It was very comfortable in the coach, though very warm. She hoped Lord Blytheland would come soon, for sitting in a coach always made her feel sleepy. However, it could not hurt to close her eyes just a little, and when he did arrive, he would no doubt wake her up. She smiled to herself. Yes, all she needed to do was tell Lord Blytheland how Cassandra really loved him, and how she wept after he left, and he would understand. He seemed to be a rather understanding gentleman, after all, at least to her. He probably would have understood Cassandra, too, if he had not been shot so full of Harry's arrows. Perhaps she would even tell Lord Blytheland about Harry . . . although Cassandra had warned her not to talk of Harry to anyone else. Psyche yawned. It would not be so bad if she closed her eyes, just a little . . . and Lord Blytheland would undoubtedly come soon.

The glow was difficult to see in the daylight even if anyone knew to look for it, and of course no one did. It hovered around the coach in which Psyche sat, hesitated, and then settled upon the groom's seat. Harry allowed himself to take form, though he kept himself invisible. He did not want Psyche to see him just yet, in case she looked out of the carriage.

He found in the month he was away, he could not help thinking of his little friend and he had wondered what she was doing, if she had done anything outrageous lately, or said anything to make anyone laugh. He had left in anger, feeling more hurt than he thought he would. She was just a human, after all, and only a child. But taking mortal form, and a young form at that, always had an effect on him, and he often reacted the way a young mortal would. It was the only way humans could understand his presence, whenever he showed himself. They often became confused when a boy acted like an old man, or vice versa. He grinned. There was no way a human could comprehend an ancient god who could take any form he wished, anyway.

But he had to return and see how Psyche Hathaway fared. While he was away, he had searched a month for his own Psyche, with no success. There were few places these days he could look—he had searched everywhere for any sign of her. He had only twenty more years to find her, before most of the ancient gods faded forever, or so Hecate the Crone, the Secret One, said. They would disappear from the minds of humans, despite the efforts of such worthy men as Sir John Hathaway to preserve the ancient stories. Artemis had already fled to the Americas, where the cities had not yet encroached upon the vast wilderness, and though Apollo had found some contentment with the German and Austrian composers of music, now Ares was strongest, for humans believed in war quite fervently, as they always had.

Many still believed in love as well, so Harry—Eros—had not lost much of his strength. But he was not as strong as he used to be, for he had lost his own love, and he was strongest when he loved as well as when he was loved. When the gods began to lose their power, he had quarreled with his Psyche, for she believed the gods lost their power because they had become too distant from mortals. She would think that, of course, because she had been mortal herself at one time. But then she had disappeared, and only the sound of her voice whispering "find me, find me" had echoed in their empty house at Olympus.

She had been right, or so Hecate had confirmed. And once he found his Psyche, it would save the gods from fading into extinction, forgotten by mortals forever.

So why did he return to Psyche Hathaway? He did not

know. She had the same name, though other mortal females had worn the name, too. Perhaps . . . perhaps she held some clue to the whereabouts of his own Psyche. Who knew why she might! She was a stubborn and argumentative child, and he did not see how she might hold a clue to saving the gods at all.

But if she did, he supposed he should stay to find it out. He had looked most everywhere, after all, and was weary of searching right now. He grinned. Besides, she was a funny child, and it amused him to tease her. It would be especially amusing to see how she went about healing the rift between Lord Blytheland and Cassandra Hathaway without his help.

Something was wrong. Psyche woke up and bumped her head against the side of the coach. It was moving!

"Well, well. The Sleeping Beauty has awakened," said a soft voice.

Psyche gave a little shriek and shrank back into a corner of the coach. "You are not Lord Blytheland!" she said, and stared at the man. He was definitely not the marquess. This man had dark hair, where Lord Blytheland had blond hair, and he was older, too.

"No, I am not. I am Lord Crawforth. And you are . . . ?"

She did not like this man. There was something . . . bad about him, about the way he looked at her. She was used to seeing what people were feeling when she looked into their eyes, but she saw no feeling in this man's eyes, and it made her afraid. But it never did any good to show one's fear, her father always said, so she would not. "I have got into the wrong coach," she said firmly. "I am very sorry, but will you stop it so I may go to the right one?"

"But you have not told me your name, little one." Psyche did not like his voice, either. He made slight hissing sounds when he talked, like a snake—or should have, for he looked at her as if he were thinking whether she should be a side dish or a main course.

"Psyche Hathaway. There! I have told you, so you must stop the coach. Now, please."

Lord Crawforth looked thoughtful. "No, I think I like company on my travels. You shall do very well. How old are you?"

She began to feel very afraid now. "I do not see why I should tell you that, especially since I do not want to go with you. You *shall* stop this coach and I *shall* leave!" She stamped her foot—it was better to be angry than afraid. "If you do not, I shall scream—loudly."

His hand came up and seized her chin, forcing her to look at him. His eyes were cold, cold as ice. "You shall do as I say. You shall indeed come with me, because I wish it. Who are you but a nobody, an insignificant thing? If you scream, I shall simply tell everyone that you are mine, that you are misbehaving. Why should they believe you, and not me?"

Psyche turned and grabbed the carriage handle, almost opening it, but Lord Crawforth pulled her roughly away. She bit him and scratched him, but he was stronger than she, and tore the ribbon from her hair and tied her hands with it.

"There now," he said, breathing heavily from his efforts. "Do be a good girl and stay still."

Psyche glared at him, refusing to cry. She wished she had left a message at home about where she had gone. At least her mother or Cassandra would have known where to start looking for her. Or Harry. She shut her eyes tightly to keep the tears from falling. She wished she hadn't argued with Harry and told him to go away. *He* would have been here with her, if she had not. That would have comforted her and perhaps they would have thought of a way for her to escape.

But perhaps . . . perhaps he had not really gone. Perhaps

he was punishing her a little by not showing himself. Oh, she hoped it was so. For he was, really, her only chance to escape from Lord Crawforth. She took a deep breath.

"Harry! Harry!" she screamed.

Immediately, Lord Crawforth's hand clamped over her mouth. "None of that, my dear. A stupid thing to do. We have traveled quite a way from where we started, and if your Harry was near then, he certainly is not now."

She bit his hand.

"Damn you!" His hand went to her throat instead. "If you do that again, I shall throttle you, depend upon it." His fingers squeezed upon her neck to prove it. "Do you understand?"

Slowly, she nodded, and he released her. He smiled. "That's a good girl. I like good, obedient girls. You will be good, won't you?"

Psyche did not want him to like her, for she felt somehow Lord Crawforth did not treat good girls well at all. In which case, she would try to be as bad as possible.

And hope and wish and pray that Harry would come to her.

Chapter 13

Cassandra was in the midst of untying her bonnet ribbons when her mother burst into the drawing room. "Did Psyche return with you?" Lady Hathaway asked.

"Why, no, Mama. I invited her to come with me to the draper's, but she refused."

Her mother's face creased in a worried frown. "She is not in this house."

A chill went through Cassandra's heart, but she made herself think sensibly. "Perhaps . . . perhaps she decided otherwise, and decided to follow me out?"

"But surely she would have *told* someone?" her mother replied. "I thought to have her do some mending, for she is very good with fine work, but she is not in her room! I knew you were going on your errands, and so assumed she was with you." She wrung her hands and paced the room. "Oh, heavens! Your father *would* be away now, and I shall scold Kenneth when next I see him for making it necessary for your father to go to Cambridge."

"Did she leave a note, or . . . or perhaps one of the servants knows?" Cassandra asked.

Lady Hathaway shook her head. "No, I found no note. The servants do not know, either, although I suppose I could ask—"

A knock on the door took her attention, and when the door opened, Thrimble and a maid entered.

"Begging your pardon, my lady, miss, but Gwennie has

just returned and has some knowledge of Miss Psyche's whereabouts," the butler said and pushed the maid forward. The girl glanced at them nervously and held out a bonnet to Lady Hathaway.

"It's Miss Psyche's bonnet, my lady. We was goin' to Lord Blytheland's 'ouse, and her bonnet flew off acos o' the wind. She asked me to fetch it for 'er, but when I came back, she was gone." The maid hung her head and began to cry. "I looked all over for 'er, I did! But she warn't anywhere! And she wot was so kind when me brother 'ad the flux! I'm afeared somethin' turrible 'as got 'er, my lady. I ran fast as I could, so as you'd know."

"Lord Blytheland!" Lady Hathaway exclaimed. Cassandra glanced at her mother and found her staring in astonishment at her.

"Mama, I have no idea why she would—" A mix of dread and embarrassment crept into her. "She said she thought . . . oh, heavens!" She turned to her mother. "She said she could help—she must have gone to his house to speak to him."

Lady Hathaway groaned. "It only needed this! And of course your father *would* be gone now when we need him! What could the girl have been thinking of?" The maid wailed louder, and Lady Hathaway waved an irritated hand at her. "Oh, for goodness sakes, do go away! And you, too, Thrimble."

"Perhaps we should go to Lord Blytheland's house," Cassandra said tentatively after the maid and butler left. "It is not as if we would enter it, after all, and it is an emergency."

Lady Hathaway shook her head. "I suppose so . . . but your father is supposed to return today. I do not know when. One of us must stay, but it is very awkward, whichever one goes—oh, what is it now?" she said when the butler returned.

Thrimble cleared his throat. " 'Tis Lord Blytheland, my lady."

"Thank goodness!" Lady Hathaway exclaimed. "Perhaps he has brought her home."

But Psyche was not with the marquess when he entered the drawing room. Lady Hathaway sank into a chair and groaned again.

Lord Blytheland strode to her side. "Ma'am, you are not well—is there something I can do to help you?"

"My lord, have you seen Psyche?" Cassandra asked. He turned to look at her, and she felt a blush rising, but gazed at him steadily. He wore a greatcoat of many capes, dressed for travel.

"No, I have not," he replied. "I came to make a last call upon you—I am leaving London."

"Leaving?" The ache that sat so heavily in Cassandra's heart of late turned to pain.

"I thought it best." Blytheland gave her a slight smile. "Country air does clear people's minds, I have heard. But come, what is this about Miss Psyche?"

"She has disappeared," Cassandra said, and wrung her hands. "The maid who accompanied her said she went to your house, and then she was lost, disappeared—I do not know! We thought perhaps you came to bring her back, but you say you never saw her. And my father is not home—he has gone to Cambridge to see to my brother's matters."

"Then you—one of you—must come with me, and we will search for her. I have my carriage outside, but I am afraid it cannot hold more than three." He looked at Cassandra for a long moment, then transferred his gaze to Lady Hathaway.

"Go, Cassandra," her mother said. "Someone must be here to inform your father should he come home early, and what if my poor child should return by herself, to find me gone?"

"I would be here, Mama, for either of them."

Lady Hathaway's lips trembled, and she put a shaking hand to her mouth. "It is not the same as having her mother—what if she should be injured? No, no, you go, Cassandra, I will stay here."

Cassandra gazed at Lord Blytheland and thought she saw hope in his eyes. She swallowed and lifted her chin. I cannot think of myself at this time, she thought. I must think of Psyche, and she must be found. She nodded. "Very well," she said. Quickly, she pulled on the pelisse she had just taken off and hurried to the door.

When they stepped out of the house, Lord Blytheland took her hand and helped her up into the carriage. There was, indeed, not much room in it. If she pushed herself to the far edge of it, she could manage not to have her leg press against his, but to do so would have been awkward. She made herself relax and think of where Psyche might be.

"Shall we start at your house, my lord, since that was where she was seen last?" she asked as calmly as she could.

He glanced at her and nodded. "That was my thought also. She might well have gone inside upon finding I was not there. That must be what happened, and we shall have your sister returned home in no time at all."

"No doubt." It was a comforting thought. She should have thought of this very sensible answer to Psyche's disappearance herself, for the maid had not mentioned asking at Lord Blytheland's house to see if Psyche had slipped inside in an attempt to see him. Cassandra sighed. But then, she hadn't been thinking very clearly lately, had she?

They rode on in silence. Cassandra clasped her hands tightly in her lap, searching the crowded London streets in front of them and feeling thankful Psyche possessed a remarkable amount of bright red hair. She would be easily seen in this crowd. But though her eyes caught every spot of red possible, none of it signaled Psyche's presence. Perhaps she was, indeed, safely in Lord Blytheland's house.

At last the marquess reined in his horses and leapt down, looping the reins upon the iron railing in front of his house. "Wait here—I shall look inside and bring her out again." Cassandra nodded.

A minute passed, then another. It could not take that long to find Psyche, could it? Cassandra bit her lower lip and stared at her hands on her lap, impatiently creasing and uncreasing a fold in her dress. She could not go in, of course, but the waiting was becoming intolerable.

"Cassandra."

She looked up, expecting the marquess, and froze. There, in front of her, delicately perched on the buckboard of Lord Blytheland's carriage, was a boy. She swallowed and felt a little dizzy. "Who . . . who are you?"

The golden-haired boy gazed at her solemnly. "I'm Harry, Psyche's friend." His wings fluttered in an impatient manner. "She needs help, quickly. My arrows are not made for what needs to be done, so you must come, and Lord Blytheland, too."

Cassandra closed her eyes, then opened them. "I *must* be imagining this."

"No, you are not." He reached over and gave her a hard pinch. "There, you see?"

She rubbed her arm—there was, indeed, a red welt on it now, and the crescent marks of two fingernails. "So you do exist," she said wonderingly. She gingerly reached out to touch his knee and felt cloth and warm skin. He allowed it, much like a disdainful cat allowing itself to be patted, tolerant only. She stared at his wings and the quiver of arrows on his back. "And not 'Harry'—Eros, I suppose?" she asked.

He grinned suddenly, a mischievous expression lighting his blue eyes, and she could not help being charmed by it. "Yes. But Harry will do." He glanced impatiently at Blytheland's house. "I wish he would hurry. When he comes, tell him to go to Green Park—they are going in that direction. It's a yellow carriage, and the crest is blue with black swords crossing over a white tower."

"Perhaps you should tell—"

"No. I dislike being seen. You are her sister, and she is in trouble, so I have made an exception in your case."

"Well, I do not see how you can say that! Anyone may see you now."

He grinned, and it was more mischievous than ever. "Only you can see me at this moment. Everyone who has seen you speak to me has been thinking how odd it is that such a lovely young lady is talking to nothing at all."

If this was what Psyche's friend usually was like, it was just as well she did *not* see or hear him, Cassandra thought, irritated. Harry glanced at the house again and made an impatient sound.

"Tell him where to go. I am going back to Psyche and see what I can do." And with a flick of his wings, his shape shimmered and he disappeared.

Cassandra could almost convince herself she had imagined it all, but her arm still hurt where Harry had pinched her. And what if it were true, and she failed to act upon it, and Psyche was hurt? She could not take the chance. She glanced at the door of the marquess's house and bit her lip. There was no time to think of proprieties now, not when her sister was in trouble. Hastily, she descended from the carriage and knocked on the door. A footman answered.

"I am Miss Cassandra Hathaway. Tell Lord Blytheland to come—I know where my sister is, and he need not search his house if that is what he is doing," she said. "Go, quickly, tell him!" The footman nodded and left.

Only a minute passed before Lord Blytheland ran out of the house, looking distracted. "Where?" he said tersely as he gathered up the reins.

"Green Park. A . . . boy saw her climb into a yellow coach and it was going in that direction."

Blytheland groaned as he shook the reins. "There must be dozens of yellow coaches going toward Green Park."

"It has a crest—blue, with two swords and a tower."

"Devil take it." Blytheland's face hardened, then he glanced at Cassandra.

"Tell me!"

"Lord Crawforth. He has . . . fast horses."

His jaw was tight and he would not look at her but stared steadily in front of him, concentrating upon his horses. There was something about Lord Crawforth he did not want to tell her, and she was sure he would not tell her no matter how she pressed him. Please let Psyche be safe, Cassandra prayed, and closed her eyes tightly. She felt a hand close over hers, and she opened her eyes to find Lord Blytheland looking at her with such warmth and kindness that she had to look away, lest the tears she felt rising inside her spill over.

"We will find her, I promise you," he said.

It was only a promise, and he had given her promises before that she did not believe. But she believed him in this now, and felt comforted.

"Psyche."

It was a whisper, and Psyche almost thought she had imagined it, obscured as it was amongst the rumble of coach wheels. But she opened her eyes and there he was, staring at her solemnly. She almost burst into tears of relief, but bit her lip hard to prevent it.

"Harry!" she exclaimed at last.

Lord Crawforth turned from his perusal out the window and stared at her. "How you do persist. Stupid girl. Have I not told you your Harry cannot hear you? If you do not stop, I shall be forced to tie up your mouth as well."

Psyche shrank into her corner of the coach and Lord Crawforth smiled pleasantly. She glanced at Harry and was glad she was not Lord Crawforth. Harry's face was stormy, and his presence seemed, oddly, too large for the coach, though he had not changed in any other way. If she had thought Harry might be dangerous when he was irritated, she had been quite right. His normal glow was pale and translucent, but now he seemed to radiate a hot, almost venomous light when he looked at Lord Crawforth. Psyche shivered. As bad as Lord Crawforth was, she was certain what punishment Harry planned for him would be worse.

But then Harry looked at Psyche, and his expression and his light softened and he smiled encouragingly at her.

"Psyche, I want you to be ill."

She raised her brows in question, not daring to speak.

"Pretend you are about to be sick in the coach. Make loud retching noises."

She looked at him, wondering what he was planning, but nodded. "Oh, dear," she said, and covered her mouth with her hand.

Lord Crawforth gave her a sharp look. "What is it now?"

Psyche closed her eyes briefly, and hoped she looked pale. "I . . . oh, no! I am afraid I feel very—" She pressed her hands against her mouth and coughed. "Ack! Urp!"

Lord Crawforth looked uneasy and moved away from her. "If you are trying some trick—"

She looked at him, making tears form in her eyes—an easy thing to do, for she had been so terribly afraid. "I—I feel ill, my lord, I truly do—Riding in coaches always— Urp!" She lurched forward, as if she were about to give up her luncheon on the coach floor. Lord Crawforth pushed himself into the side of the carriage even more, a look of disgust on his face.

"Tell him you want some milk because it always makes you feel better," Harry whispered.

"Milk? Oh, milk!" Psyche exclaimed, and leaned back in her seat, putting the back of her hand over her forehead. "Please, just a little milk, and I shall feel better."

"Milk? Where the devil would I get milk?" Lord Craw-forth said. "I would think water would be better."

"No! Milk, please. Water makes me feel worse." She widened her eyes and pressed her hands to her mouth again. "Urp!" she said, this time with more emphasis than she had before.

"Cretin," Harry muttered, looking at Lord Crawforth. "Tell him there are cows and milkmaids in Green Park, though by the gods he should know it, having passed the place every day of his worm-ridden life." Psyche almost giggled, but turned it into another convulsive lurch and another loud "urp."

"Oh, dear!" she said and heaved a deep, shuddering sigh. "If only we were at Green Park!" She pressed her hand to her mouth and shuddered again. "My mother bought some milk for me there when I felt ill, and I felt better immediately." She gazed at Lord Crawforth as mournfully as possible. "But I cannot hope for that, so I fear I shall be quite—Oh! Urp!"

"Stop!" Lord Crawforth shouted out the coach window to his groom. He gazed angrily at Psyche. "We are at Green Park now. I shall get you your damned milk, but if I find you are tricking me, it shall go very badly for you indeed." He opened the coach door, then turned back to Psyche. "You shall stay here. My groom will be watching to see if you try to escape."

As soon as Lord Crawforth left, Harry untied the ribbon from around Psyche's wrists. "What an idiot," Harry said. "He could have had the groom fetch the milk for him."

"I suspect he wished to get away, in case I should have vomited on him. And I pretended very well, didn't I?" Psyche said proudly.

"Yes. I was hoping you would." Harry grinned, then sobered. "Now, wait here. He needs to be punished."

Psyche gazed at him warily. "What are you going to do?"

The dangerous glow flickered around him again, and he stared at Lord Crawforth's retreating form. "He is a beast, and deserves only the company of beasts," Harry said grimly.

"Oh, dear." Psyche watched as her friend flew toward Lord Crawforth and draw an arrow from his quiver. He fitted the arrow to his bow, and pulled it back. She could not help herself: she covered her eyes and hoped the punishment would not be too terrible.

A plucking, a singing through the air, and then a gasp from Lord Crawforth.

"I say!" Psyche heard him exclaim. "That's a remarkably fine cow you have there." She peeked from behind her fingers.

Lord Crawforth was peering through a quizzing glass at a brown cow.

"Wecell, I daresay Bessie's a good 'un," the cowman replied proudly. "She dropped twins two year ago, and both of 'em sturdy fellows."

"Fertile, eh?" Lord Crawforth said, putting out a tentative hand and patting Bessie on the neck.

"Every year," replied the cowman. "And she never drops 'em bad, neither."

"How much?" Lord Crawforth asked, now petting the cow with more confidence.

"That'll be thrippence, sir," a milkmaid chimed in, and presented a cup of milk.

"No, no!" Lord Crawforth waved the milk aside. "I meant how much for the cow."

"The cow?" The cowman gazed, stupefied, at Lord Crawforth, then exchanged a long look with the milkmaid, who shrugged.

"Yes, the cow," Lord Crawforth replied impatiently. "For how much will you sell it—her—to me? Fifty guineas? Sixty?"

"Er, well, I dunno," the cowman said, scratching his head, but the milkmaid poked him with her elbow.

"I think four hundred guineas would be a good price," the milkmaid said. "Prime bit o' blood and bone, is Bessie."

"Four hundred!" exclaimed Lord Crawforth. "She is a fine animal, I can see, but perhaps one hundred—"

"Three hundred," the cowman interjected hastily.

They continued haggling over the cow, as Psyche watched, wide-eyed. She turned to Harry, who had returned to the coach. "Oh heavens! You have made Lord Crawforth fall in love with a cow!"

Harry grinned and twirled an arrow between his fingers. "He deserved it. At least he will not"—he gazed at Psyche and closed his mouth suddenly, then continued—"frighten girls anymore." He opened the carriage door and took Psyche's hand. "You can come out now. The groom is now madly in love with the milkmaid, and I think she will make him a good wife."

Psyche stepped down from the coach and walked away from it, and still held Harry's hand. She smiled up at him. "Thank you for coming to my rescue, Harry. I am so sorry I told you I didn't want to see you, because it wasn't true at all! I felt awful afterwards, and missed you terribly. It is a lonely thing to be in London without a true friend."

Harry looked at her and cleared his throat. She was right. However ancient one was, it was a lonely thing to be without a friend. There was nothing wrong with having a friend or two while continuing his search, after all.

"Well. Well, I missed you also. And—" He hesitated. "I am sorry, too. It was my fault, I think—the trouble between your sister and Lord Blytheland. Not all," he said. "But at least part of it. There is no accounting for how a mortal may react, after all."

"In which case, you should be careful, Harry!" Psyche

said severely, but she stopped, smiled, and shook her head. "I will *not* quarrel with you!"

"Psyche!" cried a voice from behind her.

"Cassandra!" Psyche cried joyfully. "How glad I am to see you! I did not want to walk all the way back home from here, so I am happy you have come and you have brought Lord Blytheland with you, too! How do you do, Lord Blytheland—I hope you are well?"

Cassandra almost tumbled down from the carriage in her haste to take Psyche in her arms and hug her. "You dreadful girl!" Cassandra cried. "How *could* you leave the house and not let any of us know where you were going? And to Lord Blytheland's house, too! I am *so* embarrassed!" She gave Psyche another hug. "But I am glad to see you safe—I was so afraid!"

Psyche nodded. "I was afraid, too, because Lord Crawforth is a horrid, odious man, but it is quite all right, because Harry rescued me and made Lord Crawforth fall in love with a cow! Was that not clever of him?"

Cassandra hastily glanced at Lord Blytheland, who also descended from the carriage and who looked very grim. "Yes, my dear, but let us not talk of that right now."

"If you will excuse me, ladies, I will go deal with Lord Crawforth," Lord Blytheland said.

"No!" cried Psyche and Cassandra at once.

Lord Blytheland stopped and stared at them.

"Lord Crawforth has been punished already," Psyche said. "My friend Harry did it. He will never bother me again, truly! Or anyone else. He has fallen in love with a cow, you see."

A look of profound revulsion came over Lord Blytheland's face. "Such a foul monster does not deserve to live," he said.

Psyche gave him a puzzled look. "But I think he will treat the cow very well. Only see how kind he is with it." She pointed toward Lord Crawforth. He had apparently concluded his negotiations with the cowman, who was holding a bank note in his hands and dancing in little circles on the grass. Lord Crawforth was leading the cow away, petting its cheek and murmuring into its ear.

"Please, let us go away from here," Cassandra said, touching Lord Blytheland's sleeve. "My sister is not hurt, and it is clear Lord Crawforth is . . . preoccupied." He gazed at her and his expression softened.

"Very well, if you wish it," he said, and extended his hand to Psyche. "Up you go." He lifted Psyche into his carriage, then assisted Cassandra into it as well.

Psyche sighed happily. This was precisely what she needed, her sister and Lord Blytheland together in the same place. Now she would make everything right between them again. She thought carefully over what she would say for many minutes, for this time she did not want to ruin anything between them.

"Thank you very much for finding me, Lord Blytheland," she began. "I wished to speak to you when I came to your house, but you were not there! But it is just as well, because now you and Cassandra are here together, and it is much easier telling both of you what you need to know at the same time."

"Psyche!" Cassandra exclaimed, her face becoming very pink. "Please, do not —"

"No, I will not listen, Cassandra, even though you are older than I. But I want to cry, too, whenever I see you weep, and I don't like to cry, you know."

"Psyche, please—"

Lord Blytheland held up his hand, and he looked curiously at Cassandra and Psyche. "Do go on, Miss Psyche. I suspect I am the cause of your sister's distress, and if I have been the cause of more, I wish to know how I may remedy it."

"It is not precisely because of you, my lord," Psyche said. "You see, Cassandra is very much in love with you, I know it. Harry says so, too, so it must be so. But he made a mistake and shot you too full of his arrows, and so you acted in a bad way toward her. But I made him turn you back the way you were before he shot you, and you still love Cassandra anyway, do you not?"

"Yes, of course I do," Lord Blytheland replied. "But who is this Harry?"

"He—he is Psyche's playmate," Cassandra said hastily. "You must not mind her, really."

"I do not understand how your friend can know or do such things, Miss Psyche," Lord Blytheland said, then turned to Cassandra. "But I do wish to know one thing: do you love me, Cassandra?"

He had stopped the carriage, for they were at the Hathaways' house. Cassandra stared at him, and his eyes were warm and anxious, hopeful and full of pain. She thought of what Psyche had said, remembered Harry's—Eros'—appearance before her. She knew her mythology well: the god of love could turn a man mad as well as make him fall head over heels in love. Ane love could heal as well as hurt . . . Her heart ached and the words gathered behind her lips, too numerous to choose between.

"I . . . I . . . Oh, heavens, I don't know!" Quickly, she stumbled out of the carriage and fled into the house.

"Go after her, please, Lord Blytheland," Psyche said urgently.

"She may not wish me to," he said.

"*Please* go in! She *does* love you, I know it. There is no other reason for her to feel so low when she does not see you. And if you go away without finding out, how do you know she will not marry someone and then be miserable because she loves you and no one else?"

Lord Blytheland stared at the door through which Cassandra had gone, and knew he could not bear it if she married another man. Miss Psyche had said her sister loved him. Would not a sister know, however young she was? He leaped down from the carriage.

"Here," he said, thrusting a guinea in the Hathaway footman's hand. "Hold my horses." He pushed past the footman and after questioning a few maids in the hallway, went after Cassandra.

He opened a door and found himself in a small flower-and-vegetable garden, next to the mews. Roses climbed one wall, lilies perfumed the air, and pansies crowded the edges of the walkway. He almost did not see Cassandra, for her flower-print dress blended with the colors around her, and she was sitting on a bench, in a shadowed corner of the garden, her face covered by her hands.

He walked to her and sat next to her, feeling helpless. He wished he knew what to do or say, but he had not really ever been a man for words; his music said most of what he had in his heart. But he did not have his violin with him, and he supposed his only recourse was in words . . . though they had not served him well in the past, had they? But she did not move away, and he did the only thing he could think of: He put his arms around her and held her tightly.

She did not stiffen or draw away, but sighed instead. Encouraged, he put his finger under her chin and kissed her lips, gently. "Tell me, Cassandra. Tell me what is wrong."

"I am afraid," she said. "I am afraid I will say the wrong thing, like I always do. And I was afraid you did not mean it when you said you loved me, but then Psyche said Harry shot you and made you act—Well, never mind that. But I do believe it now, and feel horrible because I said terrible things to you."

"It can't be worse than the things I said to you, and I was the one who injured you, you who are totally innocent of all the things I said to you." Lord Blytheland stroked her cheek with his finger, gazing at her with such love that it hurt to see it. She closed her eyes. "I was married once before, you know, and . . . and my wife did not love me. I was afraid,

also." He hesitated. "I do not deserve it, but will you forgive me?"

"Yes, yes of course," she said, and smiled at him.

There was silence, and then, hesitantly, the marquess
said, "Was Psyche right, Cassandra? Do you love me? For I
do wish to kiss you again, but make no mistake—if you do
admit it, I shall insist on marrying you soon. And if you
don't want that, I suggest you say no. Because, you see, I
would not like you to share your kisses with anyone else
but me, even in an experiment." There was a hint of laughter in his voice, but a question also.

She turned to him, laughing, and feeling tears as well.
"You are an odious man to bring up my experiment! It was
a stupid thing, I see it now—"

"But do you love me, Cassandra?" He held her face in
his hands, looking at her anxiously now, full of hope.

"Yes! Oh, Paul, yes!" she said at last, and put her hands
behind his neck and kissed him fiercely.

With a low groan, he pulled her to him and kissed her
with all the love he felt for her. His chest felt tight with
wanting, and his heart's defenses shattered at last, causing
him to crush her closer to him. She did not protest, but
pressed herself to him instead.

"Marry me, Cassandra, please," he murmured against her
lips, and he kissed her again, trailing his kisses from mouth
to cheek, to chin and down the long column of her throat.

"Yes," she gasped.

"Soon." He moved his hands to her waist and hips, then
pulled her onto his lap.

"Yes," she said, and kissed him again.

"Cassandra! Lord Blytheland!" Lady Hathaway's scandalized voice echoed in the garden. Cassandra looked up
and saw her mother at the door of the garden, her hands on
her hips and looking at them sternly.

Hastily, Cassandra pushed herself from Lord Blytheland's lap and blushed furiously. But Lord Blytheland took

her hand and rose from the bench and bowed to Lady Hathaway.

"It is not as bad as it seems, Lady Hathaway," he said and grinned. "You see, your daughter has just consented to become my wife."

"Is this true, Cassandra?" Lady Hathaway asked, her voice still stern.

"Yes, Mama."

"Thank God!" Lady Hathaway said, closing her eyes in heartfelt, grateful prayer. "I thought it would never happen!"

"Mama!"

"You must admit it has been a very trying thing for me, my girl! I have been trying to promote a match between you two this age, and then after that luncheon my hopes were almost completely dashed!" Lady Hathaway beamed happily at the marquess and her daughter. "I must go tell Sir John—he has just returned, Cassandra, and tell Psyche, too, for she was quite anxious about it. I have sent her up to her room to change her dress—she became dreadfully dirty, walking all the way to your house, Lord Blytheland! And thank you for your help in finding her, my lord. We are truly grateful. I *knew* you would be the perfect addition to our family." She turned to leave, then stopped. "Oh, and I should let you know, Lord Blytheland, it is not at all discreet of you to propose and kiss Cassandra in the garden here! It is in full view of the house across the alley, and I am sure any number of persons could see you from there, *and* from our house!" She turned and went back inside.

Lord Blytheland gazed at Cassandra, who was blushing to the roots of her hair, and grinned mischievously. "I suppose that means I should take you inside the house to kiss you."

Cassandra blushed more pink than ever. "Odious man!" she exclaimed, and turned toward the house. He caught her hand and pulled her to him. "Not here!" she said hastily.

"Where, then?"

"I do believe the music room is unoccupied," Cassandra said primly, then grinned and dashed into the house.

Psyche sighed as she gazed down from a guest room at her sister and Lord Blytheland in the garden. "Is that not romantic, Harry? I knew it would work out if I spoke to them. I was right, after all, you see."

Harry shrugged. "Not totally right. I think I helped, also."

Psyche stared at him. "How can you say so? You were the one who shot too many arrows into Lord Blytheland and made him act badly."

"But if I hadn't, he might not have thought of falling in love with your sister."

"You don't know that!"

"And you do?"

Psyche leaped down from her perch at the window and strode to the door of the chamber. "Oh, you odious boy! How can you say that?"

"From experience, my girl, from experience," Harry said, following her.

"Hmph!" Psyche opened the door, then crossed her arms in front of her. But she could not really stay mad at Harry. He was her best friend, after all, and she did not want to lose him again. She looked at him, unsmiling at first, and then she grinned. "Oh, never mind! I am going to the kitchens. Cook has just made up some jam tarts and I am going to get some while they are hot. I know you like them, too!"

Harry grinned. "I'll get there before you do," he said, and flew off down the hall.

"No fair flying!" Psyche called, and ran after him.